1

Gazelle in the Shadows

Michelle Peach

To Gary
Thank you for all your
encouragement way back when
this book was just a story in
my head.
                                    Michelle
3   8-11-18

A thousand thanks to the many people who have helped me during the course of writing my novel, especially my husband Richard; my children, Marcella, Emmy and John; my mother, Mary, who all put up with my erratic creative writing schedule and many all-nighters. My deepest gratitude is to my mentor and content editor, Blake Ray, who was with me from the beginning constantly encouraging me even when I doubted myself and to my British editor, Alison Burch, whose assistance in research and editing, not only the grammar but also my unique British/American expression, was invaluable. My thanks also to my friends for their support and encouragement, Gary Loudermilk, Meme Lumsden, Nicki Merck, Dr. Andrew Rathmell, and Milton Wendland, and my Beta readers Izzy, Caitlin, and Evelyn who gave me honest and crucial feedback. A huge thank you to Jeff and Janet Wylie, a most incredible artistic duo, for the illustration and graphics. Without all your support, input and encouragement this book would still be just a story in my head.

Prologue

For many years, I have wanted to write this book to leave my legacy for my children as this story is largely based on my life. There are stories in the novel that are entirely true whereas others are fictionalized.

When I traveled to Syria as a Durham student in 1992, I knew very little about the country. Many have asked me how I had the gall to jump on a plane and travel to a country where I did not even have a hotel to arrive at. My answer was that I always had a desire for wanderlust and luckily I had some experience as I was not a novice to the Arabian Peninsula. I had worked in Yemen, also a conservative Islamic country, as a junior staff member in the British Embassy operating the large radio machinery, but there, even though I learned much about the Yemeni language and culture, I solely socialized with expatriates and their families. My level of planning for Syria was rudimentary at that time as the internet search engines did not exist and only knew of one professor who had been there. I carried a travel guide book like a Bible as it was my sole fount of knowledge. It was in Syria where I wore my first hijab, an Islamic female head covering, not because I had to but rather I was keen to blend in with my Syrian friends. Another tradition, which I was aware of before I travelled to Syria, was the renown of the warmth and generosity which Arabs extend to visitors which is unparalleled in the world. I had not had the opportunity to accept such a welcome in Yemen although I had heard accounts of it from other expatriates. In Syria, from the onset, I was overwhelmed by their welcome.

The longer I stayed in Damascus and especially when I started working for Dr. Andrew Rathmell, as his Arabic translator and assistant researcher, the more I understood of Syria's tumultuous and violent history. At the time, Hafez al-Assad, the President of Syria since 1971, was at the height of his autocratic power and the country was in a state of relative calm since the end of the Gulf War in 1991. His vast security apparatus was evident on every street corner whether army, police or civilian informants. My travel guide dedicated an entire page to the various types of mukhabarat, secret police, present in the country but it also reassuringly wrote that Syria was a "safe" country for travelers. Not so obvious was the fear, paranoia and suppression which his people lived under.

My love for Syria has never been far from my thoughts and when the unrest in Syria began in 2011, my determination to start writing intensified. I was distraught and appalled by the suffering of the people and by the destruction of its historical sites in Aleppo, Palmyra, Bosra, Homs, Damascus and elsewhere. I know that many will not have the opportunity to see the sights of Syria due to the ongoing conflict, but I hope that through my story readers can enjoy the cities, landscapes and culture of Syria.

Dedication

I am honoured by the welcome and friendship I received from the Syrian people I met and dedicate this book to all the Syrian people who have lost their lives and to those still suffering since the conflict began.

One

With my legs bunched up near my chin, I buried my face into my knees and rocked. I smelled the rusty, iron scent of blood on my jeans. Strands of long hair that had been pulled out of my braid after the struggle were sticking to my neck and cheeks, held in place by sweat and blood. I reached up and felt the sore skin around my neck, where my hood had been tied. Welts had formed around my wrists, where the ropes had been. I moaned.

Who are my kidnappers? Could it be Hezbollah? The Syrian Army? Or the South Lebanese Army? God, please let it not be Hezbollah.

My heart beat in my neck at the thought of being held by a terrorist group. I squeezed my knees even tighter and whimpered from a sudden, sharp pain in my ribs.

I remembered the Sunday I broke the news to my parents that I was going to study in Damascus. Mother made me promise that I would not go to Lebanon, even saying that it's because she feared Hezbollah.

"Elizabeth, I want to hear you promise." She had insisted when I shrugged my shoulders and grinned.

I thought she was being over-protective, after all Hezbollah had ceased taking hostages three years ago and released their last captive, Terry Anderson, last year.

It can't be them.

My heart rate reduced to a dull thud. So, perhaps it's the Syrian Army? Adrien had told me during my last visit to see him at the embassy that the

11

Syrian government knew I was a former British diplomat, and even though the Syrian Army was in Lebanon, he vouched that I would be safer there than in Damascus. I trusted Adrien implicitly, as I had done so with the MI6 officer in my former embassy in Sana'a.

I prayed the Syrians had picked me up, or even the South Lebanese Army. After all, I told myself, they are on the same side. I whispered to myself Adrien's reassurance that I still had diplomatic immunity, and that this meant I would be released soon and sent to the British Embassy.

I lifted my head up and looked around the room. It was dimly lit, with one bare bulb and a fan in the centre of the ceiling. A grimy, thin mattress lay on the filthy floor, with an empty nightstand beside it. The one window the room had was crudely boarded up. I could see daylight, which seeped in from around the ill-fitting plywood. Gingerly, I stood up gripping my left side as pain seared in my ribcage and took three steps forward. Through a crack in the board, I could make out a gravel road and the bonnet of a black car. My field of vision was disappointingly limited, as I peered in all directions for any clues as to where I was. I pulled at the wood to see if it was loose, but it had been nailed to the window frame and then I discovered one, additional barrier. Like so many homes I had seen in this part of the world, windows on the first floor were barred, perhaps to keep inhabitants in rather than prevent break-ins. My hope of a possible escape route was dashed. I collapsed onto the mattress in a heap and wept.

I thought of my parents. I couldn't take my mind off the intense longing I had to see them again and put my arms around them. I had felt loneliness before, but this was different. It was an aloneness that you are somewhere in the world where your loved ones don't know, nor have any hope of finding you or even dream what is happening to you. It was an emptiness of unfathomable depth.

I reached up to the empty nightstand and pulled open its small drawer. I was surprised to find that it was full of rubbish, which I sifted through. A rush of relief washed over me, when I saw a pen and a possible scrap of paper to write on.

Then slowly, I began to write.

Two

It was a cold, rainy April day in the north of England. I was waiting for my professor to turn his attention back to me from the loose stack of papers in front of him. As I sat waiting in his office, I scanned the spines of some of his books, trying to read their titles — most of them in Arabic.

Professor Mansfield, who became known simply as The Professor, was our Arabic language and literature teacher. Most of his books were Arabic novels, poetry, and grammar books. He was one of the most knowledgeable men I had ever met, and his collection of books was impressive. Less impressive was the way he displayed them. They were stacked haphazardly: vertically, horizontally and even one pile balancing precariously on top of a small book in such a way that I wondered how long they'd last before they toppled over into the bin directly below. The spines of the books were all well-worn and used, although taken care of. I was not used to the untidiness, as our home was spotless. My mother worked tirelessly on her housework and that was just the way my father liked it. He would tell us all, "Cleanliness is next to godliness."

The Professor cleared his throat with a gruff cough. I thought that was the moment he was going to look up so that we could begin, but he just continued to read, making small noises to himself. I shifted restlessly in my seat.

I wanted to ask for a special accommodation for the year abroad that my degree required. So far, the first two semesters at the Centre for Middle Eastern and Islamic Studies in Durham University had been easier than I imagined. Just last week, the Professor walked around our desks handing out the results of a test on the first three units of our language book. When he placed mine in front of me, he said, loud enough for the entire class to hear, "One hundred percent again. You're doing really well, Elizabeth. Keep this up and you'll be in line for the Centre's Student of Excellence Award at the end of the year."

"Thanks." I looked up to smile at him, but he had already moved on, delivering the rest. I sat up straighter than before and held my head up high, feeling a tingling sensation I hadn't felt in a long time.

The Excellence Award was a coveted prize because it came with prize money as well as accolade. I was not aware that others were competing for that award until that day. I wanted to burst with joy because I had finally found a subject that I excelled in. I had never received praise from a teacher before, which honestly wasn't a surprise, as I had never excelled in any subject at school. I had concluded a long time ago that I was an average achiever. I wished I could have been more like my older brother, Jacob, who thrived in his school. Each evening, I helped mother set the dining table, laying out a white, lace tablecloth, bone china plates and silver cutlery. During dinner, Jacob and my father would get into complicated, lengthy discussions on current affairs. Occasionally I joined in, but more than often I hesitated, as it opened me up to ridicule from Jacob.

"Did you see the six o'clock news tonight, Elizabeth? The gorillas in Africa are fighting again," Jacob sneered at me from across the table.

"Shut up, Jacob. I know they're guerilla rebel fighters, not real gorillas. I'm not that stupid. Why do you keep making that joke?" My face burnt with anger.

"There's no need to use such language, Elizabeth," Father scolded me.

"But he...."

"Elizabeth, your brother is trying to explain to you the groups fighting in South Africa."

My father could not see that Jacob was being deliberately antagonistic.

It was no surprise to our parents that Jacob was accepted to Manchester University to study law, especially after he received the Debate Society County trophy, which my parents placed proudly on the mantelpiece in our living room. That mantelpiece, forever memorialising the family's achievements: a full-length photograph of me in a ballet performance when I was ten years old, and one of my father in police uniform receiving a promotion. In the hearth, a fresh flower arrangement was beautifully displayed. My mother was responsible for all the flower arrangements at our church and her talent was well-known in the village.

When it came time for me to apply to university two years later, my A-level results were not good enough for entry into any university. The universities demanded As and Bs, and I only had two Cs in maths and English and a D in French.

Jacob had attended a brand new, co-ed comprehensive school near home instead of the Boys' Catholic school across town. I once confided to my mother that I wished I had gone to the same comprehensive school as him instead of St. Agnes, the Girls' Catholic school, as I thought I would have received a better education.

"It's your father's decision that you attend the same school as me. He knows the Sisters will do an excellent job." She shrugged and that was the end of that discussion. She never defied my father's decision.

I enjoyed my years at St. Agnes, but the Sisters didn't expect much of us. My timetable included typing, cooking, Latin, and, of course, religious education classes. In sewing classes, I made a quilted bag and an apron, while my brother learned trigonometry and read the classics.

I wanted to continue my education, so I applied and was accepted at Bangor Polytechnic to do mathematics and statistics. I knew my heart was not into studying mathematics for three years. In fact, I didn't know what I wanted to do with my life. I wished I could have made it into a prestigious university like my brother. I would have pursued a degree in French, but my A-level grade was too low. I envisaged moving to the south of France and living in Cannes after my graduation. My parents were just relieved that I was going to continue my further education, no matter what subject, until I told them I wanted to enter the Foreign and Commonwealth Office as a Diplomatic Service (D.S.) grade 10, their most junior level.

Three

Professor Mansfield looked up and gave me a perfunctory smile.

"So, Elizabeth, what can I do for you? I hope you're not here to ask for an extension on the pre-Islamic poetry essay like the previous person was." He took off his reading glasses and he peered at me with a smirk.

"No. Of course not." I shifted in my seat, as I knew I was asking for much more of a favour than that.

The Professor was about the same age as my father, although there was no resemblance. He had a full head of grey hair, unlike my father who was completely bald. My father had the physique of a rugby player, probably weighing twice that of the Professor.

My father and I had a great relationship while I was growing up. He called me his Golden Princess. I thought of him as my superhero because of his police uniform. He taught me how to ride my bicycle, even bandaging a bloody knee when I fell off. I used to anticipate eagerly his return from work each evening and wrap my arms around his huge body. But as I approached my teenage years, he paid less and less attention to me.

By the time I went to secondary school, my relationship with him was distant. My girlfriends were a group of self-styled artists. In the last few years of school, they were experimenting with hair dyes and spikey, punk styles. My hair was and always had been blonde, plain and straight. When I was young, it reached my waist. As a teenager, it was cut to a shoulder-length bob. I never went shorter than a bob. Every time I cut my hair, my dad would complain, but my mother would reassure him that they were lucky to have a daughter that didn't change the colour of her hair every week. During those years, I grew much closer to my mother.

As a teenager, however, I started to notice a shift, as my father became more of a bodyguard. He dictated his opinions, rather than soliciting mine. It led to many arguments, which often placed my mother in the middle.

I remembered once, after a particularly nasty row between my father and I, going over to my friend Fiona's house and asking her to dye my hair. She was glad to oblige. I went home that evening with bright red streaks in my golden locks. My father grounded me from going to the youth club for a month and deducted four weeks of pocket money.

My defiance grew as I tried to claim my independence from his dogma. I hated how his rules were more lenient for Jacob and his judgement harsher on me. The worst judgement came when I dated one of Jacob's friends, Nigel. Nigel had been around our family for years and we knew his family well from church. For years, he and Jacob mercilessly teased me, but Nigel's jokes became flirtatious. It became obvious that we liked each other more than just friends. Jacob highly objected to his sister and friend dating, but when I was seventeen, Nigel and I kissed for the first time and it continued from there. After a while, Jacob got used to Nigel and I hanging out together and it was a time I looked back on with joy. Sadly, being together with Nigel lasted only three months. Not because we ended it, but because my father found out. I remained in complete shock for years at my father's reaction, forbidding me to see Nigel and accusing me of being a slut. Hearing him express himself so directly sent a pang of pain into my heart. A piece of me will never recover from the hurt.

After that, I dreamed of leaving home all the time. And not just leaving home, but leaving everything I knew, especially my father. From a young age, I had loved stories of travelling to mythical lands. The first I remember was *The Water Babies* by Charles Kingsley, which mother would read at bedtime. I never forgot Mrs. Doasyouwouldbedoneby and Mrs. Donebyasyoudid.

Mother had a velvet voice. I would dream of foreign and fantastical adventures. Once I started to read chapter books, I read *The Magical Adventures of the Wishing Chair* by Enid Blyton probably three times. Wanderlust set in even before puberty. I devoured C S. Lewis' *The Chronicles of Narnia*. I would lie on the grass in the sun and wander through the imaginations of great writers wishing I could just once see something more than the British suburbs I knew.

As I grew older my book collection became more sophisticated and my penchant for travelling to far-flung places became more apparent. I dived head first into *The City of Joy* by Dominique Lapierre and Freya Stark's *The Southern Gates* of Arabia. All the while, I would sneak back occasionally to *Narnia* or the tent of the sultan in *One Thousand and One Arabian Nights*.

The Professor ruffled his papers again. I anxiously bit my top lip.

Last night, as I drifted off to sleep, I had rehearsed the reasons and justifications for him to let me travel to a Middle Eastern country other than Yemen or Egypt. I was banking on Syria.

My presentation hinged on the fact that the Professor already knew I was different to the other nineteen students. He was the one who had interviewed me for a university place at Durham University, so he knew when I applied that I was working for the F.C.O. and had been posted to the British Embassy in Sana'a, Yemen Arab Republic.

I didn't have high hopes that I would be accepted with my dismal exam results, but soon after sending my application, I received a letter from The Professor requesting to interview me. As I couldn't attend in Durham, he called me at the Embassy in Sana'a. I was a bag of nerves, but when he asked me if I knew Arabic, I could utter some greetings which I had practised with my teacher.

"*Sabah al-kheir*. Good morning," I slightly stuttered.

"I'm impressed that you can speak Arabic." He had a deep voice, which suited such a man of great calibre.

"This is the first time I have interviewed a member of our dip-lo-matic service." He spoke with an air of venerability for the department .

Unconsciously, I started to wrap the long cord of my desk telephone around my index finger like a Chinese finger trap as I knew that he was taken in, in the same way my father was, by the stature that the word "diplomat" conveys. The truth is the title makes me feels uncomfortable as it more appropriately fits a career diplomat. Until I get a degree, I can't imagine that I'll be able to move up the ladder past the administrative level of this old boys' club.

"How long have you been working in the Embassy there?"

"Almost three years."

"Have you picked up any Yemeni words?"

"Maybe a couple. I have spoken to shopkeepers and taxi drivers. I don't know any Yemeni people."

"Who do you socialize with there?"

"To be honest, there's not many people here my age. I like to be with the teenager children of the senior diplomats who visit often from boarding school." I stopped. There was a silence. I pulled at the twisted telephone cord, releasing my finger and then stretched the coils out to an unsustainable position. My hands were sweaty. A thought flashed across my mind that I had blown this interview revealing too much immaturity but the truth was I liked hanging with the younger company rather than the parties I was obliged to go to with the stuffy diplomats."

"When did you join the Foreign Office?"

"Right after school in 1988. I joined as a D.S. grade 10 as my A-level results weren't good enough for a university like Durham." I pinched myself for volunteering that fact.

Ugh! Why do I do that?

"Well, that's of no importance. I have seen over the years that mature students, like yourself, who are giving up much more to attend university, have proved to be more dedicated to their studies. That being said, I would like to offer you an unconditional place at our Centre." He announced with little fanfare.

I muffled a screech of excitement.

"Really? *Shukran jazilan.* Oh my God, I'm so happy."

"My pleasure. I am looking forward to meeting you in September. Happy New Year, Elizabeth."

"Yes. See you soon and Happy New Year." As I put the receiver down, my jaw was still wide open.

Did that really happen? Am I now a student of Durham University? I danced around my dark office room clapping my hands for joy.

Sitting in The Professor's office, I had confidence that he would recall how much he believed in me, so I decided to forego my rehearsed speech and just launched straight into my question.

"Do you think it's possible for me to spend my year abroad in a different country than Yemen or Egypt?"

As part of our Arabic degree, students were required to spend the second year at school in an Arabic-speaking country. Over the years, the Centre for Middle Eastern and Islamic Studies sent its students to Tunisia, Jordan, Egypt and Yemen. The students usually went in groups to schools that CMEIS had established for their placement. Near the end of our first year we were given the option of either the International School in Sana'a or the British Council in Cairo.

"Why don't you want to go to Egypt?"

"After resigning from the F.C.O., I left Sana'a and went to Cairo before the term started in Durham. I did a month-long intensive Arabic course last July at the British Council. I lived in Zamalak while I was there. I'd like to study in a different country."

"I see." His smile faded to a look of well-practised commiseration. "I understand your predicament, but unfortunately, we don't have anywhere else to send students." He picked up another paper. I only had a second before the subject was closed.

"Do you send students to Lebanon?" I instinctively tugged my earlobe.

"Many years ago," he said pensively. "When the diplomatic service opened the Middle Eastern Centre For Arab Studies in Beirut, we sent some there, but it became known as a spy school. It was a great place for students to study as the dialect is the closest to modern standard Arabic which we teach here, but after MECAS closed, there were many kidnappings of westerners. Too dangerous for our students." He clucked his tongue.

"What about Syria?" I was pushing. I didn't want to live with the other students during the placement year.

"Well, one of our staff recently returned from Damascus, so let me talk to the rest of the faculty." He trailed off, picked up his pen, and started writing notes. I could tell that our conversation had concluded.

Days later, The Professor introduced some of the most well-known Arabic poets and authors. I must admit, I had never enjoyed my English literature classes at secondary school. Our English literature teacher, Sister Beatrice, did not spark any interest in me with any English poets or authors. Perhaps this was due to her lacklustre way of teaching the same stuff year in and year out, or perhaps, it was simply that her monotone voice put me to sleep.

The Professor was different; he had a sense of humour. On the first day, he had asked us if anyone knew any famous Arab poets or authors. Of course, almost everyone had heard of *One Thousand and One Arabian Nights*, but apart from that, there was very little response. Then he laughed.

"Hasn't anyone heard of the Prophet

Muhammed?"

That day, The Professor was discussing the work of the writer Adonis.

"Tom, pass these papers out." The Professor handed a chubby, red-faced boy a stack of papers.

I was drawn to Adonis partly due to his name, which was sexy, and partly because he had been born in Syria and lived in Lebanon.

Perhaps I could meet him if I were to go there.

"The paper you have has a list of names and some examples of their work."

I flicked through the stapled pages.

The Professor started to read about Adonis. As he read, I hoped his choice of including Adonis was a sign that I was going to go to Damascus.

"Ali Ahmad Said Esber, who is more commonly known as Adonis, wrote *The Book of Siege* shortly after the Israeli invasion into Lebanon in 1982…" The Professor kept talking and I looked down at the page, reading one of Adonis' poems. It stirred something in me Milton never had.

When class ended, The Professor motioned for me to stay behind as my classmates bumped their way clumsily through the door.

"Elizabeth, I've spoken with the rest of the lecturers about the possibility of sending you to Damascus. Actually, a couple of years ago, Mr. Dickerson attended the Arabic Teaching Institute for Foreigners in Damascus on his own reconnaissance. At that time, it was a school of good calibre, but we know nothing about it now, nor have we sent any of our students there. We are willing to allow you to go there, but…"

I clasped my hands in surprise and joy.

"But," he reiterated sternly, "you should register at the school before the beginning of the term next year. In any case, we recommend that you travel early to establish yourself."

The word "establish" concerned me. I ran possible meanings through my head: to settle and make roots, to set up and organise, to demonstrate and prove, to pronounce and declare. It was a heavy word. As mother often reminded us, "You make your bed, you sleep in it."

The worry kept me up at night. I usually slept through any disruptions from students walking home along The Bailey from college bars, but for several nights following my conversation with The Professor, the raucous shouts and loud voices jolted me from my sleep. Then, in the early hours of the morning, my tired mind wandered into fearful scenarios where I would be alone and helpless. During the day, I convinced myself they were just nightmares that were too far-fetched. For several days, I was emotionally torn between the thrill and the trepidation of the unknown.

I had never been truly alone. In fact, I had never been in charge of my own decisions. At home, of course, my father was the head of the household, although my mother would say otherwise. In Yemen, the diplomatic community was a protective bubble. In Cairo, other students had provided me with the wherewithal to live there. So now I was heading into a foreign land with barely any knowledge and as master of my own destiny. I partly relished the prospect of being untethered, but there were still lingering voices of doubt.

Now that I had the opportunity to go I had one more hurdle to jump - telling my parents. I had a sinking feeling that they would say no mainly because they thought the same as me and didn't have the confidence that I could succeed.

Once I had mentioned my dream of backpacking around Europe. Laughing, my father said I'd only last a week before I lost my passport.

"St. Anthony must be getting rich with all the things you lose and then have to pay into the poor box every Sunday."

I'm going to settle in Damascus.

I'm going to organise my tuition.

I'm going to prove I'm independent.

I'm going to declare I'm the first Durham student to do it.

Perhaps.

10 July 1992

Dear Diary,
Oh I hate this! I've got to go to dad to ask for money. It's so annoying. How can £6,000 dwindle so quickly? Of course, when I ask him he's going to give his opinion and I'm pretty sure I know what that will be. It's hard enough wrangling with my own mind, without having dad on my case. I just want his money! That sounds so bad!

He's going to ask if I've been to the library and yes I have. Only found one book on Syria and it was useless. Thank goodness for W.H. Smith bookstore. There's a travel book on Syria and Jordan by Lonely Planet. Funny, because it's called a survival kit. It's brilliant! There's nothing about the school in there, but at least it's got stuff about hotels and banks. I'll try the cheap hotels. My savings have to last a long time. Oh Lord, I have to take traveller's cheques and cash. I hope I don't get robbed! Nightmare! I'd really be stuck a long way from home. Reminder buy a bumbag!

No-one is going to believe it when I tell them I'm going to Syria! They'll probably think I'm joking or lying. I'm not even sure I can do this, but I have to now. The Professor believes in me. There's no way I can change my mind now. Anyway, I'll just move on to Cairo, if it doesn't work out in Damascus. I'm

never going back to Sana'a. Too many
memories there and John's still there.

Four

Following my talk with the Professor, I decided the best time to approach my parents was after Sunday dinner, when my father was feeling most relaxed, full from a roast dinner and hopefully humbled by the sermon from the priest.

Sundays at home had always been very traditional. Sundays were a day of rest, beginning with attending and celebrating morning Mass, followed by sports on the television, Sunday dinner and then the news. My father came from a strict Roman Catholic upbringing that he more than tried passing on to us, ushering the family to attend church every Sunday and sending me to a Catholic school. We prayed before meals, had Bibles on our bedside tables and crosses on the wall. I had not been home on a Sunday in a while, and hadn't been to Mass in longer, so my parents knew something was up.

Although I didn't need their permission to go to Syria, I was in need of monetary help. Since starting work, I had never asked for financial help and I was loathe to ask. I had always been frugal with money, but university life was expensive. From a young age, I saved every penny I could find.

"Why are you picking up that dirty penny?" Jacob would ask, as I bent down to reach into a muddy puddle for a coin.

"It's not a penny. It's 10p. I'm going to put it in my piggy bank."

"Oh, you're so rich," he snarked.

"Well, mum says that if you look after the pennies, then the pounds will look after themselves." I poked my tongue out at him. My mum instilled in me many wise words.

My savings from the F.C.O. had almost dried up paying for my first-year accommodation and tuition. I had to turn to Father.

"Mum, Dad, I need to talk to you." They were sitting comfortably on the sofa after the evening news had finished. Mother stopped folding the laundry and looked up at me. She knew something was coming and was waiting for it.

"Yes, darling. Of course." Mother was always sitting up and tugged on my father's arm. He looked as if he was about to doze off.

"The university has agreed to send me to a different country than the other students. I'm set to go to Syria."

"To Syria?" Mother looked alarmed. "Wasn't it in Syria that Hezbollah kidnapped westerners?"

"No. That was in Lebanon and they have been released now, mum. And anyway, it's no more dangerous than living in Sana'a for three years."

"Syria? On your own?" Father's sleepy eyes now opened to slits.

"Yes."

"Do you know much about the place?" Father unfolded his arms, which had been resting across his chest, coming around to full wakefulness.

"Yes. I bought a book at W.H. Smith and it's got lots of stuff for travellers." I stated gladly, proving my preparedness.

"Yes. Exactly for travellers. You can't live there!" Father stated emphatically. I had a feeling that he was questioning my capability more than my safety. I rubbed at my ear irritably.

"Why do you say that?" I raised my voice.

"Because you..." he paused for a moment. He looked across at my mother, who was frowning at him.

"You'll be unprotected. There's no diplomatic status for you as a student and that worries me."

"Oh, well, I'll be fine," I replied, lowering my voice. I hadn't expected him to be worried. "I'll check in with the British Embassy in Damascus and make sure I register with them. I'm capable of looking after myself now. I've lived in more countries than you have, and in London, so I think I will be fine. Anyway, if it doesn't work out I can join the other students in Cairo."

"Well, I don't know so much," he huffed.

"The Professor said there is a school in Damascus that Durham students went to a few years ago." I decided to bend the truth. "He said he was impressed with my studies so far this year and because I had already been to Yemen and Egypt, he was willing to let me go to the school there."

"So, you're the only student he's recommended to go to Damascus?" Father, who usually looked stern with his naturally downturned mouth, raised his eyebrows in curiosity as he reconsidered the proposal.

"Yes. He said the other students haven't travelled as much as me and I've achieved the highest grades in my spoken Arabic this year."

"Well, that's very good." My father did not waste compliments. I smiled. I wanted to elaborate on how hard I had studied at university and how I had not partied all night unlike many other students, but I stopped myself. When I called home, I rarely spoke to my father. Mother and I had long conversations on the phone in which I'd tell her how well I was doing each time. I think she shared our conversations with father, which was how most subjects were dealt with in our family.

"I'd really like to go soon, but I need to buy an airline ticket. I wondered if you could help me as I don't have enough right now." I was nervous to bring it up. Money was taboo. I had always assumed my father made a comfortable living, but talking about it was considered impolite.

At this point, my mother knew it wasn't her position to comment on loaning or granting money, so she folded some more clothes. I waited for what felt like a couple of minutes. Then he leaned down to the carpet and picked up *The Sunday Times*. My stomach sank. He shuffled the pages in silence for a moment. Then, finally he spoke.

"You know the best place to look is in the travel section here." He flicked through the sections and pulled out the travel section. "There are tons of advertisements with worldwide airfares."

"But, I thought there were just bucket shops in there. Aren't they dodgy?"

The bucket shops were known to offer the cheapest fares available. Many people were cautious about using them, in fear of being scammed, but they were known to beat all other prices offered by either travel agencies or phoning airlines directly.

"I'll make some phone calls and we'll figure out how much the ticket will be."

Mother was looking more and more worried as father perused the pages and finally she blurted out, "I don't think this is a good idea. You might get kidnapped."

"Mum, no-one has ever been kidnapped in Syria. You're thinking of Lebanon."

"Then, you have to promise me you'll never travel to Lebanon."

"I don't think I will." I shrugged my shoulders.

"Now I remember. Lebanon is where they held Terry Waite. I want to hear you say you won't there." Her voice was shrill.

Terry Waite was the assistant and emissary for the Archbishop of Canterbury in the eighties and was kidnapped in 1987 and held for five years in Lebanon.

"I won't, mother. I promise."

"Thank you, sweetheart." Comforted by my assurance, she picked up a towel and resumed her folding.

My parents had only travelled by ferry to France when they took us on a family vacation to Quimper in Brittany. They were not aware that the border between Syria and Lebanon was open because the Syrian Army occupied Lebanon. They were only passingly aware of Syria in the first place.

"What's the name of your professor?" my father asked from behind the fully spread newspaper.

"Professor Mansfield." I knew he wanted to tell his Rotary Club friends the whole story.

"Here we are." He slapped the paper. "In comparison to British Airways, Lufthansa or Air France, the cheapest ticket is with Syrian Arab Airlines," he announced. That was as close to a "yes, dear" as I was going to get.

"What about the suspension?" my mother asked. There was worry in her voice. "It was that...Hindawi Incident or Affair or some such..."

"Years ago, dear," my father said, patting her knee.

Syrian Arab Airlines had only recently resumed its services to London. It had been compelled to suspend them following tension between the UK and Syria resulting from the Hindawi Affair in 1986. It wasn't until 1991, when I was still working in the British Embassy in Yemen, that Syria backed the US-led coalition of the invasion into Iraq following Iraq's invasion of Kuwait. It was then the airlines' services to Heathrow opened again.

"Look, I could buy a return ticket directly to Damascus in two weeks for £384, but the next closest price on the other airlines is almost twice that." Father was pointing to the advertisement on the page, but I was still savouring the fact that he said "I". I was beginning to feel hopeful that he might offer to buy my ticket. "On British Airways it would cost over £800. That's probably even more expensive by the time we book your ticket."

He's going to help.

I was a young teenager when I first understood that my father's head utterly ruled his heart. As an idealistic adolescent, I dreamt of falling in love with my future husband whether he was a dustbin man or a brain surgeon. Money did not matter to me, as long as I was hopelessly in love. I thought mother and father had fallen in love that way when they first met. There must have been a time when they were deeply in love with each other. Then one day my dream was shattered. Mother was joking with father about why they got married.

"Your father fell in love with me at first sight because he thought I looked like Vera Lynn. He had a picture of her taped to his wall."

"Yes, you looked like her, but I was more interested that you were a Catholic with a respectable family name."

Mother laughed trying to convey that father was only joking, but he was being totally serious. Despite her laugh, I could see that her feelings were hurt and she was astonished that he admitted that in front of me in such a matter of fact way, instead of leaving me with the belief that her beauty captivated him. I knew that the man I would fall in love with would be utterly romantic and passionate – the complete opposite of my father.

"So, I'll call this bucket shop, Swindon Cheap Fares, tomorrow and get your ticket. It's probably better not to travel during the weekend, so we're probably looking at a Tuesday or Wednesday. That's the 24th or the 25th of August."

"Either one is fine," I grinned. The deal was sealed. Mother still looked worried, but father patted her on the knee again and flipped over to the football scores.

Five

After passing my final exams with distinction, I was ready to take my first step towards by applying for my student visa at the Embassy of the Syrian Arab Republic in London. I emerged into daylight from Knightsbridge Tube station and looked around. I knew Harrods, the prestigious and famous London store, was located here, but I was too anxious to check how far the embassy was from the Tube.

I felt disoriented and pulled out my London map. It was awkward to fold and find the right spot. I put my finger on Belgrave Square.

"Now I just need to make a right onto Sloane Street and then the third left," I reassured myself.

The terraced houses on Belgrave Square, dating back to 1820, were grand and noble. Dominated by embassies and consulates, the Square was one of the most expensive property areas in London.

As I walked along the west side of the Square, I passed mansions to the left and right. Belgrave Square Garden, in the centre, was full of trees and bushes laden with foliage and summer flowers. I noticed several flags flying from the balconies above the porticos of the houses. I read the signs: The Finnish Embassy, German Embassy, Austrian Embassy, Portuguese Embassy and then finally the Embassy of the Syrian Arab Republic. I walked up the steps past the columns and faced the black door.

It felt strange to be on the receiving end and be the applicant. Only a couple of years ago, I was the Assistant Visa Officer in the British Embassy in Yemen. On arrival, I was the Radio Communications Officer, but a year into my job, the FCO informed me that I was to undergo training in visa procedures. It came as a shock when I was instructed to attend a month-long visa course in Hanslope Gardens in Milton Keynes. It was a gruelling intensive course. We went through volumes and volumes of diplomatic service procedures.

In the end, it all boiled down to investigating the reasons and legitimacy of all applicants wanting to travel to England. We had to suspect everyone. An applicant had to have a valid return air ticket, enough money to last for the duration of their stay, a reason to return to their homeland (most commonly a job or family), and not to be listed in the Black Book. The Black Book was a ring binder with pages and pages of names, nationalities, and birth dates of people the Foreign and Commonwealth Office suspected were a threat. These people, for whatever reason, were denied visas and the visa section in our embassies worldwide would alert London of the application.

Updated pages for the binder arrived regularly in the diplomatic bag along with mail for expatriates. The diplomatic bag was our way to receive goods and letters from home and confidential, classified documents for the embassy sections. After that, it was down to intuition and detective work during an interview to determine the validity of an application.

When I started my new role in Sana'a, I soon discovered that being an Assistant Visa Officer in the YAR was nothing like the interview scenarios I had acted out in class. During the first week, I was eager and ready to apply all the Diplomatic Service Procedures I had learned, but neither the volumes of instructions, nor the regulations, nor even the interviewing practice had prepared me for how tricky some people would be.

One Monday morning, the Visa Office opened as normal and the waiting room filled up with Yemeni men. I sat beside Abu, a handsome, local man with marvellous eyes, who was speaking to a Yemeni man from behind a bulletproof glass panel. The applicant was exceedingly scruffy. He wore a suit jacket and a collared shirt that looked as though it had not been washed in months. Under the jacket he wore a *futah*, which resembled a sarong.

Abu looked over the application and checked that all the boxes were filled. He then asked about the parts that had been missed. He asked for proof, in accordance with our DSP visa procedures. When Abu asked about funds, the applicant produced a large, paper bag full of loose rials. The quantity looked, to anyone who didn't know better, like plenty of money to travel for the entire month during which the tourist visa was valid, but in fact, it only amounted to around one hundred pounds. When the man opened the bag, my nostrils were immediately invaded by the smell of the money. The unmistakable odour quickly filled the air. It was sweet with hints of oil, sweat, and earth. In the end, the applicant failed to pass muster and he sulked out of the embassy.

Abu ushered the next applicant up to the window for questioning. When he asked the new applicant about money, the man produced a paper bag. By the fourth man, it became apparent that this very same bag was being passed from one applicant to the next.

I laughed to myself standing in front of the Syrian Embassy. When the door opened, I entered a large hallway with a grand, spiral staircase. I walked into the waiting room on the left. It was spacious and light with comfortable seating. The décor was spare and nondescript. The only indication that the room was in a Syrian Embassy were a few spare posters: a Roman theatre in Bosra, a crusader's castle called Crac Des Chevaliers, the Umayyad Mosque and Islamic minarets in Damascus.

I was seen without having to wait very long and was ushered into an interview room. I sat across from a Syrian gentleman dressed in a Giovanni, grey suit and smelling of expensive aftershave. He was handsome and had jet-black hair and a chiselled, clean-shaven jaw.

He introduced himself as the vice-consular officer and shook my hand. His hand was firm and well-muscled. I handed him my application and my British passport, and he laid them in front of him on his dark, mahogany desk.

I had been asked to give up my diplomatic passport when I resigned from the Foreign and Commonwealth Office. Our own vice-consular officer, Mr. McCabe, had issued my new, non-diplomatic passport before I left my posting. The only thing different from a regular passport was a diplomatic one had an official stamp on the inside cover. I felt exposed with just a regular, citizen's passport even though it looked the same. It had a black, hard cover and a small window for the passport holder's name penned inside. It had Her Majesty's crest embossed in gold on the front. The embassy had recently received a batch of new, European Union passports with a burgundy floppy cover. Mr. McCabe had said I could have had one, but I didn't like them. Thankfully, he had kept a small batch of the black ones for staff and still, in 1991, had a couple left.

"Miss Elizabeth Booth." The Syrian vice-consular officer was disinterestedly reading the little book in front of him. He went quiet, but kept looking up at me every so often.

A moment later, he abruptly pulled his chair closer to his desk, put his chin in his left hand and leaned on his elbow. I wasn't sure if he was about to question me, or was simply thinking deeply about the meaning of my name.

"You were born in Chester." I wasn't sure if I was meant to say anything so I simply smiled and nodded. He turned to the back page. I pinched on my earlobe, hoping to hide my creeping nervousness.

"I see you have already travelled to Egypt." His finger drummed his chin.

"Yes. I took Arabic lessons there."

"Why do you want to travel to Syria?"

I twisted my stud earring.

"I'm a student at Durham University and for my second year I can study in the Middle East. I decided to go to Damascus." My ears were hot.

"And you want to travel in the next few weeks?" He was staring at me now.

"Yes. I hope to go by the end of August." I wanted to add that the other students had already left for Egypt and Yemen and that I didn't want to go with them, but decided I should not talk too much. My mother always said I talked more when I was nervous. He marked my papers.

"Where are you going to stay?"

His pen was poised to write again, but honestly, I had no idea.

"I'm going to find a hotel when I get there." I hoped I sounded convincing.

"Good. Good." He stood up and indicated the door by waving his hand towards it. The interview was over.

Back in the waiting room, I once again found myself staring at the posters and hoping I would eventually see those things in person.

I could not tell from his actions whether the vice-consular officer was going to accept or deny my application.

Before long, a lady came into the waiting room. She handed my passport to me. I was relieved. I fingered through the pages and found the month visa on the page after my Egyptian one.

Six

My alarm clock went off in the early hours of the morning. I got dressed in my comfortable, black jogging trousers and my favourite, grey sweatshirt. In the kitchen, mother was already up and had made herself her black tea with no sugar. We didn't talk as I poured milk over my bran flakes. My mind was mentally running through the list of items I had packed. I had my fluffy socks I used to pad around the house, some changes of clothes, a couple of books, and my Walkman with some tapes (most importantly my most listened-to album, *Watermark* by Enya).

It was hard to think that I would be carrying a year's supply of belongings in my rucksack. I had packed it as full as I could until the zip almost bust. I had a vague idea how cold it got in Syria, but I had barely any real information. I only knew of one person who had lived there, but being one of my lecturers he came across as unapproachable when he scurried into class and hurried out without making much eye contact with any students. I packed mostly light, loose-fitting, summery clothes: a few pairs of trousers, some long skirts, many T-shirts, and a couple of long-sleeved shirts. I could only fit in one sweatshirt and a light jacket. I knew that my attire would have to be modest in a predominantly Muslim country, so I didn't bother packing any shorts or swimming costumes.

I had decided to pack for Syria as if I were going to live in Yemen again. I had no idea whether commodities were as hard to buy there as they had been in Yemen, so just in case, I jammed in the largest tube of Colgate toothpaste, a family size bottle of

Vosene shampoo, Johnson's baby moisturiser and six rolls of toilet paper. I had only been able to resupply my clothes and toiletries in Yemen whenever I, or someone from the embassy or expat community travelled to London.

I remember when I lived in Sana'a I was excited because I discovered a grocery shop on Zubairy Street that sold a couple of recognisable brands of toothpaste. I picked up the red and white box with the Colgate logo on it, with the name also in Arabic and Chinese script.

"Kam?" I held it up and asked the shopkeeper how much it was.

"*Alf wa ishreen.*" I wasn't about to buy toothpaste for thirty pounds. Imported goods from China always had inflated prices, in addition to the extra that was added because I was a foreigner. As with all diplomats, I depended on the short trips I was given to carry the diplomatic bags on bag runs to the Foreign and Commonwealth Office in London. I managed to renew my wardrobe during those short trips and I relished the chance to browse through Boots, the chemist. I often came back to Sana'a with a suitcase full of new stuff and some for others who had asked me to buy them some familiar items. That was something I would miss in Syria, as I knew I wouldn't be coming home until the end of the academic year.

It was still dark when my mother and I pulled up to the bus station in Plymouth. The four-hour journey in the coach to London Heathrow was tedious. I wished I could have caught a train to London, but it was "too expensive". Father insisted on economy. I had booked the earliest coach from Bretonside Bus

Station direct to London Heathrow. Mother dropped me off and helped me unload my rucksack onto the tarmac beside the coach's storage compartments. I was excited to be starting my new journey. Mother's ears were burning. She smiled weakly. We hugged goodbye. I was excited, but I felt a hitch in my breathing. I was really leaving.

"Please be careful and remember to call home and let us know when you have a contact number so we can reach you. Here, take this Saint Christopher charm. It'll keep you safe while you travel." Mother handed me the small silver medallion and I slipped it on.

"Thank you, Mum. I'll write to you soon. I'm sure it's cheaper than a phone call."

"I'll look forward to your letters. I'll be thinking about you every day."

"Don't worry, Mum. I'll be fine."

I knew my mother worried a lot about me. The family called her a worrywart making fun. I knew her concern for me probably caused her sleepless nights like the ones she admitted to when Jacob went on a school exchange to Berlin with a German student for a week.

I had a nagging feeling I had forgotten something. I had ticked off all the items on my list. I remembered I didn't pack a coat because I didn't have room and hoped I would be able to get one there. According to my travel guide, the winters were harsh.

I took a window seat and as the scenery flashed by me, I daydreamed about Damascus.

Seven

As the plane taxied to the runway, the loudspeaker played the Islamic *salat*, prayer for travellers. I noticed the two men in the aisle seats opposite me were bowing their heads and clutching their *tasbih*, prayer beads, as they muttered the 99 names of Allah under their breath. I hoped their prayers were flying up to heaven and helping protect us. I had never been a nervous flyer, but every little bit helped. I smiled and ran my finger over my St. Christopher medallion.

Shortly after take off, I met eyes with the two gentlemen who had been praying and they smiled. They were businessmen. I felt strangely at ease with the passengers almost as if I was assimilating myself into the culture in preparation. Most of the passengers were Syrians: families, friends and businessmen. There were no other single women travelling.

It seemed many of the passengers knew each other as they passed up and down the aisle greeting each other like old friends and spending time chatting. It reminded me of the conversations between parishioners after a Mass. The ambience was friendly and warm. Another gentleman stopped by the two men opposite me and they shook hands and touched cheeks in a similar way to how the French greet. They had a lengthy conversation and I was surprised when the man turned to me and introduced himself.

"Hello. I'm Asim, and I am your host." He smiled. His English was perfect and with a hint of a Syrian accent. He was handsome for an older gentleman with a full head of speckled grey and black hair. He had a fit body considering his age, which I guessed was about 45 years. He wore a light grey suit and red tie. On his lapel, I noticed the Syrian Arab

Airlines motif, and then it clicked that he was working on the plane especially as I realised there were no female hostesses. He leaned in closer. I almost felt his breath on my cheek.

"Can I get you a drink and something to eat?" I wondered why he wasn't pulling a drinks trolley with him serving all the passengers. It made me feel very special.

"Yes, I'd love an orange juice," I said and then thanked him, proudly using my best Arabic pronunciation. "*Shukran.*"

"Ahhh, you speak Arabic!" He pulled away and smiled broadly like a proud father. He turned to his two friends and spoke Arabic to them. He turned back to me.

"This is Adnan and Hassan who also work for the airline," Asim gestured to the businessmen who were both leaning forward and nodding their heads at me.

"*Ana ismi* Elizabeth," I said, introducing myself. "*Ahlan wa sahlan.*"

I remembered the first time I learnt the literal meaning of the phrase *ahlan wa sahlan*, one of the most common greetings. It was during my summer in Cairo.

"*Ahlan* is the word for family and *sahlan* means a grassy piece of lowland," my teacher told the class.

"Family and a piece of land?" one student had interjected. "That is a strange way of saying welcome."

"The phrase comes from the Bedouin culture. Bedu means desert dwellers and is another name for Bedouin. The people lived in harsh, desert conditions, moving their tents to the best locations often near an oasis or flat lowlands for water."

"I get it," I asserted. "They welcomed a stranger to all that they had: their family and their tent pitched in a good spot."

"Exactly. If a traveller came across them they would never turn him away."

"But why do they still say that today?" a tall student in the back asked smirking. "City dwellers don't have tents."

"Well, the ancient Bedouin values of courage, honour, and hospitality have been passed on through generations. Today, Arabs still feel it's a moral obligation to make a guest as welcome and as comfortable as possible."

I was struck then (and again as I talked to Asim, Adnan and Hassan) by how friendly the Arab people were.

I discovered that Adnan was thirty-one years old and Hassan was forty. My new friends all lived in Damascus and were travelling back from a conference in London. In fact, they added, the reason many of the passengers knew each other was because most worked for Syrian Arab Airlines. I wondered if Adnan and Hassan were also flight attendants as there were no female attendants on the flight. Also, I never saw a drinks or food trolley the entire journey. It appeared that Asim personally served his friends and I the whole time.

Each time that Asim passed me, he smiled. He would ask if I needed anything and removed any rubbish laying on my table. I felt pampered. I took my jacket off and stepped out of my seat to place it above. Asim was quickly by my side wanting to do it for me. I sat back down and I pulled out a pair of warm socks. I placed my shoes underneath me and reflected that this was much easier than I had imagined.

"So where did you learn your Arabic?" Hassan asked.

"Oh, I'm a student. I'm studying at Durham University. This year is the year all the students get sent to the Middle East to learn the language more fluently."

"Are there more of you?" he smiled.

"No just me." I giggled slightly.

"So, you are travelling alone?" He raised his thick eyebrows.

"Yes. But when I found out I was coming to Syria, I bought the only book I could find for tourists. Even my professors didn't know much about your country."

"Well, we are more than happy to help you and welcome you to our country." He was very formal, but also reassuring. It was hard to tell if this was because he worked for the airline, or if it was just general kindness stemming from tradition.

"The Syrian people will take great care of you," Adnan added.

The conversation flowed for a few minutes as they talked about their backgrounds.

"My wife and I got married in Aleppo last year," Hassan said. "She is living there with my family, although we also have a home in Damascus. You must come and visit us in Aleppo when you get a chance."

I asked Hassan about some hotels on the list that I had picked up at the Syrian Embassy. He said that the Intercontinental was one of the best. Damascus wasn't a popular tourist destination, so there were not many hotels. Most hotels were expensive and meant for business travellers. I had hoped to find some cheap hotels that backpackers would use, but neither of my new acquaintances knew of any such places.

Asim soon joined the conversation. He seemed adamant about helping.

"There are major hotels in Damascus, but I think many of them are fully booked because of various events and conferences like the upcoming Pan Arab Games that are going on in the city." Asim stood between the rows leaning on the back of my chair. Hassan and Adnan looked up in confusion. Asim smiled at me.

"Yes. Rooms are very hard to find right now."

This revelation made me worried and I wondered whether I was going to find anywhere to sleep. I was frowning when Asim laid his hand on my shoulder.

"Don't worry. There's a woman further back in the plane who would welcome you to her home. She is a good friend of mine and you will be well taken care of." I looked back to try and see who he might be talking about, but the airline seats blocked my view.

With that reassurance, Asim left my side and as we flew into the sunset, I settled down feeling comfortable again and fell asleep.

When I woke up, we were about to start our descent into Damascus. Asim brought me a coffee and some pastries, but I could barely eat. I was so excited. On the edge of my excitement was a tinge of fear, but I pushed it down.

"It is all taken care of," Asim said. "You'll be going with Umm Shabaan and her family when you land."

I was surprised there wasn't much discussion about it. I had yet to be able to catch a glimpse of my soon-to-be host. I really wasn't going to say no given the circumstances, but then again, I wasn't given the choice. I did feel extremely honoured to be invited to someone's home when I was a complete stranger. Asim explained emphatically that my host was well respected. After all that he was doing for me on the flight and now helping me with my arrival, I wasn't about to refuse. Plus, I knew that it would have been unforgivable to refuse their hospitality.

The Arab people are known for their friendliness and generosity towards foreigners. I remember once, at the Foreign and Commonwealth Office, the ambassador told me to never openly admire something that an Arab person had in their possession because they would feel obliged by custom to give it to you even if it meant the world to them. Once, at his residence, the ambassador had met with a Yemeni tribal leader and some other Yemeni men. As usual they were chewing *qat*, which makes one feel very relaxed. During the informal conversation, he inadvertently admired the *jambiyah*, the ceremonial dagger hanging from the belt of the tribal leader, because of the exquisite embroidery and beaten silver on the handle. Naturally, the tribal leader handed it to him. The ambassador told me what a dilemma that put him in because, not only are diplomats not allowed to accept gifts, but also he knew that the handle was made of rhinoceros' horn and would therefore be illegal in any other country. He told me that it was a moment of thoughtlessness probably caused by the *qat*, the leaves of which were ever-present at Yemeni business meetings and social gatherings.

The descent into Damascus was fascinating. I was glued to the small window watching the mountains, deserts, and vast, uninhabited land draw closer and closer. Asim spoke on the overhead speaker in Arabic letting the passengers know that they needed to prepare for landing. He spoke clearly and slowly, which made his Arabic easy to follow. I wondered if that was for my benefit.

I started to feel nervous as I always did while landing. I busied myself by gathering my belongings that were spread around the empty seats next to me. I unzipped my bag and zipped it back up several times as I thought of something else I could do. I took my fluffy socks off. I reached down to find my shoes, but only found one at first. Feeling more anxiety, I fumbled around under the seats feeling crumbs and sticky substances with my fingertips. I grabbed my shoe with relief, and I slipped the pair onto my bare feet.

Remember, Elizabeth, you can do this. You will establish yourself in Damascus and prove to your family, your parents, and your teachers that you are a success. You will make your father proud. There was a distinct urge, born of habit and upbringing, to say amen after my little self-assurance. I smiled at myself. Maybe I'm more Catholic than I realise.

I looked to my friends across the aisle for reassurance. Hassan looked down at my clenched hand on the armrest. He smiled and gave me a thumbs up over the roaring back thrust of the engines.

You've already made some friends. Things are going to be okay.

Eight

As I got off the plane, the warm air hit me like opening an oven. The airport was overwhelmingly bright. The pillars were white marble, the floors were white tile, and all the other elaborate architecture was white. In contrast, I noticed that the women were all dressed in black. I was surprised to see a lady and her friends that had looked westernised on the plane, were now draped in black *abayas*, cloaks that now covered their clothes.

Many of the women in the airport also wore black *niqab*, which covered all their face only leaving a slit for their eyes. These women were most likely Shiite followers, as their adherents followed stricter dress codes. It felt more foreboding than what I had been used to in Yemen. Although a few Yemeni women were veiled and wore black, most others wore the *sitarah*, a traditional cover which was boldly coloured with blue, red and yellow. It reminded me of the material used for kaftans, African dresses. I walked past two ladies emptying rubbish bins into a cart and cleaning the floor around it. They were shrouded in black.

On my way through passport control, I noticed the large number of army personnel in green uniforms. The passport officers were dressed in black suits. There was a tense and sombre atmosphere amongst the foreign passengers waiting to pass through. As Professor Mansfield had told me, upon entering Syria, passports were checked primarily to see if the holder had travelled to Israel, which would result in an automatic denial of entry.

Asim walked just ahead of me. He was trying desperately to keep up with a woman, who I assumed

53

was Umm Shabaan, and her entourage. I was relieved when Asim turned to me and took my passport, moving us ahead of the line of foreigners quietly waiting their turns. He had a quick conversation with one of the passport control officers. Asim seemed authoritative with the officer and dramatically waved my passport at him.

I was surprised he was so daring, but it worked. Then he escorted me out of the passport hall, and we rejoined the entourage in baggage claim. I was beginning to think that Umm Shabaan was a much more important person than Asim had let on. He still had not introduced us, but she looked over at me and tilted her head in acknowledgement.

Outside, the sun had already set. My first views of Syria were of a poorly lit main road into Damascus. Asim and I were in a taxi following Umm Shabaan's car. I stared out the window, consciously trying to keep myself from pressing close enough to the glass to fog it up like a little kid.

The countryside was bleak and bare. Occasionally, out in the darkness, I saw long driveways lit up by strings of fairy lights and large buildings at the end, brightly shining with neon pink and blue lights. Later, I was told that these were restaurants. Soon, we approached the outskirts of Damascus proper. We pulled in to our destination and Asim hurried me out of the vehicle. I was grateful he paid and thanked him.

Umm Shabaan's home was beautiful. I entered a formal living room that was crowded with people. I could hear Arabic conversations all around me, but I couldn't focus on one word. They were speaking quickly and using words I could only assume were regional or slang. Lost in the fog of half-understood words, I found a place for myself out of the way.

I sat down on a beautiful high backed chair with a gold seat cover and ornate arms, that looked as if it had been styled for Louis XIV. All the furniture was gaudy and so ornate that they would look more in place in Versailles Palace. Asim brought me some sweet cardamom tea and placed it on the low table in front of me. I felt very nervous even though he was trying to make me as comfortable as possible. I smiled at everyone, hoping no one would address me in their quick dialect.

Eventually, Asim introduced me to his brother, Naguib, who looked much younger than him and at least three inches taller with an extra twenty pounds of muscle. Naguib looked to be in his mid-twenties and had black hair and a chiselled face. The room was full of other gentlemen and women who were greeting everyone arriving from the airport. The atmosphere was like a family reunion. Naguib smiled at me. His teeth were straight and white. His chin had a thin trace of a dimple above a goatee beard. I liked him instantly.

As I sipped my small cup of tea, I looked around the dining room. The furniture was elegant. There two couches, each with uniquely handcrafted wooden panels at the back and matching gold, padded seats. The side tables were made with inlaid mother-of-pearl. The floors were covered with rich, deep-red Persian carpets. A large chandelier brightly lit the room. I wished it were darker as my eyes were so tired and I was ready for bed. I still was not clear about what was being arranged for me, or where I might be sleeping. I assumed I would be staying with Umm Shabaan, but when Asim suddenly announced that he was leaving, I was taken by surprise. He and his brother gathered my heavy rucksack and told me it was time to go. The room had emptied out and friends and family were making their way to their own homes. I had not even greeted the lady of the house.

"Where am I going?"

"Do not worry. We are taking you to a very nice family who want you to live with them." I was shocked. I had thought the arraignments had already been made. Perhaps I had done something to offend. Asim was trying to reassure me as he carried my rucksack down the stone steps into the hot night air. I was so tired that I followed without asking any more questions.

Naguib and Asim drove me a few miles in Naguib's car. We appeared to be travelling from a residential neighbourhood in the suburbs of Damascus further into the heart of the city. The streets became more crowded with buildings.

When we stopped at a traffic light, I looked up to see a picture of Assad's head covering the entire side of a building. He was wearing a suit and tie. I hadn't seen a picture of him until then and noticed how unusually big his forehead was. Of course, that was an observation I was not likely to share.

The main streets were brightly lit. We passed an expensive-looking hotel and I wondered if that was one I could have stayed in. We turned again and again into smaller and smaller streets. The small shopfronts had heavy, metal shutters that were pulled down to the ground. I tried to read the Arabic on the commercial signs above them, but I was too slow. I was beginning to wonder if I really was good enough to make my way here on my own. Panic poked around the back of my mind, but my general exhaustion kept it at bay. That was a problem for the morning.

Eventually, we pulled to a stop in front of a four-storey building. There was no pavement. On the corner was a large, circular kiosk which still had its lights on and an open serving window. A few men were gathered around it, smoking and drinking tea. Waiting outside the building was a man who greeted Asim with a huge hug and handshake. He did not shake my hand, but said "welcome" to me.

"This is Abu Kersch." Asim smiled at me. "His name means 'the father of stomachs'." Asim turned to the other men and all three of them laughed together. I assumed that was his nickname and it fit him well.

Abu Kersch was a middle-aged, bald man with a pot belly that protruded from the polyester trousers clinched tightly at his waist. He was breathing heavily and I could see sweat patches under the armpits of his white T-shirt. He ushered us towards a large, black door beside a shopfront. Inside, we climbed a flight of stone steps to another door. Abu Kersch entered.

We all took our shoes off by the door. It was dark. The narrow hallway led into a small living room. In the living room, there was a woman dressed in a long, flowery dress that looked like a nightdress. Her hair was hidden under a white scarf. She rose, with some effort, from her seat. She looked a little older than my mother. She was at least a foot shorter than me and I could see her back was slightly bent.

"This is Umm Nadeen, Abu Kersch's wife," said Asim.

"*Ahlan wa sahlan.*" I held my hand out. She did not take it, but nodded with a smile.

"Welcome," she replied in Arabic. She was timid with me, but she had a warm, friendly face. I'm sure I was very different from anyone she had ever met before.

"You have much to learn about our culture, Elizabeth," Asim whispered to me.

"Why do you say that?" I asked.

"A guest is not expected to welcome the hostess until she first welcomes you."

"I remember. They welcome you to their family and piece of flat land."

"What?" Asim looked at me, bewildered.

"Oh nothing. Just something I was told in class." I brushed away my comment as quickly as I could. My ears burnt with embarrassment.

"*Ajlasi*," Abu Kersch said, pointing to a seat.

Umm Nadeen left the room, but soon reappeared with a tray of tea and fruit. She placed the bowl on a coffee table together with napkins and a knife.

"*Akli...Ashrubi*," Abu Kersch said, urging us to eat and drink. He pointed to the tray.

It was late and I was very tired. I didn't want to drink or eat. Asim nudged me, so I politely cut up an orange and ate it.

"You don't have to eat it all, but you need to take something," Asim whispered. "It would be rude not to."

"Thank you," I said both to Asim and my hosts.

Both Abu Kersch and Umm Nadeen smiled grandparents' smiles. I smiled back, wishing I understood the local dialect better. My comment about flat land earlier had shaken my confidence in the way I had been taught.

"It's late and we need to go." Asim looked at his watch, stood, and reached out to shake Abu Kersch's hand. I stood as well, but a sideways look from Asim let me know that I was staying.

Asim explained that Naguib would come to get me in the morning and then he and Naguib left me. Even though I had only known Asim for less than 24 hours, I felt apprehensive as he walked out of the door, as if a security blanket had been taken away. I was truly alone with two people I could barely talk to.

Umm Nadeen opened an adjacent door and waved me towards it. It was my bedroom. Abu Kersch placed my backpack inside and they smiled at me as they closed the door bidding me goodnight.

I'm here. I'm in Damascus. But what do you do now, Elizabeth?

The bedroom was small. There was a twin bed on a metal frame and a small side table with two drawers. The ceiling light was dim. The single window was dressed with dust-stained curtains.

Shower? I feel so grimy.

I was very tired and wanted to fall into bed and sleep, but I also wanted to wash away the long trip. While I was contemplating how exactly to ask my hosts where their shower was, the door was closed with such finality it felt awkward to open it. I heard the couple mumbling and then shutting other doors. The house fell silent. Quietly, I unzipped my bag and rummaged around for my toiletry bag. It was hard to see anything. I pulled out my pyjamas.

My pyjamas were still crisp from being dried on the washing line in our garden and smelled of home: sea air and Persil, the washing powder my mother always used. The day before I left, showers had been forecast, but mother decided we could put my clothes out to dry on the line, as long as we kept an eye on the horizon. I was glad for that as I pulled the fresh shirt over my head. It was a touch of home.

As I lay in bed, I reflected on how lucky I was to be welcomed by such kind people. I was so fortunate to have met the people on the plane and now the couple who are happy to let a stranger like me stay in their home. It struck me that my people would not be so welcoming to strangers. Father didn't even say "peace be with you" to strangers at Mass. That reminded me I would have to write to my parents in the morning.

As I drifted off to sleep quietly listening to my Walkman, I thought about the ambassador and the rhino-horn knife. There was something important about that story, but my sluggish, travel-weary mind just couldn't connect it.

Nine

My first morning in Damascus was surreal. I woke to the sounds of traffic passing below my window. Drivers occasionally sounded their horns in the narrow street as they tried to manoeuvre around parked cars. The traffic laws, if there were any, seemed chaotic.

The morning sun was filtering into the room though thin, faded, brown curtains. There was a light tap at my door before Abu Kersch opened it, smiling wide.

"*Sabah al khair*," he cheerfully greeted me.

The morning is full of light, I thought to myself. What is the response?

"*Sabah al fuul*," I replied, which I was pretty sure literally translated to "the morning is full of flowers."

My spoken Arabic was 'functional', at least that was the level that the British Council told me I had achieved after finishing the intensive course in Cairo, but accents in Syria had already been challenging. I was pleased, however, with the exchange, especially this early in the morning.

I had found the hardest part of learning Arabic, both the listening and being able to speak and respond. At university, I was taught Modern Standard Arabic and also could read *fusha* in the texts studied in our Islamic studies. Neither was especially useful though. Using *fusha* in conversation would be like speaking Shakespearian English in a pub. I hoped by living with Abu Kersch and Umm Nadeen that I would learn the Syrian dialect much quicker.

I followed my host out of my room. He pointed to the only bathroom and WC. He showed me a huge, wooden bucket with steaming hot water in it and a jug accompanied by something in the local dialect. I smiled to show I understood. I hadn't followed all the words, but had picked up the word for "bath" easily enough.

Abu Kersch picked the jug up, filled it with water from the bucket, and poured it on his arm. The water ran onto the tiled floor and flowed towards a drainage hole in the wall. He rubbed his arm with a coarse bar of soap. Then he handed me the jug and the soap. I got the message and was beginning to feel a little awkward that he felt the need to pantomime the whole process.

After Abu Kersch left, I turned to lock the door, but discovered that there was no lock. I thought perhaps I had missed it somehow as the bathroom was in semi-darkness. The light from the bulb in the ceiling was far less than I was used to. I placed my soap bag next to the door to act as a doorstop, which gave me a small sense of privacy.

The only things in the room were the steaming bucket and jug combination, a plastic stool, a small sink and a toilet. The toilet was a hole-in-the-floor type. I had come across a few in Sana'a, but only on rare occasions. Thankfully, our embassy and diplomatic houses were fitted with European toilets.

I got undressed. Then I tested the water with my finger. It was still scalding hot.

How on earth did Abu Kersch pour this on his arm?

I filled the jug with the hot water and some cold water from the sink to cool it down. I sat on the stool and wet my skin. I scrubbed myself with the ugly, green bar of soap. It smelled faintly of olive oil. As I rinsed the soap suds off, I reflected how much I would relish a proper shower with some flowery, scented shower gel, a flannel, and a fluffy towel when I got home.

I stood up in the dim light and saw a cockroach crawl beside the porcelain toilet and then another and then another. One was making its way towards me. I shuddered involuntarily.

I had first come across the horrible little beasts in Sana'a and discovered that they were fast and almost indestructible. A rolled-up newspaper was not a good enough weapon to kill them. Thinking as quickly as I could, I grabbed the plastic stool holding it high above my head. I brought it down, but missed the bug, which went scurrying off.

I grabbed my towel and wrapped it around me, picked up my clothes and made a couple of giant steps to the door. I flung it open and raced into my bedroom closing the door behind me. Once dressed, I went out into the main room.

"*Na'iman,*" Abu Kersch said. "*Allah inam aleek.*"

I didn't understand what he said, but when he invoked Allah, I remembered the phrase from a passage in the Modern Standard Arabic book. It was a blessing Muslims gave to someone who has just showered or received a haircut. I repeated the response and said thank you.

Abu Kersch handed me a pair of plastic sandals. They looked man-sized and old.

"*'Alik min fadlik,*" he said.

What does he mean, "for me"? I wondered, but I didn't want to appear rude. I thanked him in my overly-formal Arabic.

Abu Kersch laughed. Then he took one of the shoes from me and smacked it on the ground. He did it again and then looked at me to see if I had understood his action. I smiled. They were cockroach swatters. I nodded and laughed. Abu Kersch looked cross and handed me back the sandal.

I knew I would unwittingly make some blunders while staying with the old couple, and I realised I had maybe offended Abu Kersch with my laughter. I hoped he would forgive me. I had read in my tourist book that foreigners must be mindful of social etiquette and local customs, some of which I had hoped would be familiar to me because of my time in Yemen.

My host shuffled off and I put the sandals by my things in the bedroom. When I walked back out, I heard someone in the kitchen, which was open to the rest of the flat. The couple lived on top of each other.

Umm Nadeen greeted me and pulled a chair out at the small kitchen table. The table was full of plates of food. In the middle were large, circular breads, which she called *khubz arabi*, Arabic bread. They were about 10 inches in diameter and similar to pitta bread, except thicker. I recognised a plate of hummus with olive oil floating on the top, cheeses, olives, and a large bowl of fruit. She smiled as she tucked into the food with her fingers.

"*Yarja'i akli*," she said, encouraging me to join her.

She and I ate together. The cheeses were tasty with perfect saltiness, and the olives were fresh and tender. I imagined that all the food had been harvested just days ago. Abu Kersch was not with us and I assumed he had gone to work. The conversation with Umm Nadeen was simple as we ate, but the mood was gracious. She didn't want to hurry me and wanted to make sure I had eaten enough by offering more for my plate.

I helped to clear the table and she started to prepare food again, cutting vegetables. I watched her cut and slice okra and potatoes. Shortly later, she handed me a knife. I enjoyed cooking and often helped mother at home, who had taught me a lot about cooking. I was interested in learning Arabic recipes, but we only prepared vegetables. There were so many vegetables. I wondered if she was preparing dinner for a large family gathering.

We listened to Arabic music and tried making small talk. The music sounded very distant and tinny coming out of the small radio. Mostly, we chopped vegetables.

A little while later, we were interrupted by the arrival of Naguib. He had a lively conversation with Umm Nadeen. I tried to pick up some words including my name, but the conversation was fast. Suddenly, a horn sounded outside. Naguib went to the small, living-room balcony. He shouted back and forth to the people outside. I couldn't tell if he was shouting to be heard, or if something else was happening. After a couple of back and forth exchanges, things escalated, leaving no doubt that it was an argument.

I listened closely, but I couldn't glean the reason for the row. Everything was in the local dialect and so quick. I was curious who Naguib was talking to. The voice was familiar, but distorted by strong emotion.

I walked to the balcony and peered over to see Abu Kersch. He was dressed in the same sweaty T-shirt and dirty trousers he had on the day before. He was shouting up at Naguib from the street. There was another man with him. He was young and strikingly handsome. I felt my stomach tighten as I looked at him. He wore a pink polo shirt and straight-legged, blue jeans. He was shading his eyes to look up at the balcony, which made the muscles in his arm bulge, and I wondered if he could see me. I bit my lip and smoothed my hair with my hand.

Naguib turned and spoke to me in English. I snapped my attention away from the man on the street.

"Elizabeth, you can't stay here." There was no negotiation in his voice.

"Why? Did I do something?" I hoped I had not offended my hosts somehow. I turned to address Umm Nadeen, but Naguib cut me off.

"It's not you, but you can't stay here." He cut his eyes over towards Umm Nadeen. A savage look played across his face, but only for a moment. Umm Nadeen had fallen silent, but looked furious. "They are being unreasonable. We have to go."

Naguib crossed the room and entered the little bedroom I had been using. I followed him as the two men outside started arguing in quick, angry bursts.

As I walked back out through the door, I saw my host take a couple of steps, presumably to stop me, but she pulled up short. There was frustration written all over her face. I felt bad for her and torn. This couple had been kind, but I owed so much to Naguib and his brother already.

In the bedroom, Naguib was throwing the few belongings that I had pulled out back into my rucksack. He gathered my bags and made his way back to the living room. It reminded me of when I had been a child leaving for home from holiday.

"The couple does not agree with us calling on you and coming to get you," Naguib said as he made his way to the door with my things. "They used to have a daughter who is now married and living with her husband's family and they want to treat you like their daughter. You cannot leave the house if you are their daughter, as it would bring shame upon them. I tried to explain to Abu Kersch that you are not going to do that because you're a tourist, and we want to take you out to see Damascus. Unfortunately, he does not agree. It's better that you leave."

"But…" I started, as I followed behind him, "but where will I stay? There are no hotels. Your brother told me that." It was all happening very quickly, and my head was spinning.

"There's no need for you to go to a hotel. We have already found somewhere else for you to stay." Naguib opened the front door and set my bags down outside.

"But where?"

"It is a good place." He stepped outside. "We welcome you to our country and it's up to us to take care of you."

"But Abu Kersch and Umm Nadeen have been so good to me. I feel terrible. I am worried what they must think of me," I said and Naguib must have read the concern on my face.

"Don't worry. They understand."

I crossed the room and thanked Umm Nadeen in my all-too-formal Arabic. She said something to me that I didn't quite understand. The one part I thought I could make out was "Do not lose yourself in these lands." It must have been part of a traditional blessing I was unaware

Ten

Naguib opened the boot of a black car and threw my rucksack inside. The man I had seen from balcony earlier must have been in the car. Abu Kersch was standing a few feet from the car looking irate, but Naguib didn't pay him any attention. I was embarrassed by his rudeness towards Abu Kersch.

Naguib opened the door to the back seat and I stepped inside. The blue-jeaned man with the pastel-pink polo shirt was sitting in the driver's seat. I could smell his lemony cologne. He started the car as Naguib settled into the passenger seat. I stared through the dark, tinted windows at Abu Kersch as we pulled away.

"We're going to show you Damascus," Naguib said, anticipating my first question as he turned in the passenger seat to face me.

"Who's your friend?" I managed to ask in Arabic.

"Hussein."

Hussein looked in his rear-view mirror. His blue eyes peered at me for a moment. They were warm and vibrant. I was flustered by a sudden feeling of intimacy towards him, but I had no idea why it came to me. I could see his jawline and his well-trimmed beard. He was smiling. My pulse raced, and I looked away quickly.

We drove into the centre of the city. At one large roundabout, I noticed an impressive building set back behind high black railings. There was a wide pavement in front of it where a crowd of people were milling around. Some men were gathered around a man crouching on a cushion with a small stool and a typewriter in front of him. I wondered what he was doing with so many queuing up for his services.

There were several of these men dotted around the entrance to the building. In the days to come, I realised their importance. The elaborate bureaucracy of Syria was something people simply accepted in their day-to-day life. The building was the Central Bank of Syria and these clerks, without a room or a desk inside, were the beginning of the maze that led to any money transaction in the corridors inside.

Hussein pulled over on a nondescript street. Naguib jumped out of the car and disappeared down the street. My stomach was rumbling and I felt a pang of hunger.

"Naguib is getting some food," Hussein turned towards me for the first time and I met his eyes, which didn't seem to be the eyes of a stranger. He spoke with a clear, deep voice. His accent was hard to place, but easier for me to understand than the local dialect.

"You're ready to eat a donkey?" he asked with a teasing smile.

Oh, my gosh, he must have heard my stomach. How embarrassing.

I laughed.

That's funny. They use the word donkey instead of horse.

He was easy to get along with and I felt as if he knew me already. I was taken aback by how drawn I was to him. I longed to touch his face.

Naguib jumped back into the car with a handful of wraps, napkins, and water bottles.

"Falafel?" I asked.

He offered me an oversized wrap that looked as if it could feed two people. I was very thankful. I grabbed it eagerly before he had a chance to hand me a napkin. The falafel wrap was delicious. The crushed chickpea balls were still hot from the fryer and covered in a delicious sauce and salad. I ate greedily as we drove through the streets.

I was confused what the plan was, as it seemed Hussein and Naguib were driving around the city aimlessly the whole afternoon. Occasionally Hussein or Naguib would point out something of interest, but it seemed all a blur.

"This is the main *souq* in the city and that building next to it is the Umayyad Mosque." Naguib said in his heavily accented English and pointed to the Great Mosque of Syria. I had read that John the Baptist's head was buried there. I could see the ornate, golden roof of the prayer hall. I recalled seeing it on one of the posters that the Syrian Embassy had in London.

Like the *souq* in Sana'a, this *souq* was a mass of commotion and noise. The high archway entrance to the *souq* was full of Damascenes walking down it as far as the eye could see. I saw men in loose-fitting robes and veiled women with their children going about their daily chores and doing their shopping. From the back seat of the car, I wondered how long it would be before I could be one of those people in the crowd, mingling with the people.

The day ended with a long drive uphill, headed out of the city. I saw signs for Beirut, Lebanon and wondered how many miles we were from the border. We eventually parked by the side of a road that overlooked the entire city. The sun was almost setting when Hussein and Naguib finally asked me to step out of the car.

Even in the last light of the day, my eyes had a hard time adjusting to the sunlight as I had sat behind the dark, tinted windows all day. I approached a low wall and looked in amazement as the expanse of the city lay before me. I got my 35mm camera out, which I had bought at Heathrow for £20, and began taking pictures. Naguib took a picture of Hussein and I with the city behind us. He put his arm around my shoulders. I noticed his skin, the colour of coffee with cream against my pale, freckled skin. I felt my face flush.

"This is Jabal Qasioun," Hussein informed me.

The Jabal Qasioun is an impressive mountain. It gave a wide view overlooking the city, and is steeped in history. I had read in my travel guide that it was the place where Cain killed Abel, near a cave called the Cave of Blood.

Hussein pointed and I followed his finger to where two, white minarets stood together.

"That's the Saladdin Mosque," he said in English.

"You speak English?" I asked, surprised.

"Of course," he said. "I'd have to." Before I could ask why he would 'have to' speak English, he continued. "Just to the right, on top of that small hill, is the hospital where Naguib and I work."

"You both work in a hospital?" I asked.

"Naguib and I are nurses there," he said with a hint of pride.

"What kind of nurse are you?" I asked, impressed by his status.

He hesitated, as if he was finding the English word.

"I'm emergency care."

71

"It must be a rewarding job."

"Yes. It is." He smiled.

We walked a little further along the pavement. Many people were strolling around and enjoying the relative cool of the evening. The road was lined with restaurants. Many families were sitting together on the wall eating their takeaway food. We had passed some cars that had their doors open to let the night air inside.

Naguib bought us all another *khubz arabi*, Arabic bread—a pitta bread wrap, but this time it was full of kebab meat. We found a space on the low wall to sit and eat. I noticed that many cars slowed down as they passed us, and I saw many bystanders were gawking also at me. I felt very conspicuous being the only woman in western dress, with strikingly blonde hair.

I used to enjoy people-watching, especially when I was living in London. On the Tube, commuters would do anything they could to avoid making eye contact with other passengers. Here, I already found people watching me felt very different.

As we sat on the wall, passersby made eye contact with me and it was unnerving. I noticed an old couple approaching us along the wide pavement. The husband was a diminutive man in comparison to his wife, who was at least a foot taller than him. They both wore traditional garments. He wore a white *thobe*, which is long shirt, with baggy, beige cotton trousers underneath. He also wore a *keffiyah*, a male headscarf. She was in black, with a black *abaya* and *hijab*. I noticed she wore a pair of flat shoes. When they reached us, they stopped.

I was startled when the old man stood directly in front of Hussein and started to yell at him, while pointing at me. He was wagging his finger and chanting something religious. Hussein lunged to the ground by my feet and grabbed some of the bread I had torn off my wrap. I hadn't been very hungry and couldn't manage to eat it all so I threw some pieces on the ground. Perhaps he thought I was littering, but it was food so I didn't think it was technically littering. I was shocked by the commotion because the old man clearly seemed angry at me. Instead of appearing irritated by the rudeness of the old man, Hussein sounded very apologetic to him and respectfully bowed his head.

Eventually the old man finished yelling. Other people had stopped and a small mass were now staring at us all. I looked at Hussein questioningly, wanting to know what had happened.

"You can't throw bread away," he said, once the old man had moved on.

"Why?" I was puzzled. My cheeks were burning.

Hussein took the pieces and carefully placed them on the low wall beside him. I was utterly confused.

"Bread is the most sacred of all food in Islam and should never be thrown away. It must be elevated, according to Muslim custom. If you drop bread, you have the choice to eat it if it's clean, or place it on a wall so that a beggar or a bird might make use of it. It can never be abandoned."

"So sorry. I had no idea."

I felt terrible. I clearly had so much to learn.

"The Prophet, Mohammed Peace be upon Him, said 'If the food falls down, let someone take it, wipe it and eat it and don't give it to Satan,'" Hussein added.

The eyes on me felt even more intense than before. I squirmed, and my stomach tightened again. I was relieved when we all got back into the car and drove back down the mountain towards the city.

Eleven

It was nightfall when we pulled over into a dusty, dirt road. By now, I was used to being quiet and accepting the tourist route designed by my two new friends.

We all got out and walked down a small, sandy alleyway, too narrow for the car. On one side, we passed four, battered and rusty, blue, metal gates before we eventually stopped in front of a fifth. It was unlocked. Naguib pushed it open and we stepped inside. It was dark by the entrance, so I followed Hussein and Naguib tentatively. I was taken by surprise when we didn't walk into a vestibule or foyer inside someone's home. We entered a large courtyard.

All the rooms around the courtyard faced in on each other. As we headed towards the light in the centre of the courtyard, we were approached by a group of ladies. They were all wearing pretty dresses and none of them wore veils. I wondered if they were Naguib's or Hussein's family. When they saw me, they smiled and giggled. All of them were young, no older than eighteen. Not one could be a mother, but they could still be sisters, cousins or aunts.

After Hussein and Naguib were greeted excitedly by each girl, they walked towards the lit area in the centre of the courtyard. String lights were strewn around the branches of a small tree and draped across two poles. There was another girl seated on a wooden bench with her back to me. To my surprise, Asim stood up beside her.

"Hello, Elizabeth," Asim said cheerfully. "Did you have a nice day?"

"Hello, Asim. It's nice to see you again. I had a lovely day." We hugged each other.

I was happy to see Asim. It made more sense that we were visiting the family of Naguib and Asim. It was a large family. I thought he was married, so perhaps the lady next to him was his wife.

"Is this your wife?" I turned to the girl and smiled.

"No. This is Fatima. She is a friend." Asim squeezed Fatima's knee and smiled at me. I was not expecting that answer and decided that it was not my business to ask anything else. I started to blush.

"Come. Join us. We have a lot of food." He stood up and beckoned to me to take his seat next to Fatima. I sat on the hard bench next to her. In front of us there was a low table that was laden with trays of food: fruits, meats, salad, and bread. The other girls joined us and sat around the table on two other benches. They continued to smile at me and whispered in each other's ears. They were friendly, but oddly childlike. I thought perhaps it was because they had never met a western girl before.

Asim warmly embraced Naguib and Hussein, and they started talking in quick Arabic.

I was relieved when Fatima broke the silence and asked me, "*Shoo Aismik?* "

At first I didn't understand, until she said it in formal Arabic, giggling.

This was my first Syrian phrase, as well as *Shoo lounik?*, which literally means "What is your colour?" It's the Syrian Arabic for asking 'how are you?'

I introduced myself and Fatima introduced herself. She was beautiful. Her big, dark brown eyes were framed by wavy, dark brown, silky hair that reached to her waist.

She went around the table and introduced each of the girls.

"Na'imah, Meher, Samirah and Suheera." I waved across the table at them.

I wanted to ask if they were all family, but I didn't want to be embarrassed again.

The men approached us. Hussein sat next to Na'imah. Samirah and Suheera made room on their bench for Naguib to sit down. Asim joined Fatima and myself. Everyone tucked into the food with their hands. They picked up kebab meats on skewers and other meats with bread. They dipped bread into hummus and baba ganoush. I followed suit.

Meher had left her seat to go into one of the rooms. The doorway had a curtain draped across it with a bright light on. Within a few seconds she came out with a tray of plastic cups and a jug of water. She offered water to the men and then to me.

"*Ma'a?*" Fatima offered me a cup.

"*Nam.*" I accepted.

I sipped on my water and glanced around the courtyard. The courtyard was spacious. It was dark in the far back, but I could make out that it was enclosed with a high wall.

I was still trying to figure out whether I was amongst family or not. Naguib was laughing loudly with his bench companions.

Asim got up to get something from a plastic carrier bag and pulled out a beautiful, silk scarf.

"I bought this during my trip to London." He spoke to me, as he slipped it around Fatima's neck. She was overjoyed with it and she rubbed it against her cheek.

"*Shukran jasilaan,*" she said, thanking Asim for her gift.

"I often buy things for the girls: perfume, cigarettes, scarves."

"That's very generous of you."

"Do you need anything? I can get you something on my next flight. I am flying to Paris in a couple of days."

"No. I don't need anything. Thank you."

I was still confused about who all these girls were. I had my suspicions that they were not related to Naguib, Hussein or Asim, but I didn't think it was my place to ask as they were all being so kind to me.

Quietly I ate and observed my new group of friends. It was a happy group and I started to feel more at ease with the levity and welcoming ambience. I finished by having some fruit from a tray that was overflowing with cut pieces and whole pieces of fruit with a little bowl of cream to dip them in. I became extremely full, which made me more sleepy than I had been already.

Asim looked at me and seemed to be able to tell that I was tired.

"Elizabeth, you look sleepy. It's late and we need to leave." He spoke quietly to Fatima and she stood up to take my hand.

"Yes, I am very tired," I said in Arabic.

"I think you will be happy here in this home."

"Yes. Thank you so much again." I yawned.

"Fatima will show you where to sleep. Good night, Elizabeth. I hope to see you again soon."

"Will I see you tomorrow?"

"Perhaps…" He turned to Naguib and Hussein. Hussein nodded slightly. "Yes. We will see you tomorrow. Get some good sleep."

"Thank you. *Mesa' al-khayr.*" I turned to everyone and wished them all good night.

"*Mesa' al-noor,*" they each replied.

Evening of light, I thought, translating it literally in my head.

Fatima led me to one of the rooms.

"*Tsibah' al-khayr. Araki fi bukra,*" she said cheerfully. *Good night. See you tomorrow.*

"*Tsibah' al-noor,*" Fatima," I responded as I stifled a long yawn and wiped my tired eyes.

The room was entirely empty except for a thin mattress. At least at Abu Kersch's house I had a proper bed and a chest of drawers. I was so exhausted I didn't care and soon after she left I closed the door, laid my rucksack on the dusty floor and fell asleep while the conversations swirled on in the night air.

13th August 1992

A suburb of Damascus

Dear Everyone,

Hello from Damascus! I've landed! And I don't mean just on Syrian soil. I have actually landed on my feet. The steward on the flight, called Asim, told me how there were many conventions happening on my arrival day in Damascus like the upcoming Pan Arab Games and that it would be difficult to find a room in any hotel. So he took it upon himself to introduce me to a Syrian couple. The couple, Abu Kersch and Umm Nadeen, are so kind. They immediately took a liking to me. They're in their fifties. They agreed to let me lodge with them and are treating me like their daughter. They live in the city centre in a flat and I have my own bedroom. It's really going to work out well. I feel so lucky.

It's difficult to understand their dialect right now, but I'm sure my Syrian Arabic will improve much faster because neither of them can speak English, and I have no choice but to get better. I've already learnt about some cooking terms from Umm Nadeen, who wants to teach me how to cook Syrian dishes. I'll have to cook them for you, when I get home. The couple have already told me I can stay with them the whole year, and that I am already in their hearts which was so sweet. I'm really overwhelmed by their generosity, in fact everyone I've met so far has been so kind.

I haven't seen much of Damascus yet, but I'm hoping to discover and explore in the next few days and also to start looking at registering at the Institute.

15th August 1992

I have been treated so hospitably by the couple, Abu Kersch and Umm Nadeen. They have friends of the family who are showing me around the city and being my tour guides. I've had a wonderful time.

Naguib and Hussein have taken me to the old market in Damascus, called Al-Hamidiyah Souq. It's amazing. I've taken pictures and hope I can get them developed here and send them home for you to see. The friends took me to dinner last night at a restaurant in the Old City and I felt like I had stepped into a Hollywood film set. So far, I've had great food and haven't got sick at all. I must have the strong family constitution!

It's very hot here. The Syrian women are all wearing black, which I think is crazy as they must be even hotter than they need to be. I've got my long, cotton skirts and shirts to wear, which keep me cool and covered up. It's quite traditional here, but I'm being well looked after by my new friends.

I hope you and Jacob are all doing well. Love and hugs to you all,
Elizabeth

Twelve

I heard the soft whirring of a fan. Its light breeze blew my fringe over my forehead, as I lay on my back.

Oh my back! I groaned. I could feel an ache.

I rolled over to the edge of the mattress and opened an eye. My nose almost touched the dirty, tiled floor.

Where am I? My mind took a second to register that I was not waking up at home, but in a strange room.

The room was bright as there were no curtains on the two windows on either side of the door. I scanned my surroundings and saw my rucksack lying at eye level on the ground. I had no idea what time it was. I reached over and pulled out my watch. It was early, seven in the morning.

I grabbed my clothes and quickly dressed. I stepped out into an empty courtyard. The table was cleared and the benches all straightened.

Where is everyone?

Fatima appeared from the tiny galley kitchen. She was dressed in a smart skirt and blouse.

"Good morning," she cheerfully greeted me in English, which took me aback.

"Good morning. You speak English?"

"Yes, I speak a little." She seemed embarrassed, but I assured her that my Arabic needed a lot of improvement.

"*'ilaa 'ayn tadhab?*" I glanced at Fatima and asked where she was going.

"I go to work and to return in the afternoon." I didn't expect her English to be as good as it was, even though her grammar was incorrect. I wondered how she came to speak English so well and what kind of job she must have with such a skill.

"*'ayn temaliin?*" *Where do you work?*

"In doctor's office."

"*Enti mumrada 'aw tabiba?*" *You are a nurse or a doctor?* I assumed she would work as one of them.

"No, with the telephone." She gestured picking up a phone.

"*Fi aistiqbal?*" *In the reception?*

"Yes. Re-cep-tionist." She pronounced the word carefully.

"Your English is good. *Mumkin fi mustaqbal takunina tabiba.*" *Perhaps in the future you will be a doctor.*

"No." She laughed and shook her head. It was the kind of laugh that indicated that she thought I was crazy.

"I return this afternoon. You are welcome in our home." She spoke hurriedly, as she looked at her watch. She gathered her handbag and pulled out a large, colourful scarf. She wrapped it around her head and began to pin it under her chin as she headed towards the door.

"*Shukran ya* Fatima." I thanked her as she opened the door to the alleyway and was gone.

I wished I'd had more time to talk to her. She seemed so friendly. No one had been *un*friendly so far. I had prayed that I would meet good people and, so far, my prayers were being answered.

The house was empty. I must have been so tired I had slept through the noise of the other girls getting up for work.

Perhaps they also work in offices like Fatima.

It was 7.30am in the morning, which meant I had many hours to kill before anyone returned. I hoped I could find a way to fill my time.

Firstly, I decided I needed breakfast, so I headed to the kitchen. It was a narrow — probably only 8 feet by 5 feet. Along one length was a cream, Formica counter, with several circular burn marks from pans and deep grooves from cutting tools. The other side housed a collection of dated kitchen appliances: a metal sink on a pedestal, a small fridge with no freezer and a blackened, gas cooker. Some trays of fruit and bread from last night were lying on the counter, but they weren't covered so flies were landing on them.

I opened the fridge and found more leftovers. The cold kebabs did not look appetising, nor did the rice dish, which I thought had goat meat in it. In the end, I helped myself to a banana and plain yogurt, which obviously had not been pasteurized, as it was full of creamy lumps and curd. There were no cornflakes, to be sure.

Having been driven here at night, I had no idea of my exact location, but it was much quieter than the couple's house with the sound of cars on the street outside all night. I assumed I was outside the city in a smaller suburb, perhaps a village. I made a mental note to ask Fatima the name of the village.

I went out to the table and sat next to the tree for shade. The sun was already beginning to feel intense. It was completely quiet except for the buzzing of flies and the faint noise of traffic. As I ate, I noticed a lemon on the tree and then another. It wasn't as big a tree as I had thought, when I saw it lit up with fairy lights the night before. It was small and didn't give me much relief from the bright sunlight.

After eating my breakfast, I retreated to my room and dug out my sunglasses and my notebook from my rucksack. I decided there was no better time to write a letter home about my arrival in Damascus. I decided to bend the truth a little. Mother and Father would be much more at ease with me staying with an older couple that treated me as a daughter.

Once the letter was finished, I felt a pang of boredom. I wished I had someone to go exploring with. I wasn't even sure, if I left, if I would be able to find my way back to this place. I didn't have the best sense of direction. And I certainly wouldn't have been able to tell a cab driver where it was.

In lieu of getting lost in the city, I decided to learn some vocabulary. I had created an efficient study tool at university, which helped me learn the complicated grammar and long lists of vocabulary. Why not continue it?

When I first applied to university, I was apprehensive whether I was smart enough to get a degree. I had never thought I would attend as prestigious a university as Durham. Unlike the students straight out of school, who were usually not especially dedicated, I had decided I would be as I didn't want to mess up this opportunity. I soon realised that I not only enjoyed studying, but I was also successful. I achieved the top-class grade in my first-year language exam. During the following summer, I was dubious when an envelope addressed from the university arrived in the post.

I opened it to find a congratulatory letter and prize money from CMEIS for highest achievement award. I had never received recognition like that. Before, I had only just maintained average grades, even though I tried hard to revise for exams. Mathematics was regarded as a challenging subject, but I excelled in it over my other subjects. I preferred working with numbers and calculus than writing essays for social studies or literature.

Once I started to learn Arabic, I was struck by the similarity between maths and language. I saw that both had formulas. In maths, numbers are applied to a formula to calculate an answer. In Arabic, there were 28 letters in the alphabet. Ninety percent of Arabic words contained only three letters, called radicals. When it came to verbs, Arabic had up to ten forms for each verb, giving them multiple meanings. Each of the ten forms had its own "formula", which was constructed around the three radicals.

For example, the verb "to study", *da ra sa*, is form one, but if you double the second radical they used the form two pattern giving them *da ra ra sa*, which means "to teach". Also, if one added a prefix "-n" they would have constructed form seven, giving them *na da ra sa*, which means to blot out.

To commit the formulas of all ten forms to memory, I had created my own table on paper, showing all the verb formulas and taped it to the walls around my desk in my university room. They looked like tables of mathematical formulas. My walls were covered with paper with formulas for all Arabic grammar rules: numbers, *idafas*, or noun patterns, and plurals. My room resembled a student studying an engineering degree rather than a language.

I took my sunglasses and dictionary back out to the benches and settled down into my studies. I wished I had my formula sheets.

Within half an hour, I was feeling too hot. I could feel my arms beginning to burn. The hard wood I was sitting on was incredibly uncomfortable. I went back into my room and got my sun lotion out. I rubbed it into my arms, neck, face and legs.

The last time I had relaxed in the sun with my Arabic books studying was in my garden back home. It seemed a long time ago now, but it had been just a month before. My attempts at studying in my new surroundings were not going well. The heat and my uncomfortable seating were distracting.

Perhaps I could take my thin mattress outside to lie on. No, it's way too dirty out there and it's not mine. I may get in trouble. What am I going to do all day?

While I was up, I went into the kitchen to get some water. I found a glass and made my way to the tap, but stopped. I hadn't even thought, before that moment, about whether the local water was drinkable. Fortunately, there was some bottled water in the fridge. Before I had a chance to do anything else, I heard the heavy, metal gate being pushed open and Hussein and Naguib walked in.

"Hello Elizabeth. We're going to take you out for lunch."

I was so happy to see them.

My saviours! I thought, laughing to myself.

They drove me back to the heart of Damascus. I was thrilled when we parked near the Al-Hamidiyah *souq*. We strolled under the horseshoe arch I had seen yesterday and into the throng of Damascenes. I took in all my views. I looked up and saw the *souq* was shaded by a high vaulted metal roof which looked as if it had withstood gunfire and conflicts over the ages. The holes and cracks in it added to the anachronistic ambiance as shafts of sunlight lit up the dusty, dirty air of the humid, hot streets.

I heavily inhaled the aromas of coffee, spices and pan-fried pistachio nuts. There were shopkeepers selling mounds of Oriental and Persian carpets and others selling rich fabrics: silks, cottons and, the namesake of the city, intricately embroidered damascene tablecloths. Many women in black cloaks were shopping busily for their families while surrounded by children wearing western clothes.

I understand now why my travel guide stated that the souq should only be tackled by the most ardent tourist because there were hundreds of narrow alleyways feeding off the main drag. I hoped over time I would be a frequent visitor and like the *souq* in Sana'a, I would eventually have no trouble navigating my way around the maze, discovering special nooks and hidden treasures. We walked down an alleyway barely wide enough for a car. It seemed we had stepped back in time from the area we had just driven through. The modern apartment and office buildings, and bustling commercial area had morphed to whitewashed, crumbling buildings in dense, crammed streets of centuries ago. Some of the homes were leaning into each other, their balconies were almost touching.

I was walking behind my companions, when something caught my eye in a glass display cabinet at the front of a dingy store. It was bronze lantern. It was tarnished and dented, making it look antique.

How amazing is this? It could be Aladdin's lamp.

I was transported to my childhood books once again.

When I had been a little girl, I cherished visiting my grandparent's home in Manchester. Grandma always had her home-baked, vanilla cupcakes ready for us. She always arranged chocolate buttons in a dice pattern on the top. My favourite room was the library, which was really Grandad's den. It had bookcases along three sides of the room. Many were collections with many volumes. Jacob and I would pour over the pictorial encyclopaedias and atlases. When we were little, Grandma used to pick a book to read to us.

When I could read, I would choose a book and snuggle into their chocolate Labrador dog, Stoffie's, bed, which was under Grandad's desk. Sometimes Stoffie would stay beside me, which strangely made me feel comforted. It was at my grandparents that I discovered *One Thousand and One Arabian Nights* translated by Richard Burton. The volumes of brown leather covers smelled smoky from Grandad's pipe. The den was the only room in which Grandma would let him smoke. I didn't mind the smell, and in fact years later the smell of any piped tobacco reminded me of Grandad after he was no longer with us.

Among my favourite stories were "Ali Baba and the Forty Thieves," "The Seven Voyages of Sinbad the Sailor," and "Aladdin and the Wonderful Lamp." As a child, I delighted in these stories and didn't understand the deeper play between good and evil in the meandering and bizarre narratives that linked them.

While I was examining the lamp through the glass, the shopkeeper appeared from inside. He was a wizened, old man with a wiry, grey beard and a crooked back. In real life, I think Merlin would have looked like him. He spoke with a croaky voice as he slowly emerged from the shadows.

*"Bonjour...*Hello..." He recognised that I was a tourist and was hedging his bets that I was either English or French.

"Ahlan wa sahlan." I greeted him in Arabic.

"Konnichiwa. Zdravstvuyte. Ciao." I couldn't tell if he thought I was Japanese, Russian, or Italian. If he were perhaps showing off, or if we were simply playing a little language game.

I smiled and he smiled back — a charming expression despite a missing tooth.

I pointed to the lamp.

"Jamila jidan," I said. *Very beautiful.*

"American? Dollar?" I remembered that dollars and the pound sterling were a possible currency in Syria, but it's extremely risky to use the black market. I didn't want to risk it even though I did have some British money.

"La ana Britania. Eindi Lire." *No, I am British. I have Syrian pounds.*

"Ahhh yes. Yes. British." He wagged his finger as if he knew I was British all along. *"Eshreen Lires."* *Twenty Syrian pounds.*

"Ashr?" *Ten?* I had a ten-lire note in the front pocket of my bumbag I carried around my waist.

"Na'am," he agreed.

"Shukran," I replied.

I had struck my first bargain and felt so pleased with myself. I handed over my note. He opened the glass cabinet smeared with fingers prints and dirt and took the lamp out. I held it to feel its weight and turned it around. It had engraving on the bottom, which was hard to make out. I was curious where it had come from and imagined it was hundreds of years old waiting to be found.

I even had an urge to rub it. In my eagerness, I followed him inside as he got a plastic bag to put it in. I was sure Hussein and Naguib had noticed I had stopped, as frequently they had needed to usher me on as I lingered, taking in the smells and fascinating sights of the *souq*.

"Elizabeth, *Yalla!" Let's go!* I had heard each of them say at some point.

But I hadn't heard it lately and, as I stepped out of the shop, I expected to find them talking and patiently waiting for me, but they were not around. Initially I didn't panic, but walked up the street in the same direction as we were heading, hoping they would discover I wasn't with them anymore and they were retracing their steps towards me.

Within a few metres, the street split. There was still no sign of them and I didn't know whether to turn right or left. For a few moments, I was motionless, in limbo at this junction and at the mercy of a crowd of strangers who mingled around me. I simultaneously felt outlandish and almost exotic. To some, I was a curiosity as they stopped to gawk at me. To others, I was like Medusa, as mothers with children bustled by covering their eyes, not wanting their offspring to see me. To the majority, as most were men, I was Samantha Fox, a famous English pop singer, who had recently caused hysteria in a rare concert in Damascus.

"Samantha," one man jeered, as his hand brushed my hip. I had seen posters of her upcoming concert and knew of her in England, but was incredulous that she would want to perform in this city.

I prayed that Hussein and Naguib would return. Bombarded on all sides, I retreated to the side of the street only to be met with taunts from tradesmen inside their shops. They were unlike the unwelcome wolf whistles I once received from workmen when I passed by a building site in London. These taunts were hisses, as threatening as a snake lying in wait for its prey to pass. I moved away from the hisses slightly up the street, but no sooner had I taken some steps, another chorus of hisses emanated from another darkened shop front.

I didn't know where to put myself. I realised that in any spot the privacy boundaries were non-existent, as again another man passed in front of me so closely I could smell the stench of cigarettes on his clothes. I was convinced he did it on purpose. I was torn between the need to stand out so that Hussein and Naguib would spot me, and the wish I could find somewhere less conspicuous.

In the boisterous and chaotic clamour, I started to worry that there was a possibility that I was lost. It was daunting to realise that if I were truly alone then I would be unable to do anything. I had left myself completely vulnerable. At home, if we were ever lost we had a family understanding that we would rendez vous at the car, but I had no idea how to get back to their car. I could never have traced my path back.

Just as I was starting to think I needed to take a gamble and turn left, I felt a gentle hand on the back of my shoulder. Momentarily, I thought it was another man trying to brush suggestively against me, but Hussein pulled me around and I met his huge smile with beautifully straight, white teeth. I was so relieved. I forgot where I was and hugged him. He took a modest step back.

"We were looking everywhere for you. You should not be alone." There was a paternal tone of chastisement mixed up with relief in his voice. I had heard it many times as a child, but didn't place it. It was simply familiar, and that was something extremely comforting.

"I'm sorry. I thought you saw me stop to buy something."

"No, but, thanks to Allah, we have found you."

Hussein turned right and we walked on. I stayed close by his side. I liked that I was walking beside him, as I felt protected and happy that no other men would dare touch me accidentally or not.

We turned into a restaurant. Above the front window I saw the name *Abu Karim Mathaf*. It was small, rather like a Chinese takeaway inside. I couldn't see any seating area, so I thought we were picking up sandwiches again. There was a large serving counter on one side with plates of food on display. On the adjacent wall, there was a large painting of Hafiz al-Assad. I had noticed his picture on the walls of many shops. Behind the counter there was a large piece of meat rotating on a skewer and a high pile of fresh *khubz arabi*, Arabic bread. The room smelled good enough to make my mouth start watering.

Naguib and Hussein met with a man and shook hands with him. He wore a black suit and tie and appeared to be the owner. He ushered us all immediately upstairs. The white, stone stairs were narrow with shiny, white marbled tiles on either side. They spiralled around to a second flight. At the top, the stairs were flanked by two large, white, alabaster columns. Then, the room opened out into a large dining area with numerous tables beautifully adorned with white tablecloths, silverware and napkins and smelled of apple smoke from the *narguiles*, the water pipes.

It was a complete contrast to the small café downstairs with the stone, unswept floor and white ceramic tiles on the walls. One façade of this room, behind some musicians, was made of intricately carved wood. Around the rest of the room, the walls were tiled. The shiny, white tiles were interspersed with fifteenth-century Mamluk tiles. The tiles had pale-and-dark blue floral and geometric designs on white backgrounds. Some were hexagonal-shaped, others were square and some had gold borders, while others were plain.

We walked past the group of musicians, who were playing on drums and a sitar on a low, wooden stage. The suited man showed us to a table and pulled a chair out for me to sit. There were not many others there for lunch. In fact, the waiters outnumbered the guests, which meant that we all received excellent service from multiple waiters.

Fortunately, as I was incredibly hungry, plates of food appeared very quickly. Hussein and Naguib talked to each other, and I wished I could join in. I couldn't hear anything over the music and, unless they spoke much slower, I didn't have a chance of understanding them. It would have been nice to have Fatima here to speak to. Perhaps I could trade her some English lessons.

I soon felt very full. I didn't know what to do. I got out my notebook and randomly started writing to myself. I felt impatient to leave the restaurant and re-enter the labyrinth, but I was obviously on my two male friends' time. It was more than a little annoying, but at least we weren't in the car for another whole day.

Eventually, after another lively conversation with the owner during which he gestured to me more than once, Hussein turned to face me.

"How was your food, Elizabeth?" he asked in his rich, baritone voice. The way he said my name brought up goose pimples on my arm and brushed away my irritation.

"Yes. It was excellent. Do you need to go back to work after lunch?"

"I'm actually in mourning right now," Hussein said sadly.

"I'm so sorry for your loss." I searched for an Arabic condolence, but none sprung to mind.

"My father died this week and our family is grieving." He held his hand to his heart as he spoke of his father and said something in Arabic, which sounded like a short prayer that he spoke in a whisper, much like the way my father softly murmured as he blessed the body of Christ and held the host above his head at the altar.

"I know how hard it is when you lose a loved one. I lost my only uncle last year. He was very dear to me and, as a little girl, I used to tell him I was going to marry him."

"I'm grateful for you as you have brought light to my day." He smiled at me.

I loved the way Hussein expressed himself. His words were so eloquent and he treated me so differently from boys I knew who dated my friends. Boys back home were immature and bad-mannered in comparison to Hussein's respectful behaviour and way of speaking.

Naguib left us to return to his work.

"Let's go back to the *souq*. Stay close to me. I don't want my Gazelle to get lost again." Hussein smiled. His smile was captivating. I noticed the fine lines around his eyes wrinkle.

"I promise." I smiled back. "But there is so much to see here."

"We have plenty of time to come back and I'll show you much more of my ancient city."

A passage I had read while studying in the university library bubbled into my brain. It was written by Mark Twain about Damascus, when he visited in 1860.

"To Damascus, years are only moments, decades are only flitting trifles of time. She measures time, not by days and months and years, but by the empires she has seen rise, and prosper and crumble to ruin. She is a type of immortality." Without realising it, I had spoken it out loud.

"Well put."

Hussein grinned at me and together we headed back through the serpentine alleyways towards the covered market. I felt as if I were in another time, visiting an ancient metropolis with a protective friend by my side. In the distance, one by one, I could hear the minarets come to life as the afternoon call to prayer began. The muezzin began the *adhan* prayer. Until a friend in Yemen explained it to me, I never realised that the prayer was the same at the beginning of each call to prayer because it sounded so different in each mosque. The voice of the muezzin could be tuneful and almost singing, or it could be a monotonous chant from a scratchy voice.

"It's *Asr*," Hussein explained. "The afternoon prayer time."

As he was talking, the loudspeakers above us crackled and the muezzin from the nearby Great Mosque of Damascus began his song. Goosebumps ran up my arms. It was beautiful.

"Can we go in the Umayyad Mosque?" I asked Hussein.

He shook his head.

"Please can we go?" I asked again coyly. I was dying to see it. I pictured the poster I had seen in the Syrian Embassy in London and couldn't believe I was now feet away from the real thing. I longed to visit the Shrine of John the Baptist and the Tomb of Al-Hussein ibn Ali, a grandson of the Prophet Muhammed, and a martyr venerated by the Shiite Muslims.

"It'll be hard to go at prayer time. We will come back soon." Hussein smiled reassuringly.

For ten minutes, I was transported into a whimsical trance as I thought of how I was walking in the steps of caliphs from the eighth century. I felt like no one but me was in wonder as the muezzin continued to sing. Some shopkeepers continued their business as usual, while others laid their prayer mats on the ground towards Mecca in prayer, and still others walked by us loudly clicking their prayer beads and muttering under their breath.

I stayed close to Hussein's side as we passed shopkeepers on either side shouting out to the crowds about their wares. A teenage boy was pushing a cart of merchandise in the midst of all the pedestrians and hit me on the shin. Some of the chewing gum and sweets he was selling were scattered on the ground. A few people around us hissed and tutted in disapproval, which appeared to make Hussein upset as he reprimanded the boy. I was thankful Hussein was there.

We meandered on through the market, slowly making our way back to the car. Hussein and I talked and laughed as we walked. I wished I could have taken his hand, but I thought about the way he had stepped back quickly when I hugged him.

As we were making our way out of the *souq*, one shopkeeper, spotting a foreigner and a good potential sale, shouted at me as I passed him.

"Hello. Come buy here. Good shop. Good price." He tried very hard to get my attention, but didn't notice that I was not alone. Hussein made a quip at him I didn't quite understand, but that immediately stopped the shopkeeper's incessant calls. The man, ever the salesman, offered to make a good deal to Hussein to amend the insult to his woman. The shopkeeper was standing in front of his shop, which was selling women's fashion and traditional Islamic wear.

"Elizabeth, do you need any clothes?"

"No, I'm fine."

The *jilbabs*, *kaftans* and *abayas* came in all the colours of the rainbow, bold patterns and sparkly adornments, some of which were displayed on mannequins.

Hussein spoke to the shopkeeper who left to fetch something. He showed Hussein some *hijabs*. After a short discussion, the shopkeeper embraced Hussein, slapping him on the back in friendly camaraderie and Hussein turned to me and presented me with a headscarf.

"This is for you, so you feel more comfortable in public."

"Thank you." I blushed.

It was a white *hijab* and it was perfect. He had got me something I didn't even realise I needed. I tried to wrap it around my head and Hussein shook his head. He and the shopkeeper laughed.

"I think one of the girls had better show you how to wrap and pin it," Hussein said, adjusting it for me.

I felt a surge of desire that shook me to the core.

Thirteen

For the first week living with the girls, Hussein and I saw each other every day. I spent the first part of my morning sitting by the lemon tree, studying my vocabulary and then, by lunchtime, Hussein would come to pick me up. Occasionally, he took me along when he had things to do or buy, but he also took great care to ask if I needed anything done. He took me to the post office where I posted my first letter home. I wished I could have included some photos, but I hadn't finished my roll of film yet.

I also mentioned that I needed some sunglasses. I had lost the pair I had brought with me and needed some new ones.

That day, after eating a falafel sandwich for lunch, Hussein took me to a small street kiosk that sold sunglasses. The small space was laden with racks upon racks of cheap pairs made in China.

"Are these what you need?"

"Yes." I took a pair and slipped them on waiting for him to tell me whether they suited me or not.

"Here." Hussein picked a different pair. "put these on."

They were brown imitation tortoise shell frames. I put them on and looked at him with a huge smile.

"*Jamila.*" *Beautiful.* He looked at the young boy running the stand. "Eh?"

The young boy agreed with him and was complimentary. In small ways, Hussein told me daily that I was beautiful, whether it was my hair, my clothes, my voice, or my eyes. At first it was hard to accept compliments as I couldn't remember the last time I had received even one. He made me feel more beautiful than I had ever felt before.

Within five minutes, Hussein had negotiated a price.

"Keep them on. You are beautiful." He brought his face close to mine. I was flustered again by his sudden intimacy.

Back at the girls' house that evening Hussein and I were relaxing on the bench. It was my favourite part of the day as the temperature had cooled off and we reminisced on the day we had just spent together. It was also the time of day we talked most about ourselves.

The night after Hussein bought me the sunglasses, we started to talk about the differences in our upbringing. It was the first clear indication that I had that maybe Hussein felt the same way about me as I felt about him.

"Tell me about your family," he said.

"My mother is a teacher and my father is a police officer. I have one brother who's older than me."

"Did your father treat you differently than your brother when you were growing up?"

"Yes. My brother had more freedom than I did."

"Did that bother you?"

"It did, but my father treated me differently because I am his only daughter."

"How was it different?"

"Well, my brother dated as a teenager. He also had more independence, as he could get away from the house because he had a motorbike. It was quite isolating for me, as we lived in the countryside in a small village a long way from town. I had to rely on my parents to take me anywhere."

"So, your father forbade you to date?" Hussein asked pointedly.

"Is there a hidden reason why you want to know about who I dated?" I tried to sound coy, but felt a little awkward asking.

"I would like to know more of who Elizabeth is."

I was happy that he wanted to know me more and I wanted to know more about him. In the back of my mind, I could hear my mother's voice telling me I had not even known him a month. I brushed it away.

"Well, to answer your question, it wasn't that he forbade me to date, although he tried. He was strict and the family's reputation and respect were extremely important to him."

"As is a father's duty."

"I was brought up in a Christian family." I paused, as I tried to discern his reaction. I wanted to figure out if it was a good time to discuss religion as we hadn't broached it until now. I knew he was a Muslim as he went to prayer often, but I didn't know how devout he was. I had heard that devout Muslims were forbidden from having relationships with someone other than another Muslim.

"Islam and Christianity are similar in many ways," he replied. "After all, we both have to respect our parents and believe in one God."

I was relieved.

"Tell me about your family." The door had been opened, but religion was a tricky subject no matter what. The fact that I had been raised in a devout Catholic family was something I felt I didn't want to share at this moment

He paused.

"As you know, my father died just recently. Now, it's my responsibility to take care of my mother and my sisters. We live not far from here in a city called Duma'a."

"I am so sorry for you and your family's loss. Are you the only son?"

"Yes. I have just two sisters, Aysha and Moina. Their lives are similar to yours as they rely on me to drive them places and they cannot date before marriage. Their reputation is important too, just like it was for your father."

"It's not that I couldn't date," I clarified.

He smiled a fleeting smile.

"Of course," he said and patted my hand. A thrill ran up my arm.

Fourteen

On Fridays, I enjoyed seeing more of the girls as it was the Holy day and, like a Sunday for me, it was their day off work. In the evenings, we always had company for dinner, but on Fridays it was just the girls. They told me it was because the men spent the day at the mosque and with their own families. Fridays was the day the girls caught up on chores around the house.

One Friday, I woke to the sound of Arabic music being played on a cassette player. I got up and joined the girls who were all enjoying their Holy day. It was a hive of activity: some were cleaning the house doing various chores, and others were cleaning themselves.

I was happy when Fatima suggested that we should wash our clothes. I had watched the others wash clothes, and it had come to the point that I could no longer last without doing my own, although laundry was my least favourite chore growing up. There's only so many pairs of knickers one can pack.

It was not the kind of clothes washing I was used to at home. This required much more effort. Fatima and I headed over to the far corner of the house, where there was an outside tap and hose. She filled two large buckets with water. She added washing powder to one and left the other one for rinsing. We sat next to a large, smooth, grey washing stone about the size of a footstool, which I had seen the girls use to massage stubborn stains out of clothes.

The cassette player started to play a familiar song, which I had heard several times from that tape. The song had a long introduction with a catchy drumbeat, before the singer started. Fatima started to sing. She had a beautiful voice. She seemed to swoon over the song and the lyrics. Although it's often hard to hear words in songs, I could understand that it was about love.

"Who sings that song?" I asked her, after it finished.

"Kathem al-Saher. He is a very good singer. This song is called *Ghazal*, Gazelle."

"I like it. You're also a good singer. I can't sing at all."

"Thank you. He is also very handsome." She walked over to the cassette player and picked up a tape box. There was a picture of Kathem al-Saher on the cover.

"This is him." She showed me and sighed. "He's very popular and a new artist."

"He is handsome, but not as handsome as Hussein." I smiled.

There were a few seconds of silence.

"So, do you like Hussein?" she asked guardedly. She focused on a stain on one of her blouses.

"Yes," I replied excitedly, as I submerged my underwear in the soapy water. I had never had a sister for these sorts of conversations and I was excited. I had always wanted a sister for as long as I could remember. When I was small, probably about five or six years old, I remember mother saying we were going to a nursery. The only kind of nursery I knew was the one we used to attend in the school where she worked. All the way in the car, I was excited because I thought it meant we were going to pick up a sister for me. When we stepped out of the car into a garden nursery, I asked mother where my new sister was. It dawned on my mother that I was confused and she gently explained to me that there are two kinds of nurseries: one for young children, and one for plants. I cried all the way home.

"Hussein has been so kind to me and I really like him a lot," I said excitedly.

I had talked to Fatima several times over the last couple of weeks, but we had never talked about Hussein. I felt as if my heart was going to burst, now that I had the opportunity to let out all my emotions.

"I feel like I have got to know him really well," I continued to gush. "And he is so dreadfully handsome."

I anticipated Fatima's response would be equally excited. I wanted to ask her, if she knew whether Hussein liked me.

"I don't think you know him at all." Fatima took her blouse out of the soapy water and was now pummelling it vigorously against the stone.

I felt a little taken aback by her response.

"But we've been together every day and even in the evenings, talking so much," I replied defensively.

"Please be careful and don't lose yourself." She didn't make eye contact with me, as she continued to work out the stain on her blouse.

"Is there something I should know about him?" I had stopped washing my knickers and looked directly at Fatima, hoping to glean something from her reaction. This conversation was not going the way I thought it would. I remembered what Umm Nadeen had said to me—something similar, when I last saw her.

"Just be careful that's all."

After we finished washing our clothes, I remained unsettled from my conversation with Fatima.

Why is she telling me to be careful? Does she think he will break my heart?

Some of the girls were not so friendly, but Fatima had been from the very beginning. She showed me how to work the gas stove and how to work the dilapidated shower, which I appreciated, after seeing how much worse it could be. She was the person in the house whose company I enjoyed the most. She taught me about the music she loved and I reciprocated, playing one of my favourite tapes which I had brought with me–*The Watermark* by Enya. She had really taken me under her wing.

I had grown to trust Fatima, over the course of time that I'd been with the girls, but she could be over-cautious, I thought. She had advised me to be wary of the girls. When one of the girls, Samireh, asked to borrow my floral skirt, Fatima intervened and told her she couldn't, and told me later that the girl was a thief and not ever to lend things as they would never be given back.

Perhaps Fatima is untrusting of friends in general.

25 August 1992

Somewhere in Damascus

Dear Diary,

I'm so lucky! I've met so many kind people already. I have been treated with so much hospitality and friendship.

I really like this girl called Fatima. She's much friendlier than the other four girls. She's just a bit older than me. She comes from a village outside Damascus and came to live and work here. She's clever too as she speaks some English, but I'm talking as much Syrian as I can with her. I feel like my Arabic is already getting better!

Wow! There was a huge commotion in the house yesterday. Everyone was wailing and crying. I thought someone had died for sure. I couldn't figure out what anyone was saying. Fatima told me that Suheera was shunned by her family. Suheera's entire village believes she has AIDS which Fatima said is a complete lie. She'll never be able to go back to home. I guess the only good thing is that she has her girlfriends and a home here where she can feel safe.

I told Hussein about Suheera. Guess what? He told me I had to get an AIDS test asap. All foreigners are required by law to be tested. I went to do it today. I don't like needles and what if the needles are dirty!? That scared me more than anything. I knew I wouldn't have it. I was so nervous when Hussein opened the paper. He pretended I was positive and for a few seconds I believed *him til he laughed. Such a joker! Look out Hussein I'm going to get you back.*

Fifteen

"Tomorrow morning, we are going on a road trip to Hama," Hussein declared, the day after my conversation with Fatima. We sat on the bench, under the tree. Fatima shot a look at me from a few feet away. I ignored her.

I was excited to hear that we were going on an excursion out of Damascus.

"I would love to visit another city," I responded excitedly.

Hussein told me Hama was famous for its ancient water wheels. I decided to put on my tourist hat and get ready for my first road trip out of Damascus.

That next morning was hot and sweltering. I decided to wear my long, pink, floral skirt and the white *hijab* that Hussein had given me. I looked at myself in the small mirror in my wash bag. It was strange to see myself with a headscarf. It reminded me of old age pensioners in the UK, who were the only people I knew who wore headscarves. Still, I knew it would be different here and the scarf would help me feel less conspicuous.

"Very pretty," Hussein said, from the doorway.

"Thank you." I blushed a little.

I looked forward to seeing him so much each morning, that I took a little more time to get ready. I had only brought a small amount of makeup as I didn't wear much back home. I wanted to look pretty for Hussein, so I applied my blue eyeliner and mascara.

I was surprised to see Fatima had not gone to work when I went into the courtyard.

"Good morning, Elizabeth," she said brightly, as she was busy doing her hair. "I'm going with you to Hama."

"Oh, excellent," I said nonchalantly. I had thought it was going to be just Hussein and I. I was upset that she wasn't happier for me and Hussein, and doubted that Hussein was sincere.

"Elizabeth, your *hijab* is not right," she said looking at my scarf. "I will show you how to do it this afternoon."

I took it off.

Naguib arrived to pick us up. When we were ready to leave, Fatima, and not Hussein, sat next to Naguib, while Hussein and I sat in the back.

"We are all going to have a great day together," Fatima said cheerfully. I thought she might be guarded towards Hussein, but she seemed amicable.

I decided to put my worries behind me and focus on the trip. I was nervous and excited to sit next to Hussein, wondering what lay ahead.

Fatima and Naguib started flirting in the front seat, like boyfriend and girlfriend. I was surprised and confused by the way they were acting. It made more sense for Fatima to be involved with Naguib than his married brother, Asim, but I didn't understand Fatima's heart. Ultimately, I thought, if she was being carefree with Naguib, I need not pay attention to what she had said about Hussein.

The drive to Hama was two hours. Heading north out of Damascus, and away from the Anti-Lebanon Mountains, the landscape was unremarkably arid and rocky. Occasionally, we drove through a linear village that consisted of a few shabby buildings, with workshops and garages, grocery stalls and dusty restaurants with plastic tables and chairs outside. Each village looked as poor and neglected as the last one. The land between the villages was too hard and rocky and I reflected that it must be very difficult for people to even grow their own vegetables or keep their own animals. Occasionally, I saw a boy shepherding a herd of goats, or a group of men languishing in the sun in the middle of nowhere.

We stopped at a small stall and Hussein jumped out to get some bottles of water for the rest of the drive. I watched him, as he shook hands with the shopkeeper, as if he had known him all his life.

He's so friendly to everyone.

He was smiling when he got back in. He leaned to the front to give a couple of water bottles to Fatima and Naguib. He was telling Naguib something and gave him brotherly pats on his back. They were both laughing, but I wasn't able to understand the joke, although Fatima was jokingly looking mad at their playfulness. He leaned back and handed me some water. His hand lingered on mine as I took the bottle from him and then he rested it on my knee. I could feel the heat from his palm through my light, cotton skirt. A tingle ran through my entire body, but we sat motionless with our thighs touching. I didn't know what I should do next.

Should I move my hand?

I was trying to figure it out, when he turned to me. He reached over with his other hand and cupped my face. His hand covered from my chin and up behind my ear. He pulled me towards him and we kissed. It was a gentle and lingering kiss. I had never kissed a man with a full beard. The bristles of his moustache lay softly around my lips.

After all the days of driving around the streets of Damascus alone in the backseat, I easily succumbed to the passion that had built up inside me.

Gently, Hussein manoeuvered me across his body. I wriggled into a position straddling his lap. My head was touching the roof of the car, as I faced the back window. I could see the empty mountain road twisting behind us, as we drove on towards an unknown city.

I heard Fatima cough behind me.

He's not going to break my heart Fatima.

I giggled awkwardly because of the position I was in. I tried to pull myself off his lap, but Hussein tenderly held me in place. I mildly resisted, but was easily persuaded to embrace longer.

I need to stop.

I pleaded with the judgmental voice in my head.

He may break your heart in the end.

It was my mother's voice now.

I dismissed the voice.

Hussein buried his face in my chest, as he held me on his lap. The deep feeling of desire stirred like it had never done before. All other thoughts dissipated.

It wasn't until we entered the populated suburbs of the city that we released our embrace. We sat back in our seats and we tenderly held hands. My cheeks were burning, but not from embarrassment this time. We passed along leafy boulevards where the lanes were separated by lush trees. We pulled into a small car park and I peered out of the window. Before I could even see the *norias*, I could hear them.

"Is that noise the Water Wheels? They are so creaking and squeaking so loudly."

"Elizabeth, you would be making creaky noises if you were from the fourteenth century." Hussein said.

113

Fatima snorted loudly.

These ancient wheels, which scooped water up approximately 20 metres, used to provide water to the mosque and houses and irrigate the farm fields, but were now just a tourist attraction. Apparently, their appeal was not widespread, as the car park was empty. We appeared to be the only tourists.

Once out of the air-conditioned car, the midday heat hit me full in the chest. Then, I looked up and was shocked to see the immense size of the ancient Water Wheels looming above us.

Wow. They are humungous. I can't believe they've been turning non-stop for hundreds of years.

We took pictures of each other with my cheap camera. First Naguib and Fatima posed together and then Hussein and I hugged each other in front of one of the second-largest *Norias, the Al-Mamuriyya*. Fatima was dressed in jeans and a T-shirt with no headscarf, while the men both had chinos and polo shirts on. We resembled a happy foursome on a romantic getaway in Europe.

We continued our tour along the Orontes River and into Old Hama. I was not expecting to see that some of the buildings showed signs of damage by bullets and rockets and most of the *souq* had been destroyed.

"What happened here in Hama?" I asked Hussein. He seemed reticent to answer. All of my company fell silent, and a sadness prevailed. There must have been a tragedy here. I knew it was not the right time to push for answers. I wished I knew more about Syrian history.

We moved onto four other *norias* near the Mosque Al-Nuri, which had a striking minaret banded with black basalt and yellow limestone. Although Hussein and I could not hold hands in public, I sensed the electricity between us. On our return to the car, we meandered towards a low hill with a large plateau that stood out from above the city. I had noticed it when we first arrived and wondered what it was.

"That is the citadel," Naguib said. "It has a park and a popular picnic area."

The sun was oppressive as we walked with no shade along a path on the edge of the Citadel Mound. Some families sat on the grass eating and drinking as young children played. The women were covered from head to foot in black and I thought they must be melting in those dark clothes as I was drenched from the dry heat in my baggy, cotton, pastel T-shirt and loose skirt. I stopped various times to snap pictures of the view of Hama below and the sites that we had just visited. My photo film was almost finished as I had taken 30 pictures since arriving.

I turned my camera and noticed that Hussein was strolling with Fatima. They were having a heated discourse just feet away from me. Hussein was doing all the talking. Even though he had raised his voice, I couldn't understand anything as Hussein was speaking very quickly to her. Usually when he knew I was listening, or when he was speaking Arabic to me, he slowed his speech down, but it was evident that they were having a private conversation albeit in public. Their conversation abruptly ended and Hussein joined me as Naguib, who had walked ahead, waited for Fatima to join him. They walked to the car and got in.

"What happened between you and Fatima?" I asked Hussein.

"Nothing. It was something that happened some time ago which needed to be fixed." I was no wiser as to what had happened and thought perhaps Fatima would tell me more later.

"I'll take a picture of you, if you like." Hussein changed the subject.

"I've only got six photos left and I want to save them for something spectacular in this city."

"You are the most spectacular thing here, Elizabeth."

I was embarrassed and didn't know what to say and I smiled at him. My cheeks burnt.

"Remind me to buy you a film and get that one developed for you next time we're shopping." He smiled. "Let's go back to the car to get out of the sun."

We returned to the car to find Naguib and Fatima in the back seat. Hussein opened the front door for me. I noticed that Fatima was fixing her hair calmly and then reached to drink some of her water. Naguib, on the other hand, was flustered. There was no doubt that there had been some intimacy between them. Hussein got behind the wheel and smirked in the rear-view mirror at Naguib.

The journey home was lighthearted. The radio was playing and Fatima sang along to one of the songs. She and Naguib appeared to be happy together.

I kept looking over at Hussein and he'd catch me staring. We laughed together and squeezed hands. I was feeling ecstatic. It seemed as if Fatima and Hussein had got over their small fight. We arrived home in time for the men to perform evening prayer.

Sixteen

The intimacy we had shared during our trip had reinforced my feelings for Hussein. It was difficult to study my vocabulary as I was impatient to see Hussein arrive to go for our daily lunch. We embraced each other every morning knowing that we would have to stay apart as soon as we stepped out into public and conformed to society.

"Hello my darling." I loved to greet him with kiss.

"*Ya habibiti,* my baby." It made me laugh because his words were barely audible as they were squashed between two pairs of lips.

One day, in the late afternoon, Fatima, Suheera and Na'imah came home early from work. They excitedly told me they were taking me to their Turkish bath, the *hammam,* nearby.

"What do I need to take?" I asked.

"Shoes, shampoo, soap," Fatima said.

It was only a five-minute drive from the house and Hussein drove us all in his car. We turned right off the main road into a small side street. Hussein stopped in front of a sandy, brick building with two floors and a large, brick dome. It was nothing like the impressive Roman Baths, which I had visited in Bath, England. There was not even a sign outside the building, rendering it indistinguishable from the rest of the buildings on the street.

"This is for ladies only." Hussein smiled. "I'll be back to take you all home."

We entered the reception area through a heavy, dark curtain used for privacy from passersby in the street. The room opened out unexpectedly into a cavernous space. There were seats along the walls furnished with rich, although threadbare, oriental carpets. In the centre, directly under the dome, there was an octagon fountain inlaid with blue, mosaic tiles. From the inside, the dome was transformed into a light show. Cracks within the bricks allowed shafts of sunlight to shine through. The illumination made me feel relaxed. Unfortunately, it didn't smell as relaxing, as the vapoury air invaded my nostrils with tobacco and must from wet carpets.

There were two women who were assisting us in the lobby area. One of them, a plump, short woman, was dressed in a long, black robe and colourful *hijab*. She handed out some *minshafa*, thin towels. The other, a tall, slim woman, handed us glasses of rose water.

"Get undressed," Fatima told me. "And wrap this around you."

I timidly undressed feeling embarrassed by my body. I wished I had packed my swimsuit now. I clung onto the towel as I awkwardly struggled to pull my clothes off and then wrapped it tightly around me. I was relieved that it was large enough to cover me from my breasts to my knees. Na'imah and Suheera disrobed, unabashed by their nakedness and tied the towels around their waists.

I was freezing as I stood almost naked in the lobby area. Fatima saw my chattering teeth.

"This is the *barrani* chamber, the coolest room. Let's go into the next one which is warmer."

I happily followed her into the next, warmer chamber. Suheera and Na'iamah stayed in the *barrani* chamber. I sat on the wet, stone floor next to Fatima and felt the sweat run from every pore in my body. Fatima took out some soap and face cloths, which she had brought, and began to wash herself. I began to scrub myself as well.

In the steamy mist, I saw other women in the room. Many small groups were chatting and socializing while washing their hair and bodies. They walked around without towels. I was shocked at how open they were with each other. I couldn't help but reflect on the two extremes of womenfolk: being concealed in the homes and covered in black when out in the street compared to the freedom and nudity in the *hammam*. I could understand how they must cherish the time they spent together and the community it helped them create.

I was eager to chat about Hama with Fatima and hear about her and Naguib. I hadn't had a chance to catch up with her. I hoped she had changed her mind about Hussein. After all, she seemed to have enjoyed her time with Naguib.

"The trip to Hama was great," I said. "I hope we can go on another with Naguib and Hussein."

"I had a good time, but I don't think I'll have time to go again."

"Is that because Naguib and you have to work?"

Fatima paused and looked thoughtfully at me.

"Yes."

"I'm so glad that Hussein can spend so much time with me." I suddenly realised how insensitive that sounded and corrected myself. "I mean, I'm not glad that his father died, but I'm glad he is not working right now."

"What do you mean?" she asked.

"Isn't he still in mourning?" I wasn't entirely sure how long he would be in mourning, and I had supposed he still was.

"I don't know," she said, but her tone was abrupt. It was strange that she didn't know about Hussein's father and I sensed she didn't really care to talk about Hussein.

I bit my lip, frustrated. Fatima got up and gathered her things.

"Let's move onto the *jouwani*, the hottest chamber."

I had thought we were already in the hottest one, but I was extremely mistaken. The third room was like a kiln. The furnace was situated in this room. Heat and smoke passed in pipes under the floor from there into the other middle room. I realised I had not drunk enough, as I felt very thirsty and had probably lost a pint of sweat already.

Fatima was listening in on some women talking. She was bemused by their conversation. The women were cackling loudly at each other. There were four of them, all middle-aged, round and fat. They sat in a huddle, washing each other with a clay substance. I had noticed that they occasionally looked at me and cackled more.

"What are they talking about?" I asked, thinking they had made a joke about me, and hoped Fatima had heard them.

"Those women are gossiping about a girl that the mother is arranging for her son to marry."

"What's so funny?" I asked.

"She brought her here."

"Why?"

"Mothers-in-law always like to check out the bride-to-be. She wants to make sure she's not got any serious, physical faults," she explained. "One of her friends thinks the girl is too ugly for her son."

"That's awful," I said, but I laughed anyway.

"Then the mother asked if they noticed anything about the body of the bride-to-be being ugly, and one of them said she thought she saw she had three nipples."

"No," I splurted. "That's so funny."

"I don't think it's true, but they love spreading rumours." Fatima was laughing hard.

After that room, Fatima took me into a cold one, which I disliked very much. It was meant to cool you down, but I found it too chilly. The stone was slippery. We returned to the middle chamber to find Suheera and Na'imah. The second lady from the reception was sitting with them, still dressed in her black robe. She was scrubbing Suheera down with a black scrubbing cloth made of goat's hair.

"Elizabeth, you need to be scrubbed by the *muqashshara*," Fatima said, indicating the woman with the cloth.

The darkly clothed exfoliator beckoned me over. Her pruned and puckered hands were covered in henna designs and her nails were orange. It seemed ominous, as I lay, almost naked, in her shadow, on a rubber mat. I thought I had washed myself and scrubbed my skin, but she scrubbed harder, so hard that I could feel my skin sting.

"*Baqraa qadhra. Ya shamootah. Ajnabia qabiha.*"

Dirty cow, I translated. *Prostitute. Ugly foreigner.*

She doused me in hot water and lathered my skin with soap. Then she pummelled my skin, squeezed my muscles and pinched my flesh. I felt like a rag doll in the hands of a mischievous toddler.

I wanted to respond to her insults, but honestly, I didn't have the energy, or feel in a position to defend myself with barely any clothes on. When she had finished with one side of my body, she slapped me on the arm and indicated to turn over.

The women around us clucked like hens, as they watched me squirm and gasp while I was vigorously scoured like a burnt frying pan. Strings of black dirt accumulated on my stomach, arms and legs. Obviously, I hadn't washed myself as efficiently as I had thought. I was embarrassed, but not surprised by all the grime as I hadn't had a decent shower since I arrived. When the woman had finished inflicting pain, both verbally and physically, I felt like a freed convict and rushed to the cold chamber to rinse off.

"She was so rude to me," I commented to Fatima, as I rinsed.

"I am sorry for what she said. She is not used to seeing foreigners in this *hammam*."

My spirit was somewhat bruised, but I stroked my fresh and clean skin while getting dressed. Within a few minutes of waiting, Hussein arrived to pick us up and deliver us back to the house.

31 August 1992

In love
In Damascus

Dear Diary,

I've never really considered myself to be pretty, but now I do. Hussein tells me daily how beautiful I am. *Enti jamila!* It's not just the words though, it's the way he says them. He whispers them sexily to me, and his beard tickles my neck. He calls me his Gazelle. I love that term of endearment because it makes me feel dainty, sweet and lovable.

From the moment I met Hussein, I liked him. I really think it was love at first sight and he said that it was the same for him. I was struck by his eyes, so vibrant and kind. I have not met a Middle-Eastern man with blue eyes, and his are a subtle, light blue with long, black lashes. Like any girl, I'm jealous of them! Mine are blue but not as blue as his! When he smiles, I smile and his laugh is contagious. I have never met someone as handsome as he is. Fit, tall, and at the same time an air of elegance that I didn't expect I would like in a man. He's exotic!

I can safely say I have never dated anyone like Hussein. I haven't dated much in any case. In fact, I've only had two boyfriends. (I don't count William!). There's Colin, my brother's friend, which was weird from the beginning. And Nigel, who I went out with for almost two years. We ended up having a long-distance relationship.

I went on a few dates with Colin, but I don't really count him either as we were too nervous and I think he only thought of me as Jacob's little sis. Nigel was a strict Catholic and didn't want to "go all the way" until after marriage. I was okay with that. Even if we hadn't moved away from each other, I don't think we would have ever married.

Hussein was the first I was with. He told me that I was his first. It wasn't awkward at all with him. I've never felt so close, so emotional and so in harmony with someone. I cried at the end overwhelmed by our love making. I'll never regret giving myself to him.

Hussein is completely different. He's manly and commanding, but also gentle and comforting. I longed to give myself to him like a gazelle would eventually succumb to the lion.

Well, Guess what? When we got back to the house after our Hama trip, we made love. I felt sexy, beautiful and in love. We were passionate, at times intense and then we lay together laughing and cuddling. It felt wonderful to be holding each other at last.

I never expected to fall in love with someone while studying in Damascus. Now that it has happened, I don't want to change anything. I feel as if this was meant to be and I hope that we can stay together in the future wherever that may lead us.

Seventeen

The Saturday after our trip, I asked Hussein if I could go to the British Embassy as it was bothering me that I had not yet registered. I knew our embassies always advised expatriates, wherever they may be, to register with their local British Embassy.

The vice consul in Sana'a, Barry Cole, was always complaining that some of the British expatriates, even friends we hung out with, had not registered with the embassy. He thought it was reckless not to register where they were residing in Yemen. Addresses were usually the only way of contacting them, although many addresses were hard to write down as most roads had no names and most houses had no numbers. Many people relied on physical descriptions to explain where they lived.

"If you're heading north, I'm the third street on the right off Haddah Road. It's the dirt road opposite the Ajlil grocery and the fifth house with the overlapping balcony with blue railings."

Telephone lines in homes were rare. Some expatriates had business telephone numbers, but even those phone lines weren't totally reliable. Ultimately, expatriates never imagined that they may need to be contacted urgently by family or friends from home, whether for a personal reason or for national security. Yet embassies rely on contact details as they are responsible for evacuating their citizens in the case of a dangerous situation.

Yemen was a very safe country for foreigners until the Gulf War broke out in August 1990. Before that, conflicts happened, but they mostly involved infighting between tribes in the countryside outside of Sana'a. What threats that did occur, rarely endangered

125

foreigners. We received reports from the American Embassy from time to time that an American 'oily', an employee for an American oil company, Hunt Oil, had had their car hijacked by a tribe. The driver of the car, usually a Toyota Land Cruiser, was always unharmed. In fact, the tribesmen would provide him with a taxi to return him back to his base. Hunt Oil had lost many Toyotas but never had any employee been harmed. The incidents were so harmless they were light entertainment at dinner tables.

One such story from 1989 had always stuck with me. A group of German tourists on a package holiday were visiting various historical cities in Yemen, including Shibam, Kawkaban and Ta'izz. They travelled in a small convoy of Toyota, four-wheel-drive Land Cruisers from city to city. During their excursion to Ma'rib, an ancient Sabaean city, and most probable seat of the Queen of Sheba lying to the north-east of Sana'a, they were abducted by tribesmen in the middle of the arid, volcanic countryside. Their disappearance caused grave alarm to the German Embassy, as news of their disappearance spread around the expatriate community.

It was the first time we had heard of such a kidnapping. The tourists were missing for a day, when they suddenly arrived back at the Taj Hotel in Sana'a in taxis. Instead of stories of horror, the German tourists were enraptured by their experience and told the press when it eventually got wind of the story that their captors had treated them as honoured guests. A lamb was slaughtered for them by the tribesmen to show their esteem and served along with a feast of delicious, Yemeni dishes. The punchline was that the expatriates joked that the company should put the abduction on every guided tour in future, as it was the highlight of the tourists' adventure.

The embassy was open on a Saturday, adhering to the Muslim working week so Hussein agreed to take me there that afternoon. I sensed that Hussein was in a strange mood when I jumped into the car to head there.

"Is everything okay?" I looked over at him, as he drove.

"Yes…" He looked over at me and reassured me that he was fine, but his eyes told me otherwise. His eyes, the blue of cornflowers, were always shining with joy when we were together, but they greyed with darkness inside his weak smile. When he pulled over to the curb, opposite the building, he pulled down the sun visor. He acted as if he didn't want to be seen, but I only saw the Syrian guards, who were posted at the entrance to the embassy.

Is he embarrassed to be seen with me?

"Be quick," he said, as I opened the door. I wanted to ask him if he was sure he was okay again, but he had put the car in gear and was ready to pull away.

"I'll be back here for you soon."

I didn't have a chance to say goodbye.

The British Embassy was surrounded by a high white wall and I saw the familiar embassy plaque above the gate and the Union Jack flying on a flagpole on the roof. I entered through the visitors' entrance.

"I've come to register as a British Citizen," I informed the pale, red-headed receptionist behind the glass partition.

Moments later, a side door opened and the receptionist led me to another office. It was there that I met Adrien Osbourne.

"Miss Elizabeth Booth." Adrien was a very distinguished gentleman, with a deep voice that sounded like the BBC presenter, David Attenborough, whom I enjoyed listening to when he narrated natural history programmes. He stood almost to attention in front of me, with his hands behind his back and just a slight tilt of his head towards me. He wore a dark-blue, double-breasted suit, buttoned up. Underneath, he had a white shirt and tartan tie. With his brown brogue shoes snapped together, he looked like a soldier. He did not have the appearance of a stereotypical, English man with pasty skin and light brown hair. He was naturally tanned, with a shock of dark, thick hair, cut very short. I thought he looked Mediterranean. He held his hand out and firmly shook mine.

"I'm Adrien Osbourne, the information officer in the embassy. I understand that you are here to register."

My ears pricked as soon as he said he was the information officer. I was well aware that the information officer, John Ellis, in the embassy in Sana'a was the MI6 officer. In fact, the man in front of me looked more like a James Bond character than John had.

I know it. He's the spook here.

"Yes. I'd like to register."

"Good. Please take a seat."

"Thank you." I sat on a small sofa with a glass table beside it, which had a few magazines and newspapers on it. He took a seat behind his desk.

"Here's the consular form for you to fill out and we'll need a copy of your passport." He pushed the form to me across his desk. I was curious why I was in his office receiving the form, when the front desk could have dealt with the situation.

"Where are you staying in Damascus?" he asked, getting straight to business.

"Actually, I am temporarily living with an old Syrian couple, but I don't know the exact address yet."

I lied instinctively. I wasn't even sure of the address of the place I was staying, and decided to keep it simple and say I was still with the old couple.

"How did you find them?"

"I was introduced to them during my flight over. It's only temporary, until I start school. I hope to find my own place soon."

"That would be a good idea. You may find a place with another student. The Christian Quarter of the Old City is very popular with students. So, where are you studying?"

"I am from Durham University. I'm in the second year of my Arabic degree, doing the study abroad year. I'm going to register at the Arabic Teaching Institute for Foreigners."

"Are you the only Durham student here? We've had students from Cambridge and Exeter Universities in the past, but none this year so far."

"I'm the only one from Durham. The others went to Yemen and Egypt."

"The only student," he said with a sniff. "That's extremely unusual. The universities send students in groups to ensure their safety. Why would they allow you to come alone?"

"Actually, I used to work for the Foreign and Commonwealth Office," I said with a fleeting touch of pride. "I did a tour to Sana'a for three years and then I lived in Cairo for a few months. My professors knew that I didn't want to go back to either country with the other students, so they agreed I could go to Syria."

"What did you do in Cairo?" He asked, raising his eyebrows.

"I studied Arabic with the British Council."

"You joined Durham already with a knowledge of Arabic?"

"Yes."

"When was your tour to Sana'a?" Adrien asked.

"From 1988 to 1991."

"What did you do there?"

"I was the radio communications officer and I did some visa work."

"It must have been an eventful tour. Unification, the invasion of Kuwait by Iraq. I always hoped to be posted to Yemen."

"Yes. I was one of the staff left behind during the war."

Adrien nodded thoughtfully. He stood again.

"Miss Booth, I'm impressed. You are certainly different to any other student I have met."

He stopped talking for a minute and appeared to be trying to remember something. He looked thoughtfully at nothing in particular across the room.

"So let me see. You were there with Mark McCabe, the ambassador."

"Yes, and Barry Cole, the vice consul and," I continued with a small smile, "John Ellis, the information officer." I stressed 'information'.

"Let me ask also, have you told anyone about your former time in the Foreign and Commonwealth Office?"

"No. I haven't mentioned it to anyone."

"I strongly advise you to continue to keep that confidential from everyone, in particular the Syrian government and the Institute."

"I understand."

He paused, as if he was not sure whether to continue. He sat again and knitted his fingers together. "This is strictly confidential, you know. As you have probably gathered, I am John's equivalent here in Damascus."

"Yes. You kind of gave it away when you said information officer." I was relieved he had said it finally. It cleared the air.

"It's coincidental that we have the same positions," Adrien said officially. He smiled, but it seemed a calculated gesture. "There are officers in many different roles."

"Of course," I agreed.

"There needs to be an understanding that this information is strictly confidential. I shall be clearing this with London." He was back to being more serious.

Adrien's desk phone rang. While he took the call, I glanced around his room.

His room was very sparse. Also, I noticed his desk was completely empty of any papers. All that was on it was a coffee mug with a logo from Rothman's International. I found that unusual.

Some pictures hung on the wall beside his desk. They were framed photographs of landscapes and portraits of people. As I scanned them, one stood out more than the others. It was a black and white close-up photograph of a Muslim woman wearing a *hijab*. The background of the photo was slightly blurred, which only added to the artistic appeal. Part of her face was in the shade and the other side was lit by sunlight, illuminating delicate wrinkles on her face.

"My mother," Adrien said, when he caught me staring at the photo. He had hung up while I was not paying attention.

"She's beautiful. Where is she from?"

"She's from Algiers, Algeria. She and her entire family moved to Marseilles after the Algerian War of Independence. I think her brother, who was a Harki soldier, was killed by the FLN."

"But you are British?" I questioned him, even though it seemed obvious as he was working in the British Embassy without a hint of a French accent.

"Of course. My father met my mother when he was doing his gap year before university, travelling on the trains through Europe. I guess they fell in love at first sight." Adrien smiled his quick, official smile again. He was back to business. "Do you know much about the Arabic Teaching Institute for Foreigners?"

"The university told me a little about the school, but not much really. I know it's in Mezzeh, but I don't know where that is exactly."

"How were you proposing to get there, if you don't know where it is? You seem to have arrived here without any preparation."

I pulled at my ear. I was more than a little embarrassed. I had every intention of organising myself, but I hadn't anticipated that I would meet the love of my life. How could I tell him that it was because I was in love with Hussein so soon, and he was taking care of showing me around Damascus?

"I was planning on getting a taxi. I thought the driver would know where the school is," I lied again, leaving out any mention of Hussein. I wasn't sure why.

"A taxi without knowing the address?" Adrien raised his eyebrows. "The Mezzeh district is on the west side of the city." He opened a drawer and handed me a street map of Damascus.

A map. At last, I have a map of Damascus and its suburbs.

It didn't dawn on me to wonder why Hussein had never offered to pick up one for me.

"This is where it is." He pointed to the location of the school, took his pen and circled it. "You can show a taxi driver this map."

"Thank you." I took it from him before he even had a chance to tell me to keep it.

"It's a popular school with many foreigners: Europeans, Japanese, Australians and Africans." He cleared his throat. "But there's more that you need to know about the school." He sounded a little ominous. "The Institute is run by the brother of the Interior Minister, Sayyed Al-Ibrahim Al-Tahiri. You know all teachers will report back about each foreign student straight to him?"

"I read about the paranoia here."

"Yes?"

"Also, the Ministry of Interior will have students placed in the school to report on the foreigners too."

"Really?"

"Yes. It's different now that you're not a diplomat. I suppose in Yemen, you didn't interact with the Yemenis much."

"Not at all."

"You're in a unique situation, Miss Booth, and I would like to take advantage of that. We have limited intelligence and would like you to be an unofficial informant."

"What would I have to do?" I twisted my earring. This was a lot to take in.

"It would be helpful for us to know the names of students, nationalities of students and teachers, and any fraternising that you see going on between students or teachers." His demeanour became even more serious. He leaned forwards, looking soberly at me.

I looked away instinctively.

"But I don't want you to draw attention to yourself."

"Of course." I was taken by surprise.

"So, this is something you can help us with?" he asked pointedly.

"Yes."

"Good. Good. Just notes. No questions. Okay?" He hesitated. "The government is watching everyone and in particular the foreign students. I can assure you, they will already have tabs on all who have entered the country, including you."

"I understand."

"You must be careful, wherever you are. The men in suits, that I'm sure you've noticed, are the *mukhabarat,* the secret police. There are several internal intelligence organisations and it's no exaggeration that they are all over the place. One protects the President's palace in the city."

He pointed to a place in the Muhandeseen district on the map, just below the Jabal Quasioun, the range of mountains overlooking Damascus, where I had been with Hussein and Naguib.

"I passed that place and was told not to point at any buildings." I recalled that Hussein had said to be careful at the roundabout where I saw a barrier across a side road and men in black.

"Yes. Those would be the Presidential secret police," he informed me. "Well, Elizabeth, we are always at your service." I sensed the conversation was ending.

"You can come back to see me whenever you have anything. Perhaps after you have settled into your classes. Is this agreeable to you?"

"Yes. I can do it," I replied as I scratched the side of my neck.

"Good. By the way, don't forget that once you have registered at the school, you will need to go to the Ministry of Interior to apply for an extended visa. I presume your one-month tourist visa will expire soon. When did you arrive?"

"August 12. So, what do I need to do? I'm not sure."

Hussein never mentioned this to me. I hope he knows what to do.

"You will need to go to the Ministry of Interior in the Muhandeseen district within a calendar month of your arrival. Let me warn you, that you will be there for many hours collecting a list full of signatures. One official is not enough to sign off on a student visa."

Adrien stood up from his desk, picked up his coffee mug and headed towards the door.

"Good luck with your visa." He extended his hand.

"Thank you."

I stood, shook his hand, then followed him out.

Outside, I saw Hussein's black car parked on the opposite side of the road. I looked around the street and noted how many members of the Syrian army I saw. My mindset had shifted. I felt I was being watched.

Hussein seemed in a better mood when I jumped in the car, but I was pensive about the conversation with Adrien.

"Did it go well? Are you registered?"

"Yes."

"You seem distracted." He was surprisingly intuitive.

"No. I'm fine."

"Did you talk to anyone else?" Hussein asked.

"No. Just the receptionist."

It wasn't that I distrusted Hussein. I was trying to digest the content of Adrien's request.

I noticed I felt nauseated from hunger.

"Could we go and eat?"

"Of course."

"I picked up your developed film and have another one for your camera. We can stop at the Post Office to get stamps for you afterwards."

"The receptionist photocopied my passport and said something to me about my tourist visa running out. Do you know what I need to do?"

"Yes. I was going to say we need to go to the Ministry of Interior to get you an extension to stay."

"A student extension?"

"Sure. We'll do that very soon."

Eighteen

My tourist visa was going to expire on September 12, so we had two days to apply for my extension from the Ministry of Interior.

Hussein picked me up early the next morning to take me there. We knew it would be a long day, so we grabbed a quick breakfast and left the house.

The sandstone, brick building was five floors. Large cement blocks were placed strategically at the front, in order to prevent cars from parking alongside it. The paved area in front of the building was crowded with men, most in army uniform. There were various large groups of them standing around, as well as some seated underneath the few trees, which offered the only relief from the heat. Young lads were pushing carts around, selling cigarettes, sweets and newspapers.

We drove around the building to another street, where Hussein found a place to park directly in front of a bakery. As we walked along the pavement, we passed cafes and street traders selling fruit juice. There were just as many men on this side of the building as the other: socialising and drinking tea, smoking *narguiles* in front of the cafes, in no apparent hurry to get anywhere. It seemed as if no one had a job to go to even though they were in fatigues.

I walked very closely to Hussein, making sure there was no doubt I was with him. I didn't want anyone thinking I was alone. In the sea of faces, I didn't see any other westerners around. I checked my head scarf as I followed Hussein to an entrance. There was a huge Syrian flag above it, with a sign in English and Arabic stating it was the Visa and Immigration Office. I wondered why so many Syrians were going in and out of the building for the Immigration Office, but

137

discovered it was situated on the first floor, and the huge Ministry housed many departments.

We stood momentarily in a small crowd by the narrow door, until an armed guard dressed in a pale-khaki uniform gestured to Hussein to come forward. Hussein's hand brushed mine as we pushed forward to the front. It was as much affection as he had showed me in public, and I was grateful for it.

Hussein spoke hastily to the guard. I couldn't follow and bit my lip in irritation. Lately I had been having to remind him that he needed to slow down. I wasn't as if I needed him to slow down much. I had improved greatly, especially with my Syrian dialect. I was sounding less and less like a news presenter on Egyptian TV and more like a local. I found I could pick out every other word or two and end up getting the gist of conversations, but sometimes Hussein didn't seem to want me to understand him. Hussein asked me to get my passport out and then handed it to the guard. He looked through the pages and handed it back.

We entered a tight hallway and walked up a dark, stone staircase that led to another waiting area. I expected to see some foreigners amongst everyone, trying to do the same as me and get a visa extension, but the room was packed with Syrian men. It was daunting to think of getting through the jammed crowd. I stayed at Hussein's side, as he cleared the way for me. Again, almost instinctively, I checked that my *hijab* was covering all my hair and looked at the ground.

The employees sat behind a counter with a large, glass window reaching to the ceiling that separated them from the chaos in the waiting room.

There was neither order, nor queues. Instead it boiled down to who could manage to get the officials' attention. Some applicants waved their papers in the air above everyone's head, while others flashed a handful of notes at the window.

"Why are there so many people here?"

"A lot goes on at the Ministry of Interior: traffic offences, crime…citizenship." Hussein said absently as he read the signs above the window, trying to ascertain where to go.

"This place is crazy." I was feeling very uncomfortable with so many men staring at me and bumping me. I felt some men brush past me a little too close for comfort, giving me direct eye contact as I stood beside Hussein.

Thankfully, we pushed our way into a smaller room. This room was full of women and children, and nowhere near as crowded. It was also less oppressive, without the dense smoke. I looked at Hussein questioningly.

"We're in the family room," he said, reading my mind.

Before we even took a seat, a soldier came up to us and spoke with Hussein.

I heard the guard question Hussein whether I was family.

"No." He went on to explain to the guard, but turned away from me and lowered his voice as he spoke to the guard. The guard peered at me over Hussein's shoulder. I heard him say some new Arabic words as he smirked at me, making me feel uneasy. I kept repeating the words in my head, hoping to remember them. I had learned a lot of Syrian slang this way. If I didn't have my notebook handy, I'd just keep it fresh in my mind to write down later and hopefully ask either Hussein or the girls to explain it.

Nikah mut'a muwaqqat.

"Elizabeth, follow this man. I'll wait here for you."

This was the most nervous I had felt so far. Adrien's words rang in my ears.

"The government is watching everyone."

The environment of mistrust was beginning to take its toll on me. The Syrian people are afraid of the *mukhabarat*, and I easily felt that I should be afraid of them too. I didn't suppose they would just give you a fine, if you were found to have done something wrong. I knew that, every day, people reported on each other, motivated by money, spite or governmental persuasion.

Being in an official building and surrounded by soldiers was nerve-wracking. The soldier directed me through a side door, into a hallway. He ordered me to stop at a doorway, where a few other soldiers were sitting idly, smoking and drinking glasses of tea at small tables. The soldier I had followed knocked on the slightly ajar door and entered. In a moment, he reappeared and opened it wide, ushering me in. My eyes had to adjust to the brightness in the room after the windowless hallway.

I approached a Syrian officer at the far end. He was middle-aged and stocky with thinning, black hair. He wore a darker green uniform than the other soldiers, with medals on his chest. He sat behind a large, grey, metal desk that had scores of scratches and dents on the side panels. The sun's rays lit up particles of dust and plumes of smoke coming from his desk, which was full of papers, an ashtray full of cigarette butts, and a framed picture of President Hafez Al-Assad. I was getting used to seeing their president all over Damascus. The people had to display their love for him wherever possible. From car stickers saying I "heart" Assad, to framed pictures of him, and sometimes his family, on walls, in shops and homes and huge posters and statues around the city. It was almost as if they had an intimate relationship with him as a family member. I could not imagine the laughs my fellow British friends would have had, if I stuck a bumper sticker on my car declaring my love for our Queen.

"Come take a seat," the officer said in English.

I sat on one of two metal chairs, which reminded me of school furniture.

"Welcome. I'm General Bashir Al-Saidi." He was not smiling and didn't seem very welcoming at all. "Your passport, please."

I passed it to him. He proceeded to flick through the pages. I couldn't miss seeing a large, tacky, gold-framed picture on the wall behind him of President Hafez Al-Assad in his military attire. He had been superimposed onto the foreground, while the background depicted a dramatic war scene with jet fighters flying overhead, tanks rolling over bunkers and explosions. It made him look like a hero of a 1950s, classic Hollywood movie. General Bashir proceeded to flick through the pages.

"Elizabeth Mary Booth." He read my name aloud, tapping a pen on the metal desk.

"Are your parents from Syria?"

"No. They're both English."

"Your name is Arabic. Ab-booth."

I stared back at him blankly.

I have no idea what he's talking about. My name is English, not Arabic.

A soldier came scurrying in without knocking and approached the General. The General immediately handed him my passport without a word and the soldier hustled back out with it.

"Why are you here?" he asked. He put his pen down and folded his arms.

"I'm studying Arabic at university in England."

"How do you like Syria?" Now he grinned at me.

"It's a beautiful country, with beautiful, kind people," I politely responded in Arabic.

A soldier walked in with a tray and placed a steaming, hot glass of sweet tea on the edge of the desk next to me then set down one for his General.

The General interrupted our conversation to talk to the soldier, as if he were scolding him for something he did. The soldier retreated out the room.

"So, you like Syria?" He lit a cigarette, as another soldier entered. This soldier appeared nervous and hovered at the door, waiting for the General to make eye contact.

"*Nam?*" He beckoned the soldier to him.

"Yes?" He raised his voice, asking the soldier again what he had to say for himself.

The nervous soldier spoke quickly to the General. The General listened for a moment and then aggressively blew out a large puff of smoke.

He drummed his finger on his desk and sternly spoke to the soldier. I could not gather what he was saying, but undoubtedly he was not happy with him.

At this point, I didn't think the General was the least bit interested in me answering his last question. The soldier retreated. The General turned his attention back to me.

"So, you like our country?"

As I was about to say I did very much so, another soldier popped out from behind the door.

This time the General shouted at the soldier and didn't beckon him to step into the room. The soldier left. Within a moment another came walking in with my passport and placed it on the General's desk.

The General flicked through my passport one more time and then handed it back to me.

Finally, he said, "I'm glad you like our country. I hope you enjoy your stay with us."

I took my passport from him and paused. I didn't think it would be processed so quickly. I wondered if Hussein had helped with a bribe. There seemed to be a culture of that.

That was so much faster than what Adrien had told me and only one signature.

A soldier held the door open for me. I made my way out into the dark corridor. The soldier accompanied me to an exit on the side of the building. I recognized that the bakery was just around the other side and Hussein's car was parked in front. I was excited to tell Hussein how quickly I got my visa. As I rounded the corner, I saw Hussein sitting outside one of the cafes with another man a few hundred feet away. They were deep in conversation. Hussein looked up. He grimaced.

"*Ahlan.* Hi." I smiled.

Hussein made one definite nod to the man who immediately got up and walked off in the opposite direction. I had seen the "one nod" many times in Syria. It was not a downward nod to the chin, which I would associate with a yes, but an upward jerk. I've seen it used with a myriad of meanings mostly between men;

it was a greeting, an affirmative yes, an order to leave, and a dismissive "I don't know."

"Hi, that was sooner than I expected," Hussein said once I had reached him.

"Yes."

"Is your passport stamped?"

"Yes. It's done."

Hussein looked through it and saw on the last page that there was indeed an extension visa.

"Very good." He passed it back to me. Our exchange was strained somehow, and I couldn't help feeling uneasy.

Nineteen

A few days before I was going to start at the Institute, Hussein came to the house in the late morning. He was pale, his eyes were wild, and his hair was unkempt. I had never seen Hussein look like that.

"What's wrong?"

"It's Naguib," Hussein said, frowning deeply.

"What's happened?" I asked.

"Naguib was taken away by the Police this morning. They arrested two others with him."

"Oh no!" I cried out. The thought of what prison must be like here flickered across the back of my mind. "Did you see it? What did he do?"

"I did not see it myself. I was told. He was accused of stealing from the hospital."

"That's terrible."

"I have to go to the police station for his family and find out more."

"I'll go with you," I said gathering myself up. Hussein looked at me sternly.

"Of course not."

"Hussein," I said, trying my best to imitate the stern voice my mother used when she really needed to put her foot down with my father. "Naguib is my friend. He has been kind to me. I am coming to help."

"I do not have time for this," Hussein said turning. "I only came so you could tell Fatima."

I stepped between him and the door. Anger flashed across his face, taking me by surprise. I stepped back instinctively. Hussein immediately softened.

"Fine, come along then."

We left for the police station near to the hospital. The building was swarming with Syrian men in their army fatigues. All of a sudden, I felt overwhelmed.

"Would you like to stay in the car?" Hussein asked, obviously noticing the look on my face. "I'll only be a few minutes."

I nodded sheepishly. I didn't want to deal with the sea of men at such close quarters. I wrapped and pinned on my hijab, even though I was in a car with darkened windows, which gave me an added sense of being camouflaged, and got out my vocabulary list for the day.

Within twenty minutes, as Hussein had promised, he was back.

"He's not there. They have no record of his arrest at the desk."

"That's worrying. Now what?"

"Sayyeb prison."

Hussein didn't waste any time and started the engine.

"I have to find him for his family. Asim is overseas and his family needs me."

Hussein ran his hand roughly through his hair. His anxiety fed into me. This was not exactly the laying low that Adrien would have wanted.

"Hussein, are you sure it's a good idea to go to the prison?"

"Do not worry, Mary," he said, and then corrected himself. "Elizabeth."

"Who is Mary?" I asked him. I had never heard him talk about anyone by that name.

"No one. I have no idea where that came from."

In my gut, I knew there was much more to this situation than Hussein was telling me.

We pulled up to the police prison. In the car park was a large sign, *Al-Sijn Sayyeb*. Sayyeb Prison. Underneath the name, we read the visiting hours:

Saturday 8a.m. to noon for relatives
Monday 8a.m. to noon for official visitors
Male visitors daily 10a.m. to 1p.m.
Female visitors daily 2p.m.to 4p.m.

"It's too late for me to go in," Hussein said, looking pointedly at me.

"It's 2 o'clock already," I said, looking at my watch.

"Yes. Exactly. I can't go in. You will need to go in by yourself."

"I can't do that," I said as I clasped my hands together almost in prayer. "Why don't you just come back tomorrow, when men can visit?"

"It's safer for you to go in, anyway," Hussein said, eyeing the prison.

"What do you mean?"

"If I went, they may question me and determine that I'm a collaborator with his crime and detain me, but if you go, you could pose as an aid worker or even a member of the embassy."

"I have no idea how to do that."

"Trust me. They won't question you. Do it for me and for Naguib. You do want to find him, don't you?"

"Yes. Of course, I do." Something inside me was telling me not to agree to it, but I wanted to make sure Naguib was safe.

My brow furrowed. Hussein saw the doubt in me.

"Trust me. It'll work. Don't mention his name, just say you are checking prisons for your embassy. And take off your scarf so you will be more Western."

I took my scarf off. I had become accustomed to it, and it was surprising how vulnerable I felt, once I took it off. The gravity of the situation unnerved me.

In the building, I joined some other women who were waiting for the visit to begin. They were complaining to the guard that they were late opening the gate. We were instructed to hand over contraband: food, drink, cigarettes and cameras. Then we were ushered through a gate past armed guards.

To my surprise, the guards did not ask any of the women, including myself, who they were visiting. I had my story ready, that I was an embassy consular assistant evaluating the prison conditions. I thought at the very least I would have to sign in or show my passport, but I moved through the security gate along with the small crowd.

I could see the prison yard when we stepped outside. We were told to stand in a designated area, behind a high fence. It looked out across a concrete yard, surrounded by an additional, high-wire fence probably about 12 feet high and topped with razor wire. Between the two fences there was a buffer area 6 feet wide for guards to patrol the circumference of the yard, and on each corner, towers were manned by more security. I broke out in a sweat.

The inmates began to emerge from the building into the yard. Within a couple of minutes, the yard was brimming with men. They wore different-coloured jumpsuits: purple, blue and red. I wondered what the significance was.

"Why do all the colours mean?" I asked one of the women in Arabic.

"Blue is for the convicted," she said. "Purple is for those not convicted yet."

"What about red?" I asked.

"Death penalty," she replied.

I looked around the prisoners, the majority of which were young men, and sadly saw quite a number in red. Tears pricked my eyes. I felt as if I was staring at animals in a zoo. I couldn't take my eyes off them. Some were barefoot—their feet black with dirt, while others had plastic shoes or sandals. Their uniforms were ill-fitting and dishevelled. The hardest thing to acclimatise to was their shaven heads.

Some prisoners gathered close to their fence and wrapped their fingers around the wire. Others were aimlessly sauntering around the periphery of the yard, alone or in groups. All the conversations between the women and the inmates were shouted across the patrol path. The men were shouting, non-stop, jeering and begging for contraband.

"Give us cigarettes," they shouted.

"Money," shouted others.

I scanned the faces of the hundred or so men.

"Who are you looking for?" asked a toothless woman in a black *abaya*.

"Naguib." I only knew his first name.

"Any of you donkeys know Naguib?" the woman yelled.

There was a chorus of voices as the question rippled through the men, but no one recognised his name.

"Do you have money?"

"No."

I wasn't about to give her anything as I was afraid of being caught.

After twenty minutes, the guards came and opened the exit gate for us to leave. I walked out to meet Hussein by the car.

"I'm so sorry. He wasn't there."

Hussein was silent. He stared into the distance. His beautiful eyes were cold and hard.

"What can we do now?" I asked.

"I'm not sure. I'll take you home."

He dropped me off at the house.

"I'm going to Naguib's family to let them know he wasn't at the prison."

"Okay. I hope he turns up."

Hussein drove away after barely saying his goodbyes.

I didn't expect to see Hussein until the next day. The next morning, Hussein picked me up as usual. To my surprise, Naguib was in the passenger seat.

"*Ahlan,* Naguib. How are you?" I said, as I got into the car.

"Hello, Elizabeth," Naguib said, but his demeanour was depressed. "Please accept a thousand thanks for all that you did looking for me."

Naguib was wearing a baseball cap. From the back seat, I could tell that his head had been shaved. The back of his head and his neck had nicks and scabs. It sent chills through my body. Naguib was my friend, and I easily could have never seen him again.

I didn't want to pry, although I wondered which prison he had been in, and I wished I knew how he managed to get released after such a short time. I was happy that he was with us and safe though.

When we stopped to get some fruit juice at a fruit seller, I noticed that Naguib stayed in the car and did not jump out to get the drinks. I got out with Hussein and ordered my drink.

Halib wa ananas.

I ordered my favourite combination of milk and bananas. I turned to Hussein.

"Where did you find him?"

"Later," he said, as we approached the car.

The lunch we shared was brief and awkward. We dropped Naguib off at the hospital, before heading back to the house. After we left the hospital, I pressed Hussein and he reluctantly gave me the details as he knew them.

It had started when one of the clerks from his office had been caught stealing supplies from the storeroom and trying to sell them. Once the administrator had been apprehended, the authorities wanted to know if he was working with others to sell the stolen merchandise, and he was interrogated for hours to give up the names of his accomplices. The man swore to the police that he had worked alone, but under severe interrogation he gave up some names. Naguib's name was one, and he was immediately taken into custody.

Naguib had been interrogated, along with the others, for hours. The police took them from the police station to a prison. They held him for 24 hours in an overcrowded cell, but he was eventually released, although he had no idea why.

Naguib sunk further into his car seat because of the shame he would face with his head shaved in public. People were well aware of the significance of a shorn scalp. Not only would the public get that message, but it would also bring shame to his family. Luckily for Naguib, he had been welcomed back by Hussein, his other friends, and his family.

The whole incident made me look more warily at the people around me.

14 September 1992

A Damascene
Damascus

Dear Diary,

I definitely don't think of myself as tourist, because tourists are people who get a guided tour and pass through several cities in a matter of days. I wouldn't classify myself as a traveller either. Travellers don't settle in one place. No, I'm a participant in Syrian life.

Because I'm with Hussein I've been able to talk to the Syrian people and the Damascenes and witness their daily lives. I feel safe in Damascus, even though I know I must be careful. It's hard being judged all the time for being a westerner, but then each and every person is being judged. Living under the watchful eye of so many police, soldiers, and officials would make anyone paranoid. It's sad when you can't even trust family members, members of your own neighbourhood, or work colleagues.

No one can openly oppose or criticise the regime and you can't mention the word 'Alawi', the Shiite minority sect the President's family is from. Can you imagine being really afraid to criticise John Major in front of your friends or family? So crazy!

I think about what happened to Suheera and how her family abandoned her, and also Naguib being accused by his work colleague, and the rift between Samirah and Fatima. It's all based on mistrust.

I hope Hussein knows he can trust me. I don't want to get to the stage where I am living in fear, and not being able to trust my loved ones. What an awful way to live. It does make me thankful for my family, friends, and home.

Twenty

On the day before school was to start, Hussein drove me to the Institute to register. We pulled up near a large building that was unmistakably a school, although it didn't look like schools back home. The entrance into the grounds was gated. There was a huge sign above the gate in English and Arabic that read, 'Arabic Teaching Institute for Foreigners.'

The heavily barred main gates were locked together with a large, black padlock and chain. We walked through the side gates for pedestrians. The high, cement walls that surrounded the grounds were topped with railings that made them even more impressively high. I felt like we had entered another prison.

Inside, the walls along the school's corridors were whitewashed and blank. I had read that the school doubled as a secondary school, attended by Syrian children in the morning, so I was surprised that there were neither posters and pictures of the pupils' work, nor were there plaques or memorabilia on display in the corridors. Overall, the school seemed devoid of character and empty.

At St. Agnes school, many walls around the reception and corridors were full of various types of wall hangings; one entire wall was dedicated to headshots of all the staff. My friends and I used to wish we could draw moustaches on the glass.

Hussein and I saw a gathering of foreign students in the reception area. I estimated thirty students of different ethnicities and nationalities. Some were obviously European from their western dress, and a few white females who wore *hijabs* appeared to be from eastern Europe or Russia. Others seemed to be from Asia and Africa. Many were chatting with each other while waiting in line. Hussein and I joined the line. Hussein had asked me to wear my *hijab* before coming to school, but I had told him I didn't need to, if I was amongst foreign students.

"You see there are students with *hijabs* on." He pointed out the Muslim women.

"I see, but I prefer not to wear it in the school," I said firmly. Hussein looked crossly at me.

Staff members were seated behind tables where the students lined up. There were three female teachers who wore headscarves and were dressed in black, as well as three male teachers in suits. One student stepped forward at a time, when a teacher beckoned the next in line to approach.

I pulled at my ear.

"You'll be fine," Hussein said in Arabic. It was reassuring how used to the language I had become.

The teachers took notes as they interviewed the students. Then they asked all the students to go down the left corridor to the classrooms. The corridor to the right, with its glistening, clean floor was empty, which gave me a foreboding feeling.

Perhaps that's where the administration rooms and Principal Al-Tahiri's office are.

As I reached the front of the queue, a teacher waved me forward to him.

"I'll be in the car when you've finished," Hussein said, as I stepped forward to the table.

A grey-haired Syrian man, who gruffly asked me my name and nationality, and then asked for my passport, greeted me in English. He verified all my information and turned to the page in the passport with the visa extension. He made notes and then handed me a piece of paper and told me to head to classroom three. I felt even more nervous than before, because I didn't like taking tests.

I paced down the corridor, listening to my tread fall upon the white, marble floor to the classrooms. The number of each classroom was displayed on a sign above the door. I stopped at classroom number three, where about twelve students stood outside.

This is a co-ed class. I was relieved.

"Hi, I'm Elizabeth." I introduced myself immediately, hoping to make a good impression.

"Hi, I'm Elina," a student replied enthusiastically. Elina was a striking blonde with bright, blue eyes. She had an incredible smile.

"Where are you from?" I asked her.

"We're from Norway." She was speaking of her friend, beside her. "This is Astrid." Astrid had strawberry-blonde, curly hair and seemed much shyer than Elina.

As the introductions went around the group, I also met an Icelandic student called Magnus, two German students named Hans and Ingrid who seemed to be a couple, and a student from Kenya, Kaleem, who seemed shy like Astrid.

"Do you know what this test is for?" I asked.

"I think they are determining our level in Arabic." Elina seemed to know much more about what was going on than everyone else.

"What classes are there here?" I inquired.

"They have beginners, intermediate, and advanced," Elina said. "I hope I make the advanced level, but I'll probably be in the intermediate one. The beginners class is way too easy."

"I really hope I'm in the same as you Elina," Astrid said. She didn't make eye contact, when she spoke to anyone. I began to wonder whether they were friends before they came, or if they had just met.

While I was thinking about all of that, someone shouted down the hall in Arabic, and we all filed in. It was an old-fashioned room, with rows of wooden desks with wooden chairs behind them. At the front of the classroom, a female teacher was busy working at her large, wooden desk in front of a blackboard that spanned the whole length of the room. She didn't pay any attention to the students entering the room.

"Begin the test." The teacher never looked up at the class.

I took a seat and opened the small test booklet that sat on the desk. The test paper was in Arabic and English. Finally, the teacher acknowledged the class. She seemed surprised to see so many students in her classroom.

"Those of you who score the highest will go to the advanced class." She spoke in Arabic.

The beginning was easy, with simple vocabulary questions. Page two was a series of grammar questions asking for the verb, adjective, predicate and object to be underlined. I found this relatively easy as well. I had a better understanding of written Arabic than spoken. I had been drilled very hard on vocabulary and grammar during the first year at Durham University.

I moved onto the third page, which had a comprehension passage with several questions. There was no English on this page. I read the passage and understood the news story about the Syrian government. It praised Hafiz al-Assad and his generosity towards his people and foreigners.

A couple of students finished and passed their papers to the teacher, who placed them on the corner of her desk. I had finished third, but I hesitated to hand my paper in until a few more were added to the pile. I didn't want to be moved into the advanced class.

When I eventually handed in my paper, I saw that many students had already left the building. I walked out and I met up with Hussein, having not said goodbye to anyone. I was just glad to see him and that the test was over.

"How did it go?" he asked.

"Great, I think." I wanted to hug him, but I knew we couldn't touch each other in public.

"Did you meet other students?"

"Yes. I met quite a few Europeans and an African. There was a Japanese girl there, too."

"I bet you were the best student." He smiled like a parent. "Did you do well?"

"Yes. My Arabic is really good. Thanks to you, of course, as I get lots of practice. By the way, I'm starving." I grinned.

"Come on, let's go get some lunch." He gave me a big, cheesy smile back.

We left the school and headed back into town.

20th September 1992

Damascus

Dear Mum and Dad,

Hi from Damascus!

I can't believe I've been here for a month already!!

Reassuring you all that I am doing well and I have settled into a good routine.

I wanted to tell you all about my trip to Hama. I don't know if you've heard of this city but it's famous for the water wheels that date back to the 8th century! The water wheels are still moving, although they aren't providing water to the city anymore. They are very loud and creaky.

I went there with some Syrian friends, Hussein, Fatima and Naguib. Fatima has become my close girlfriend here. In fact, she is like the sister I never had. She speaks English, but I talk to her in Syrian. We help each other out with our languages.

Also, I wanted to tell you I have registered with the Institute. There are a lot of foreign students there: German, Icelandic, French, Moroccan, Turkish, American and Japanese. I met a few of them when I took my placement test last week.

I'm working hard and really starting to see the benefits of being with my Syrian friends, as opposed to being with the Western students. I definitely did the right thing coming to Syria, instead of Yemen or Egypt with the other Durham students.

The weather is still really hot. I don't spend much time outside. I guess it's still warm at home too. I hope you're having an Indian summer. Thinking of you all and hoping you are all well.

I'll write again soon.

I've enclosed some photos from my first film. I've written on the backs of them. They are of my friends when we visited Hama and some of the market, the Al-Hamidiyah in the Old City. It feels like I have walked into a Hollywood film set of Lawrence of Arabia or something.

Love,

Elizabeth

Twenty-one

It was strange that the first day of school was a Sunday. I guess I'll have to get used to that. I thought of one of my favourite songs by the Boomtown Rats *I don't like Mondays*, but now as the Islamic day of rest is a Friday and Saturday is a day off, I will have to get used to starting my week on a Sunday and 'not liking Sundays'. When Hussein and I arrived, students were gathering in small knots outside at the back entrance of the school. It was a covered porch area, with wide steps along the length of the wall. Others sat on low, concrete walls, but everyone was generally milling around from group to group.

"Hi again," I said, as I approached the Norwegian girls.

"Hi, Elizabeth," Elina said cheerfully.

"How did you do on the test?" I ventured.

"It seemed quite simple." Elina's English was perfect and her Arabic have must been excellent, as she was the second person to hand her paper in.

"I found it hard." Astrid added, looking in our general direction.

"I was able to do the vocabulary and grammar pages, but it was difficult to do the last page," I said. Astrid nodded her agreement, but did not say anything.

The porch was getting crowded, as more students arrived and were getting to know each other.

"Where are you staying?" I was trying to be polite, but part of me wondered if I had perhaps internalised Adrien's advice.

"But I don't want you to draw attention to yourself and be careful what you reveal of yourself to others. It's my

belief that the less information there is of you out there the better."

"We've got a house in the Old City. It's incredible. We live off Straight Street near Baab Touma," Elina replied.

"I wouldn't live anywhere else. Living in the Old City is like living in the dark ages. The Christian and Greek Orthodox churches are all there." Astrid suddenly became animated.

"Do you live together?" I had seen parts of the Christian Quarter in the Old City with Hussein, but I knew it would be so different if I lived there.

"Yes. We are here with our university studying for our degree. You'll have to come and see us."

"Yes, please come." A quiet voice spoke up. Astrid was looking at me directly and I saw her smile for the first time, which lit up her face.

"Thank you. I'd love to." I thought of Hussein briefly and wondered what he would think of me making a visit, but I brushed the thought away. Of course, he wouldn't mind.

I picked up on a male voice with a British accent nearby. I looked around to see who it could be and had no trouble identifying the English guy in question, as soon as I spotted the white ankle socks and sandals. He also wore a white, collared, starched shirt and long, beige, dress trousers. He appeared to be in his late twenties and quite plain, with mousy hair and a chubby figure.

"I flew with British Airways from Heathrow. The flight was hit by air turbulence."

He's definitely English. How am I going to introduce myself?

Before I could think much longer, he approached us three blondes.

"Hello. Let me introduce myself. I'm Matthew Marshall."

"Hi, I'm Elina Nilsson from Oslo."

"Hi, I'm Elizabeth Booth." I didn't need to tell him I was English.

Astrid fell sullen again. She's friendly and then aloof. She puzzled me. She seemed complicated, but also vulnerable.

"We were talking about where we live. Have you found a place yet?"

"Yes. I've got a flat near the Assad Library by the Omayyad Square. It's the top-floor flat. I enjoy a cup of Earl Grey tea in the morning, watching the sun come up above the rooftops of buildings. It's quite fabulous and a wonderful way to start my day."

I couldn't tell if he was serious or joking, but I liked him immediately.

"Who's the guy I saw you with?" asked Matthew.

"That's Hussein. He's a friend." I was flummoxed. I had always been a bit shy about matters of the heart.

"Are you staying with him?" he asked.

"I'm staying with some friends." I dodged the real push of the question. Matthew seemed curious for an Englishman.

"I bet your Arabic is great," Matthew said, with a chuckle. "Mine is atrocious."

"Staying with locals has really helped my Syrian dialect a lot."

Before long, a teacher asked us to go to our classrooms. I saw Matthew head towards the beginners' classroom.

"I'll see you all later," Matthew said with a wave.

"Don't you want to check where you're placed?" I asked.

"I think I know, my friends." Matthew chuckled again and ducked into the beginners' classroom.

For the rest of us, our class assignments were listed on a paper, hanging in the hall. All the students crowded around the paper. I was relieved to find out that I was in the intermediate class. Hans and Elina went next door to the advanced class. Astrid was desperately upset as she didn't make it into the advanced class with Elina.

"I am just as good as Elina. I should be in the advanced class with her." She scowled darkly.

"Well you may move up to it, if you do well," I said trying to console her.

"I guess, at least Kaleem is in class with me," Astrid reflected. "And you are, of course." I was glad she included me, and I smiled at her as we made our way in.

The teacher in our classroom didn't waste any time and handed out large, black, ring-bound books, full of Arabic passages. As I flipped through, I noticed there was not one single translated word in the entire book. It was daunting.

The teacher started by introducing herself and talking about the school.

"*Ana ismi Ustatha Ad-Din.*" Her name was Professor Ad-Din.

"There will be nothing but Arabic spoken in this class," Professor Ad-Din warned in Arabic. "Anyone caught speaking another language will be forced to leave the school. You can speak to each other in other languages during the ten-minute break."

Professor Ad-Din opened the book to the first chapter. I scanned the words, as she started to read. I recognised that it was a passage by Taha Hussein, from his collection, *Al-Ayam*. It was a passage in which he talks to his young daughter about her innocence and sweet heart, hoping to spare her of the deprived and tragic life that he had experienced. Each paragraph the teacher stopped to write vocabulary on the board, which she described and even occasionally mimed the meaning, until the majority of the class grasped it. She was a middle-aged lady with an ample figure. Her antics often generated laughs with the students and I was glad to see she had a sense of humour. I scribbled what I thought were the translations in my book.

I was relieved when the short break came because my head was aching.

After the break, the second half of the class was dismally boring, as my headache worsened. Professor Ad-Din tried to explain grammatical rules and there's no way to act out whether an accusative or genitive rules the phrase or not. I was elated when we were dismissed and made my way quickly to meet Hussein.

"How was your first class?" Hussein asked, as I climbed into the car.

"I'm in the intermediate class."

"Really? I thought you'd be in the advanced class."

"I must have just missed it," I said.

"Did you talk to other students?"

"Of course."

"We should go to eat with them sometime," Hussein said.

"You would like to meet the other students?" I was puzzled.

"Why not? Or invite them to dinner sometime."

I didn't expect Hussein to want to know any of the other students. I suppose he just wanted to know my friends. Something about the way he said it left me with a nagging feeling, that he wanted to know what I was doing without him around, more than him wanting to get to know the other students. I had an urge to hold my new friendships closer to me.

Twenty-two

At the end of the first week, all the students were ushered into the canteen. The teachers stood sternly with their backs against the walls, watching all the students mingle and talk. Our chatter was interrupted by a high-pitched screech over the loudspeakers and then the Syrian national anthem started to play. The teachers mouthed all the words and even some of the students joined in.

Principal Al-Tahiri then came in to address us all. He was a smart-looking man, mustachioed with thinning hair that was swept over his bald patch. He spoke about Arab pride and Islamic achievements. He also told us that students were not permitted to leave the premises or miss a day of school.

After the speech, the teachers dismissed us and we walked to our classrooms. My teacher began a new passage about Hama, which spoke of all the criminals and terrorists who killed the people by the thousands, and how the Syrian government had saved the inhabitants.

When I met Hussein outside in the evening, I was interested to talk to him about our text on Hama.

"I read about Hama in class today and it reminded me of our trip there."

Hussein was in a sullen mood and merely nodded in response.

"I wish you would wear your hijab when you come out of school." He scowled deeply gazing at the dashboard.

"But I didn't wear it in class. It doesn't seem worthwhile putting it on as I'm just getting in the car."

"I would like you to do it for me." He smiled thinly, but didn't look at me focusing rather on the road ahead.

"I can do that."

"*Shukran*." He thanked me still concentrating on the traffic.

"So how was your afternoon?" I tried to lighten the conversation.

"It was full of errands for my mother."

Our conversation petered out. We drove to the house in silence. Silence had not felt uncomfortable with Hussein until this point. Something was wrong.

That evening, Hussein took me out to eat. He seemed to have got over his bad mood.

"I know this restaurant that serves the most delicious sheep's brain. Have you ever eaten a brain before?"

"Yuk! That's awful. What is it like?"

"It's tasteless actually. The best thing is it makes you smarter than you are." He laughed.

"Well, if that's the case I'll try some." I laughed too. I was so glad that he was back to himself.

In the restaurant, we continued to chat. Hussein ordered sheep's brain much to my objection. When it was served, there was no doubt that it was a brain by the greyish folds and wrinkles on its surface. Hussein sliced a sliver of it for me. He watched me squirm with a mouthful of sheep's brain. It was tasteless, but the most revolting thing was the smooth texture, like eating liquid velvet. I managed to swallow it, but declined a second spoonful.

"You don't seem to be a devout Christian," Hussein observed between bites. "Do you follow your faith?"

"I used to, when I was younger, living with my family, but I don't practise anymore. I still believe in God and Jesus though."

"You know, Jesus is revered in the Qur'an, as are many prophets like Noah and Abraham. All are holy men and messengers of Allah's word."

"How devout are you as a Muslim?"

"I'm the same as you. I follow my faith, but not strictly."

"In Islam, do you have to marry a Muslim?"

"Not necessarily, although it makes life a bit easier for the couple, if it is not a mixed marriage here in Syria. It would probably be different in Europe."

"Perhaps, one day you will experience western societies in the same way that I am experiencing Middle Eastern life in Syria." I smiled to let him know what I was implying. His eyes lit up.

"Well, let me ask you. Would you marry a Muslim?"

"I might." I giggled.

"Would you convert to Islam?"

"I don't know enough about it." That was a heavier question than I had anticipated. I had thought we were flirting more than anything else.

"I'd be honoured to answer any questions, or tell you about my faith."

"How easy is it to convert? Would I have to be baptised or something?"

"No, nothing like that. You could become one, right here, just by saying the Shahada."

"Is that *la ilaha illa'llah muhammadur-rasūlu-llāh?*" I tried to pronounce the words clearly, knowing that they were sacred to Hussein, in the way the Lord's Prayer had been for me as a young Catholic.

"Yes, and now you are a Muslim."

"What?"

"I'm joking, but in reality, you can convert simply by reciting the Shahada in front of at least two witnesses."

"That is amazingly simple."

It eased my mind to know that Hussein had an open mind about other religions and western women. For a moment, I toyed with the idea and it wasn't beyond the realms of possibility that I could become his wife and even a Muslim.

Twenty-three

One Thursday evening, when the girls were looking forward to the beginning of their weekend, I came home from school to find the house was a hive of activity. The girls were rushing around preening themselves. Fatima emerged from her bedroom wearing a glamorous, red dress, bedazzled with sequins. Her hair was teased high above her forehead and her makeup was bolder and heavier than usual.

"Are you going somewhere nice?" I asked.

"It's a party tonight. We have all been invited."

"What kind of party?"

"It's a celebration for one of Hussein and Naguib's friends."

"Am I invited to go?"

"Did Hussein not tell you about the party?" Ever since the trip to Hama, Fatima had been distant with me. Outwardly she was still friendly, but things were different.

"No," I said, concerned.

Why wouldn't he tell me about a party with his friends?

I didn't have any sparkly dresses in my rucksack, but changed into one of my skirts.

Fatima came to me with some dangly earrings.

"Here, you can wear these."

"Thank you." They were so long they grazed my shoulders.

Hussein arrived. Fatima smiled at Hussein, but he didn't return the gesture.

"What are you doing?"

"Fatima told me we were all going to a party," I said, trying not to be too confrontational.

171

"Of course, of course. I thought I had told you. Elizabeth, my friend is getting married in two days. We have been invited to his party."

"Are you sure? I can stay here if you want me to."

"No, we have all been invited."

"Don't men and women attend wedding celebrations separately here?" I asked.

"Normally, yes, but this is a special friend and a private venue, so we are all going." Hussein seemed irritated.

"*Mumtaz*. Great." I grinned.

Naguib arrived shortly after Hussein with two other men I had occasionally seen at the house before with Na'imah and Meher. He looked more cheerful than when I had seen him on the morning of his release. His hair was beginning to grow back and he was smiling.

Hussein and I drove separately to the party. The drive took us out of Damascus towards the airport. It seemed strange to be driving along that road again. It felt like such a long time since I was first driven into Damascus. Things felt very different this time.

We approached a large, white, stucco building that looked Mediterranean in style with its red-tiled roof and pulled into a crowded car park. A pink, neon sign above an arched doorway read "*Mat'aam Al-Karim*". The Generous Restaurant.

Everyone moved on into the restaurant, which had a beautifully manicured courtyard. Fragrant bushes and flagstone pathways separated tables. Fairy lights were strung all around the trees. In the middle of the courtyard, there was a large table with seats for up to twenty or so guests. It was laden with platters of fruit and food. Some guests had already seated themselves and were settling in, as waiters buzzed around serving water.

The girls went to sit at one end of the table and joined a few other ladies. Fatima came to me and led me to a seat amongst those women.

"Fatima, I would prefer to sit with Hussein."

"You must stay with the women," Fatima insisted.

Hussein had already left my side and was making his way around the other end of the table greeting all the men. Greeting was a lengthy affair. Embraces consisted of cheek touching with air kisses, handshakes and slaps on backs, all happening simultaneously.

I acquiesced and followed Fatima. I politely greeted the ladies, who I hadn't met before. There was an Asian woman, who barely acknowledged me only raising an eyebrow as she continued a conversation with another lady.

"*Ahlan wa sahan, bismi* Nadia," another woman said, unsmiling. A short, buxom girl with jet-black hair introduced herself. She looked like a teenager. Her makeup was caked on, as if she had been practising with it for the first time. She wore a black, sequinned dress, which didn't fit her properly.

I felt awkward taking a seat amongst the women. They didn't appear to be enjoying the celebration particularly. They watched the men haughtily, most barely speaking to each other.

It reminded me of school discos, where the girls and boys stood on opposite walls, not wanting to socialise from sheer awkwardness and embarrassment, but this was markedly different, as these women were not school children, and their behaviour was not because of embarrassment.

I surveyed the other end of the table. Occasionally, one of the men made eye contact with the women, who never stopped staring at them. Samirah got up to join one of men and sat beside him. The music became louder and more vibrant, and soon belly dancers appeared. The first was in a beautiful red costume with sequins and beads. Her top was exquisite, with gold embroidery interlaced in the velvet material.

As I watched her make her way around the table, another dancer entered the courtyard area. She had cymbals on her fingers and she moved her arms as if they were snakes. Both had lush, black hair, which they flung back and forth, as their bodies twisted and twirled to the rhythm of the drum beat. The girls made loud noises with their tongue, which Hussein had once called zillzilling. The belly dancers wound their way around the table, as clapping exploded. One danced by Hussein, who was grinning as he puffed on a *narguiles*, a water pipe. She was incredibly talented. I was mesmerised watching her belly undulate and inflate rhythmically from her ribcage to her pelvic bone. She could isolate all parts of her body, moving her hips independently of the top half of her body. Hussein and Naguib threw some money which fluttered to the ground around her bare feet. I felt a pang of jealousy.

The waiters continued to circle the guests, this time with hot coals for their *narguiles*. More food was delivered: *kebeh*, fried meat balls with pistachios and bulgur wheat; *kofta* and *tabbouleh* smothered with parsley and zesty lemon juice; and my favourite dessert, *kunafeh* which is made with phyllo pastry stuffed with mild white cheese and soaked in sugary syrup.

I noticed Fatima having a heated conversation with Nadia, who was seated next to her. I couldn't hear them over the music. They were blustering at each other so close their noses almost touched. Fatima glanced anxiously over to the men and saw that one or two of them were paying attention to the commotion. She tried to hush Nadia, who was getting more and more agitated. Suddenly, Nadia got up and left the table.

"I'm sorry." Fatima walked over and turned to me.

"What are you two rowing about?"

"Listen, you don't belong here," she said abruptly.

"I know. I wish I had stayed at the house." I felt intensely out of place.

"*You* should not be here with us." Her tone laid a cautionary emphasis on "you".

"Why am I separated from Hussein?" I believed I would be more comfortable moving to his end of the table.

"We are not considered girlfriends, nor are any of us wives."

"Fatima, do you mean to say we are some kind of accessory to the men?"

"Yes. What you may call..." She searched for the word in English. "Escorts." Fatima was talking in a hushed voice, under her breath. I could tell this was not something she wanted to disclose.

"Am I considered one sitting here with you? I need to sit with Hussein." I got up to leave, but Fatima held my arm.

"Wait. Don't leave yet." Her eyes were darting around the table. I could sense she was extremely anxious. I reluctantly sat back down.

"Is your relationship with Naguib real?" I asked, as pointedly as I could muster.

"No."

"Are you one?" I felt ashamed to ask her such a vulgar question. A torrent of images flashed through my mind. The evidence had been right in front of me.

How could I have been so unaware? The gifts. The food. The visitors.

"Elizabeth, I had no choice. I brought *irdh* — shame — to my family," she whispered. "I can never be married."

"Why?"

"They do not believe I was a virgin, when I didn't bleed on my wedding day. I was to be stoned, but my uncle is connected and had me sent to Damascus. I should be dead." She had one tear forming in the corner of her eye, but remained stoic. I could only imagine the depth of her horror.

"I'm so sorry." I wanted to console her, but she was putting on a brave face. She hadn't answered my question though. "Fatima, am I considered an escort because I am living with you?"

Fatima fell silent, after she glanced again to see who was watching her. She collected herself and turned away from me to eat from her plate.

"I have to go to Hussein now," I informed her, even though she was no longer listening to me. I got up and walked around the seated guests to the end of the large table.

The reality of my situation hit me. I was overwhelmed by Fatima's story and that I was living amongst a group of prostitutes. The word brought up a sense of burning embarrassment I hadn't felt since Catholic school. I looked at the men in the room with disgust, but I was comforted by the fact that Hussein was different. Even though these men probably looked upon me as an easy, western woman who had no morals, I knew that Hussein knew me better and respected me.

I crossed the room and stood beside Hussein, but he was talking to a small group of men. He acknowledged me and nodded his head, as if to indicate that he would be a few minutes while he finished his conversation. My mother used to do the same, when she met a friend while shopping in the supermarket and I wanted to go home. She would acknowledge me with a stern look, and I knew I had to wait patiently for her to end her conversation, which did sometimes run into half an hour.

I left Hussein. I needed to hide for a moment.

The bathroom had three stalls. It was unsanitary, but I didn't care about the stench and filth. I leaned up against a grimy, white-tiled wall, with my head in my hands. I was feeling foolish for having missed so many signs. I was also upset with Hussein for not telling me who I was living with.

I heard a sound from one of the stalls. The door opened and Nadia came out. She was still looking wide-eyed and irritated after her argument with Fatima.

"Are you okay?" I asked her in Arabic

"Hussein *ayze nikah mut'ah*."

"I don't understand." I struggled to understand her dialect. I recognised the words, but didn't know what they meant.

177

Nadia repeated them ardently, hoping the meaning would become clear to me.

She desperately searched for a way to convey the meaning.

"*Enti.* You. Hussein. *La.* No." Nadia pointed to me, wagging her finger and shaking her head. "*La, la, la.*"

Fatima appeared in the bathroom.

"Fatima, Nadia is trying to tell me something about Hussein. What is it?"

"It's a temporary marriage." She knew immediately and I realised this was the root of their earlier fray.

"What does that mean?" I asked Fatima.

"You must be careful. It's a marriage for pleasure only."

"He hasn't even mentioned marriage." Of course, he had. I felt my face burning. I tugged at my ear, suddenly intensely aware of the weight of the earring that hung there.

"He will."

"Do you mean Hussein wants to marry me just for *pleasure*?"

"Yes, and maybe to get a visa for England."

"That can't be true!" My pulse raced.

"Once you take him to Europe, he will have all he wants. You will be done."

"But what of his family? He'd never leave his mother and sisters."

"Elizabeth, he has no family here." Fatima shook her head.

"But Hussein is in mourning for the death of his father."

"After the loss of a family member, Muslim women grieve for four months and ten days. It's very specific. But male relatives only mourn for three days."

My devastation was palpable. Nadia put a hand on my shoulder, reading the conversation on my face. I shrugged it off.

"I have to get away," I declared. I had an overwhelming need to flee, but I didn't know where to. That feeling scared me more than anything.

"Elizabeth, you must be careful. Don't do anything now. I will try to help you find a way out." With that, she and Nadia left the bathroom.

Fatima's last words echoed in my brain. If this were all true, I had to be careful.

Three days. They only mourn for three days.

I pulled myself together and washed my hands. I looked into the blurry mirror, speckled with black splotches on the glass. In the distorted image, I saw my blotchy, reddened face concealing fireworks and rage, love and frustration, ambition and fear. I brushed away the dust and grime on my T-shirt from leaning on the wall and walked out to joined Hussein at his table.

"Hey, you look sad," he said.

"No. I'm just tired."

Did he ever love me?

At this point, I didn't know who to believe, Fatima or Hussein.

After the party, I had fitful night tossing and turning in my sleep. I dreamed I was on the roof of a tall skyscraper. I was enjoying the views of the city below and the expanse of the panoramic horizon. As I glanced around, I spotted a fire in the far distance. I walked around the roof to another side of the building, still enjoying the sights and then I saw another fire. It started to worry me that there were now two, and before I had time to think if I should alert someone, I saw three more, and then two more. The sky turned to night and the fires blazed and grew and I tried to find the door to get down from the building. Then I woke up in the darkness of the night. I was sweating on the thin mattress I had got used to, in the room that was not my own. I didn't sleep the rest of the night.

Twenty-four

In the morning, the images of my dream lingered for hours. I'd had anxiety dreams before: finding myself facing a test at school that I had not prepared for, or being partially naked in public. But this dream was different. It felt like a warning.

I was exhausted. At least, being a Friday, it was not a school day. I would not have been able to stay awake in class. I rolled out of bed and dug into my rucksack for something to wear. Fatima had procured a small table and chair for me so I could do my studies and a rectangular, unframed mirror to hang on my wall. I felt disconcerted, as I gazed into the mirror to brush my hair. A pretty girl stared back at me, but she didn't have the same confidence she used to. She looked sad, no longer the fresh-faced optimist I saw in the mirror back in England. I tied back my hair and applied a little makeup.

I continued listlessly with my routine and set about translating a large text from one of Ghassan Kanafani's novels for my next class. For the first time, the walls of my room felt like a trap, which I had voluntarily walked into. My fellow inmates did not choose their imprisonment. I had the capability to change my situation, but their options were zero. I recalled Fatima's heart-wrenching story, and how she must have lived through so much I could not begin to understand. Her fate was in the hands of others. As was mine, for now.

I went over the plan I had formulated in the early hours of the morning, when my mind was unable to drift off to sleep. I gave myself a day, two at the maximum.

I have to start fresh.

Hussein arrived in the late morning to take me to lunch. We headed towards Al-Hamidiyah market and parked by a different entrance. He tried to talk to me, but I could tell he could feel the distance between us. I kept thinking about what Fatima had said and the lies Hussein had been feeding me.

You should have known, Elizabeth, I chided myself. *If something seems too good to be true…*

I could barely look at him. It made me flush with anger and embarrassment. I settled for looking out the window, until we came to a stop.

The road through the market was crowded, with stalls selling kitchen utensils, pots, pans, tools and machinery. We walked through various sections of the *souq*. Men with heavy machinery were working on various metal components; sparks from a welding machine leapt up in the air as we passed. Some groups of Syrian women were shopping for material amongst bolts of cloth that were stacked precariously high in the tiny stalls. Then we entered a gloriously lit area.

We walked along a concrete path that looked as if it had been swept clean recently. It was unmistakably the jewellery section. The glistening, glass cabinets displayed exquisite, bright yellow, gold pieces. The necklaces were hung to show off the intricate workmanship of the artisans who had created them. I wanted to stop and look at some of the displays. I pondered how it would be to meander around the *souq* by myself. Then I remembered my first time in the *souq*, when I had lost Hussein. In the back of my mind, there was an impulse to press myself close to him. I dismissed it.

Before long, we entered a shop with some glass cabinets that sold many different items: electronics, kitchenware, household utensils and miscellaneous knick-knacks. In a way, it reminded me of a tiny department store. It wasn't clear to me what Hussein wanted in here. I aimlessly walked to the back of the shop, browsing high shelves stacked full of merchandise: radios, cameras, toys, a silly Hello Kitty alarm clock. I became more and more confused about what he could be buying. That thought brought the fact that I didn't truly know Hussein slamming into the forefront of my mind. I thought about the fires from my dream again.

Hussein was talking to the shopkeeper, a man about Hussein's age, who was behind the register near the front of the shop. Before long, Hussein handed some money to the shopkeeper and received a small, plastic bag, which he put in his pocket.

"Elizabeth, we can leave now." Hussein waved me over.

I had noticed a poster about a book fair on the wall by the shop and pointed it out to Hussein. I decided I would take the next morning off studies and go by taxi to check out what was there.

"This looks interesting. I think I'll go tomorrow morning. I might pick up an Arabic novel that's easy to read."

"I'll drive you there," he replied, as we made our way through the market.

"I don't mind catching a taxi. There's an address on the flyer and, in fact, I really want to go by myself."

"No. It's *mamnoor*."

"Forbidden. Why?"

"It's an Islamic book fair and women are not welcome alone, as they cannot buy books without a male relative."

"I'm a tourist. I don't think it'll apply to me."

"It's our law." He raised his voice. "If you were my wife, you would have to be respectful and obey the laws."

I gritted my teeth. I was frustrated, as I didn't know how to verify what he had said but I felt in my bones that he was lying.

We continued to walk on and soon entered a restaurant. It was lunchtime and I was grateful for a break and a chance to eat. Hussein ordered a specialty dish from Damascus called *fatteh*, made with hummus, whole chick peas and yoghurt in a bowl. It was delicious.

"I noticed you don't wear jewellery, Elizabeth," Hussein said, between bites. His enthusiasm for the food, a cute quirk two days ago, now played on my nerves.

"No. I'm not a jewellery kind of person."

"I hope one day I will buy you some."

"A necklace, or earrings perhaps."

"Perhaps a ring, if you agree to sign a *Katb el-Kitab* contract?"

"I don't know what that is." I hadn't come across it in my vocabulary, although the root, *katb*, came from the verb to write.

"It's a marriage contract."

"Marriage?" I wasn't smiling. "I can't get married."

"It's as simple as converting to Islam. There doesn't need to be a wedding. There only needs to be two, male witnesses. If the bride-to-be says 'I agree' three times to her fiancé, officially they would be married according to Islamic law."

Did he not know that girls dream of the day they will get married from a young age? I had images of my white dress and red roses. I wasn't about to get married without my father giving me away, and being surrounded by family, and certainly not with two strangers as my only witnesses. Certainly not to this man.

I felt sick to my stomach. I hoped I wasn't showing what my mind was thinking, that I had just one or two days to get through, and then I could say goodbye to him forever.

"Wedding is a holy sacrament in my religion," I said.

"We can still marry here, and then over there, and get married again."

"You mean you would marry in a Catholic church?"

He hesitated.

"Yes. If it means so much to you — or you could become a Muslim."

Again, I knew I had caught him in a lie after the book fair one. I had learnt in my studies during my first year, that a Muslim cannot marry a Christian — not a Muslim man as devout as Hussein was beginning to demonstrate at least.

I tried desperately to keep my composure.

"You must love me very much."

"*Ghazali.*" My gazelle. I shuddered at the name.

Twenty-five

It was a sobering revelation to admit that I had dreamt of marrying Hussein, but the fairy tale had been shattered. It wasn't a dream anymore. The thought of being married to Hussein was evolving into a nightmare. I had once pictured my parents' faces, relishing what their reaction would be when I told them I had fallen in love with a man here in Damascus. I knew the news would have shocked them. It wouldn't have been the first time I dated someone against my father's wishes.

One such time was with a boy who lived in our village. He was called William and was the same age as me. We had known each other since we were in primary school. He had two younger brothers and an older sister. His father, Ron West, was a lorry driver who irritated my father almost every morning on his way to work. Once I started high school, I witnessed how berserk Mr. West made him each morning father took me to school. The huge West lorry would clog up the narrow village road making it hard for cars to pass often resulting in long delays. Father would shout and curse Mr. West into damnation for making him late. Father was a very impatient and punctual man.

It's no exaggeration to say that my father considered Mr. West and his entire family below him. That snobbery rubbed off on Jacob and I growing up because we were staunch enemies of all the Wests' children. We and our gang of friends would often declare war on the Wests' gang down in the woods. We strategised our war plans from our secret treehouse, deep in the woods between our houses. We would battle from morning to afternoon for days and come home muddy, bruised and scratched from our outdoor play.

William, his brothers and sister attended the same local, comprehensive school as Jacob. I saw the West family at church, every Sunday, but William rarely went. My father never acknowledged William's parents at church and always arrived early, so he didn't come across them in the foyer. One day before Mass began, a commotion stirred in the subdued hush of the congregation. As I knelt in prayer, I heard tutting and gasps. I looked up to see my father frowning at a teenager standing at the back of the church with a red Mohican, black leather jacket with chains and studs. Many heads were turned back to stare at the menacing figure. Some parents tried to distract their young children from pointing while older couples were shaking their heads disapprovingly. It was William and he had become a punk.

"How dare he turn up to church looking like that," Father snarled under his breath. Of course, his children — that is me and Jacob — were 'model children', as far as the rest of the congregation were concerned.

When the congregation filed out after Mass, my father greeted the priest and socialised with some of his church friends. I was standing as usual with my youth club friends, when William approached us by the youth club door. Although William didn't come to Mass anymore, he did make the odd appearance at the youth club on Fridays. I hadn't spoken to him in four years.

"Hey, Elizabeth. Long time no see." He stood confidently among the group.

"Hi William." My cheeks blazed.

I felt a rush of excitement because he addressed me first in the group.

I knew that it would annoy my father that I was talking to him, but I didn't care. I wanted to be like William and shock my elders.

"I like your Mohican." I reached out to touch it. It was brittle. "Gosh, it's so hard."

"Yep. Took a bar of soap and a can of spray to keep it up." He smoothed one side of his head.

I could see Father approaching us and he looked angry. I knew if he reached us he was going to say something embarrassing to William.

"Got to go." I quickly walked towards father intercepting him.

"Time to go home." Father scowled.

"William, come to the club next Friday." I shouted back at William knowing full well that father would hear.

"Yep. Maybe." He grinned and coolly blew rings of smoke from his cigarette.

I was right. Father was infuriated, but I just thought he was a snob. In defiance of my father, I met William a few times at our youth club and down in the woods. Even though I kept it secret from my parents, I felt like a rebel. We dated for less than a month.

That evening after the market, as the sun was setting behind the high wall, I sat alone, deep in thought on the bench in the courtyard. I didn't expect to be thinking about my father and William, but my defiance towards my father felt familiar. My desire to shock him felt familiar. My reason to date William was driven by the hope of hurting my father and it was wrong. Was my relationship with Hussein based on love? It felt no more solid than my relationship with William.

Instead of focusing on the book in my lap, I watched the shadows creep across the ground and reach my feet. Minute by minute, they edged up my body darkening everything in their path. I thought of shaking the melancholy away by helping the girls prepare dinner, but inertia had totally taken over my body.

"You seem distant," Hussein interrupted me. I had almost forgotten he was there.

"I have a test tomorrow, and I need to study," I responded curtly.

"I wanted to talk to you for a moment. Is that okay?" He spoke tenderly. I closed my textbook to indicate that I was ready to listen.

"I wondered whether you had thought any further about saying the *Shahada*?"

"Why do you ask? I didn't think it mattered to you that I am Christian."

"If you decide to convert to Islam, we can also be married." As he spoke, he fumbled in his trouser pocket.

"I bought this ring, when we were in the *souq*." He grinned, not noticing the disappointment in my face.

He held up a ring, no thicker than a paperclip, between his thumb and index finger. It had no diamond nor detail, except the band was bent into a small infinity loop on the top. This could not possibly be the ring, the moment, the place he chose to propose to me. It was devoid of intimacy, romance and affection.

"Is this a proposal?" I couldn't summon a smile.

"Do you remember what *Katb el-Kitab* is?" He then reached into his other pocket and pulled out a piece of paper.

I was speechless.

"This is it." He unfolded the paper. "Our wedding contract."

He handed it to me. "We can be married tonight." I read the stamped document from the Ministry of Interior. Sure enough, it had my name, Elizabeth Booth, and his name, Hussein Ali Al-Hambali.

"There are two male witnesses here, Ahmed and Salim." He pointed to two of the men, sitting with the girls, whom I had never met before.

He stroked my head, as if he was trying to brush away my bad thoughts.

"Why the hurry, Hussein?" I had no intention of accepting his proposal.

"You are the love of my life. I long for you to be mine." He spoke as tenderly as he had done when we travelled to Hama and he had whispered in my ear, but the words sounded empty to me now.

The words that came back to me were Nadia's and Fatima's.

It's a temporary marriage.

I knew I had to maintain my composure and endure his declaration of love, but I wanted to run far away. I only wished I had somewhere to run to.

He continued to implore me to say the *Shahada*. My throat was constricted. No words could come out, even if I had wanted them to. My mind raced in a million directions.

"Please accept, Elizabeth. You can say 'I accept' three times, and we will be married." He held my hand, stroking it and my ring finger. The thought of him placing that ring on my finger was abhorrent. I withdrew my hand from his.

"I need to talk to my parents first." I summoned up a half-smile, hoping to convince him that I was on board to accept his proposal, but as a good daughter I had to speak to my father.

"I understand," Hussein said softly. "Of course, you need to speak with your father."

In the morning of the following day, Hussein and I headed to the hospital where Hussein said I could call home. I was grateful to have the opportunity to make an international call as my travel book said that calls were not cheap as they had to be made in five-star hotels or telecom offices and could take up to two hours to place.

"You will be able to make a short call to your parents," Hussein said, as he ushered me into the car.

I longed to speak to them, particularly to my mother as she was my emotional anchor. While living in London, I used to chat on the phone with mother often. I desperately wanted to talk to her today. I needed her reassurance that everything would be okay.

The large, white hospital building loomed on the top of a small hill. We parked and walked up some wide steps, where above the entrance I read Hospital Hafez Al-Assad in large, gold lettering. Inside, the corridors were wide and spacious. Naguib showed me into a room with hospital equipment and a hospital bed. He went into a smaller office and talked to a man there. Soon he beckoned me into the smaller room and pointed to the rotary black phone on the man's desk.

They told me the international code for England again, and I dialled my parents' number.

The man exited the room to give me some privacy, but Hussein lingered by the threshold pretending to be engaged in a conversation with Naguib.

I had to go through the motions of speaking to my father, so that Hussein did not suspect how my heart had changed.

"Plymouth 8652110. Who's speaking please?" All our family answered the phone the same way.

"Hi, mother. It's me."

"Elizabeth, darling."

It sounded so great to hear her voice and I was instantly homesick. I knew that I was on the brink of crying. I wanted to tell her everything. I wanted to be comforted and sob into her arms. I had given my heart and my body to a man who did not love me. I felt ashamed.

"How are you?" she asked, optimistically. Mother sounded happy to hear from me, although I knew she must have spent many nights worried about me being hundreds of miles away and out of touch.

"I'm doing fine," I said, trying my hardest to be as convincing as possible. I looked up from the dial on the phone, at which I had been staring, and saw Hussein's head tilted towards the threshold.

What am I going to do? Can he hear me on the phone? Are they listening to the call, somehow? Think. Think.

The mistrust I held was engulfing me. I needed to keep up the façade that I was talking about the marriage approval. I pretended to look as if I was answering their questions and reacting to their responses, but acting was not my strongest skill. It was

192

telling how impossible it was to say anything to them about the marriage, even if it were true. The fact that I couldn't even mention him in any capacity was undeniable proof to me that it was over between us. I felt devastated, but also scared about how I would tell him and how he would react.

Hussein approached me to let me know I had to get off the phone. Naguib's colleague would get in trouble if I spent too much time on an international call.

"Mother, I'll call you again soon," I said sadly. My mother could tell my voice was broken.

"Are you sure you're okay, darling?"

I visualised my mother on the kitchen telephone by the wall. I longed for the simplicity of life back home.

"I'm fine, mother. It's going really well for me here."

"Okay. Let us know if you need anything. We love you, sweetheart."

"I love you both."

"Call us again soon."

"I will when I get the chance. Bye mother."

"Bye darling."

I put the receiver down slowly, not wanting to end the call and feeling so far from home.

"Elizabeth, we're leaving," said Hussein. He sounded stern, as he often did lately.

"Yes, I'm ready." I followed Hussein out of the hospital. We passed many small rooms, which I could see were full of hospital beds. We passed doctors in white lab coats, but Hussein did not greet them and they passed him without any recognition.

"Do you know those doctors?" I ventured to ask Hussein.

"No, I work in a different wing."

"Did you ask your parents?" Hussein asked me, while we were walking to his car.

I couldn't answer.

How can I tell him I never even asked?

"Yes, but my father was upset. I am his only daughter. He wants to be part of the wedding and to meet you. He forbids me from doing it." I tried to sound sufficiently distraught by my father's position.

"So, you do not accept me?"

"I'm sorry, Hussein." With crocodile tears in my eyes, I said simply, "He forbids it."

Hussein was silent.

He opened the car door for me to climb in and shut it loudly. I had an empty feeling that ached in the pit of my stomach.

"I'm returning to work tomorrow," Hussein announced, as he climbed in the driver's side.

"At the hospital?" I asked.

"Yes. I begin night shifts tonight. I don't think I will be able to see you during the day either, as I have family responsibilities as well as sleep."

"Why is it so sudden?"

"My grieving period is over."

We drove home, mostly in silence. I mentioned finding a new place to stay and Hussein said that was for the best. We pulled up outside the house and I climbed out of the car. Hussein stayed behind the steering wheel, barely acknowledging me.

"Well it's goodbye for now, Elizabeth." He was cold, as if he were saying goodbye to an acquaintance.

"Goodbye, Hussein. Perhaps we will meet again." I wanted to say, "good riddance," but I had been brought up better than that.

1 October 1992

Middle of the night
Damascus

Dear Diary,
This first night without Hussein visiting feels
odd. I feel as anxious now as I did when I first
arrived in Damascus. I'm writing now
because I can't sleep. My mind won't switch
off. I read about the hotels again in my travel
guide and the map of showing where they all
are. I can't help feeling nervous again. I feel
foolish for letting myself rely so heavily on
Hussein to the point where I'm now feeling
unprepared and no better off than when I
first arrived.

Plus I'm stuck in my room as I don't
want to face the girls right now. I know what
they really do for a living and it's not that
I'm judging them as I know they didn't have
a choice in the matter, it's just that it feels
awkward here and I feel vulnerable. I'm so
ready to leave.

Of course, I'll miss my friendship with
Fatima. I cried yesterday when I told her
that I was leaving. I don't know if I will ever
come back to visit her as I never want to
bump into Hussein again.

Fatima was so sorry for telling me
about Hussein's real motive behind proposing
to me but she's really saved me from a
terrible situation. Without her help, things
could have turned out differently. Actually,

the thought of how things could have turned out makes my stomach churn.

The weird thing is that I told her he was back to working night shifts at the hospital and she didn't say anything. I'm pretty sure that's because he must have told me another lie.

I'm going to miss Fatima, my little sis.

Twenty-six

I spent the morning packing my rucksack and gathering my things, once everyone had left for work. I decided, if I didn't find a bed with one of my fellow students, I would check into a hotel. I didn't want to return to the girls' house again and risk the chance of seeing Hussein.

I managed to flag down a taxi and directed the driver to take me to the central bus depot. I felt overwhelmed, when he pulled into the crowded station. Blue and white buses were coming and going from bus bays that were teaming with passengers. I remembered hearing from the students that the number 60 was the bus to school, and had the destination Ad-Deira on the front. School started at 2p.m., which was straight after all the schoolchildren had left the building for the day.

I arrived with half an hour to spare, so that I could buy a strip of tickets from the kiosk. I saw Hans and Ingrid and made my way to them through the crowd.

"We haven't seen you here before," Hans said with a grin on his face.

"I'm catching the bus from now on."

"Where's the guy you were with?" Ingrid asked.

"He can't take me anymore. I have to leave the family I'm living with."

"Sorry to hear that," Hans said, and Ingrid nodded.

"I'll just have to find somewhere else," I said and smiled. I hoped my expression was convincing.

I was relieved to be with people I knew on my first day catching a bus in the chaos. It was a good thing too. While standing at the correct bus stop trying to watch out for the number 60, Ingrid and Hans suddenly started to race towards a bus that looked packed already. I chased after them, and the moving bus. The bus driver had decided there was nowhere to pull up to pick up passengers. A bus with a different destination had taken its spot, so the driver of number 60 decided to keep moving on out of the depot. The three of us ran with our arms waving in the air almost directly in front of the bonnet, and the driver stopped to let us on.

The single-deck bus looked vintage—similar to an old school bus from the 1960s. There were double seats on either side of the aisle. The blue, shiny, faux-leather padding was cracked and flaking. Every seat was taken. Some passengers were already standing and holding onto the metal frames on the top of each seat when we got on. Schoolchildren had filled the back, women with smaller children and babies were in the front. We filed into the middle and stood holding the frames to keep steady. I grabbed a bar and found myself next to a stout man with a bald head. His head was level with my stomach and I felt especially uncomfortable when a passenger squeezed past me and my rucksack and my stomach had to lunge forward into his face. He didn't move and I avoided eye contact, as I didn't want to see what his reaction was.

The thirty-minute bus ride to Mezze was bumpy and long. It stopped countless times to let passengers off and on. Hans, Ingrid and I moved further and further towards the back of the bus, as more people stepped on. The driver did not necessarily stop at the designated stops, and often the passengers would yell at him angrily for missing their stop, even though they had rung the bell overhead.

Astrid and Elina got onto the bus a couple of stops later. They stood near the front. Elina saw me and waved, looking surprised. Astrid had her head in her book and didn't look up.

I hoped I would be able to move in with them, rather than trying the hotels I had narrowed down from the travel guide.

When we finished class that day, a small group of us walked out of the grounds together towards the bus stop. Matthew, Hans, Ingrid, Kaleem and a few others walked along in a loose knot. Everyone was discussing which restaurant to go to for dinner. They were all talking about places I had not heard about or seen. They had discovered so much about the city already. Of course, I knew some restaurants that Hussein had taken me to, but I had no idea of the addresses, or even the names, so I kept quiet. They decided on a restaurant in the Old City, which made me anxious. I wondered if it was one I had been to with Hussein.

"Elizabeth, you're carrying a rucksack. What's going on?" Matthew asked motioning for me to hand the bag to him. I did so gladly, thankful not to carry the weight.

"I've left the Syrian family. Things didn't work out," I replied.

"I'm sorry to hear that. It was going so well for you and your Arabic."

I was grateful to Matthew. Feeling somewhat homesick and disillusioned with my Syrian friends, I was comforted by his accent and his kind concern.

"You're welcome to come to dinner with us," he offered.

Elina interrupted us. "Yes. That would be great. We're heading to the Old City, where Astrid and I live."

"You know, if you want, you can sleep at ours. Kaleem is already sleeping over too, but he is on a mattress outside. He says he loves the starry sky." Astrid looked across at him and smiled broadly.

"I would like that very much. Thank you."

Our bus pulled over, amidst a hub of buses and taxis circling a roundabout. In the centre, I saw Baab Touma, the Gate of Thomas. This gate, one of seven around the city, was named after Thomas the Apostle. It was a monument from Roman times and was originally connected to the walls of the city, which had long since disappeared. The girls told me it was the gate leading into the Christian quarter.

The main street was potholed and crudely tarmacked in patches, leaving cobbled stone protruding from some areas. A line of cars was parked along the street. There was only room for one-way traffic, but that didn't stop cars coming in either direction.

It was dark by the time we got off the bus and filed along a narrow pavement, brushing by a black car. I noticed some familiar scratches along the passenger door, which reminded me of Hussein's car. It was the same make as his car. The passenger door's dark window slightly cracked open, as a puff of cigarette smoke billowed out. Prickles went up my spine, as I had a feeling someone inside was watching me.

As soon as we had passed the car, the window closed and it pulled away. There were many black saloon cars on the road, but I knew, in the back of my mind, that it was Hussein. I was oddly certain. I had no idea why he would want to spy on me, and I didn't want to think about it, so I tried to dismiss the thought and I kept up my pace with my new friends, as we turned off that narrow road.

Above me, some houses had wooden balconies protruding into the street with latticed wooden shutters. They were precariously supported by wooden mounts, sunk into the walls of the houses. Some buildings looked as if they were made of wattle and daub, scarcely modern. Other homes resembled Tudor homes, with the black-and-white strips on their facades. Taking a few steps, I faced a Roman column and archway. A few more, and I passed a small passageway that turned into a Byzantine, tiled nook. Behind the doorways of eras gone by, were shops, churches and houses.

The cobbled pavement was cracked and uneven. I had to focus on my feet the entire way, as the surface was lethal. I knew we couldn't be far from Straight Street, *Sharee al Mustaqueem*, a Roman street mentioned by St. Paul in the Acts of the Apostles. It was astonishing that the streets in the Old City dated back to biblical times. Modernity met history, as wires and pipes draped in knots and webs along the sides and roofs of the houses zigzagged across the streets, carrying electricity, water and telephone to the community.

Eating dinner with my new friends was refreshing. We laughed and talked. I barely thought about Hussein, and I was grateful for that.

Afterwards, Astrid and Elina invited anyone else who wanted to come to their house. I followed them, as they navigated through a labyrinth of small streets. Some streets were wide, and others were hardly wide enough for a mule. One appeared to end in a brick wall, but we skirted beside it down a small alleyway into the next street. It was impossible to tell what kind of house was behind each door, embedded in the high walls. They could hide a humble Damascene home, or a large, Ottoman palace. So many looked the same. Even in daylight, I could never have found my way back and now in the darkness it was virtually impossible.

Once we made it to their house, I discovered that Matthew had left us. As he was the only other British person in our party, I was sad that he wasn't joining us. We were down to five: myself, Astrid, Elina, Hans and Kaleem. Eventually, Hans also left.

"I hope you don't mind Kaleem staying with us," Elina apologised. "He doesn't have anywhere because he hasn't found a place that he can afford yet. We told him he can sleep outside."

"It's okay with me. You are so kind to take us both in." I was thankful for a place to stay, without having to find a hotel room. Kaleem didn't bother me, although he did occasionally seem sullen and was often quiet.

Astrid told me I would be sleeping with her, as it was the only bed available. It was a king-sized bed, with a wooden frame and a thick, luxurious mattress. I was excited, as I had not enjoyed sleeping on the thin mattress back at the girls' house. I crawled into the bed after changing and was soon asleep. I did not dream.

London – Two English girls, 14 and 15, were tricked by their father into marriage in far-off North Yemen seven years ago, and therein lies one of the season's more curious tales, one that might yet have a happy ending.

—Chicago Tribune, January 07, 1988, *Sisters Try to Cancel Their "Sale"* by Peter Slevin, Knight-Ridder newspapers

Twenty-seven

Days passed in my new routine. I was comfortable and free, although I spotted Hussein's car twice more. It was sitting, parked outside school, as I walked in. Something was wrong, but I wasn't sure what to do.

Instead of studying one morning, I decided I needed to see Adrien at the Embassy. I wanted to update him on the students I had met so far and I hoped I would have the chance to call home from his office.

"Hello, Miss Booth." Adrien again stood almost to attention as I was ushered into his office.

"Hello, Adrien."

We shook hands.

"I'm glad you're here." He seemed serious, as if there was some weight on his mind. "But first things first, how are things? Tell me how school is going at the Institute."

Although his questions were casual, I noticed his sombre demeanour.

"Has something happened? Something grave?"

"Please, first tell me what you have come to tell me."

"Well, I have met some students," I crossed my arms tightly, sensing that he had more pressing news to tell me, but I proceeded. He took notes of the nationalities and names of the students I mentioned, but didn't follow up with any questions about them.

"I'm staying with the Norwegian girls in the Old City."

"So, you've left the..." he cleared his throat. "Syrian couple?"

I swallowed hard and my face burnt with embarrassment. Had he known I wasn't staying where I had said?

"I had a feeling you would find a place with other students," he continued. He smiled; this news seemed to please him. "And what else?"

"I'm in the intermediate level. So far, we've learnt about ancient Syria. There was one text about an ancient sea port on the Mediterranean coast that dates to the Stone Age. I forget the name." I shrugged my shoulders.

"I've visited Ugarit or Ras Shamra, as it's known today. The archaeology site is fascinating. It was there that the earliest-known tablet carved with an alphabet was found. Syria is full of so many historical treasures." There was an earnestness in his voice I found endearing.

"I really want to see much more of the country."

"And anything else?" The glint in his eye disappeared.

"We also learnt about a famous Arabic poet Al-Mutanabbi and Arabic authors. We read an extract from *Men in the Sun* by Ghassan Kanafani, where emigrants were left in the water tank of a lorry and died." My words trailed off as I watched his grave expression return.

"Not such a great story to read about." He frowned. "Any political history, or economics?"

"We read about the Hama massacre, where the Syrian government saved the people."

"Not exactly. That's their version of history." Adrien furrowed his brow. "The most brutal carnage known in recent Syrian history happened there, but it was under Assad's orders that the town was besieged and massacred."

"Why would he slaughter his own people?"

"It was an uprising. That he won't tolerate. It's probably best not to bring the subject up."

"I understand. Sometimes politics comes up during our discussions, at the end of class. Some students debate with the teacher and it occasionally gets heated, with anti-American, or anti-Israeli opinions. I don't get involved."

"Good. Steer clear of politics, in any discussion with anyone. Have you seen the Principal come into the school?"

"Yes, Al-Tahiri addressed all the teachers and students on National Day. It's the first time I've seen him."

"With the *mukhabarat*, I expect?"

"Yes." I had noticed the men in suits who had been roaming stealthily around the building. "They played the national anthem and then Al-Tahiri made a political speech, which went on and on. It was hard to understand it all. He did say we should be grateful to the President for allowing us into the country."

Adrien cleared his throat.

"Thank you for your input," Adrien said, with an air of finality. He changed the subject abruptly. "There has been important intelligence that has just come in. It's from John, in your old embassy in Sana'a." I felt my eyes go wide. I hadn't expected to hear John's name. "Yes, John is still there. I think it's his last year of tour there."

I rubbed behind my ear as he continued.

"The CIA is working closely with MI6. They have informed us about a Peace Corps female volunteer, who was working in Sana'a and has recently disappeared."

"Why would the CIA be involved?" I wondered aloud. "When I was at the F.C.O., we had a high-profile, consular case of two, British girls being married off to Yemeni men, but it was handled by our consular section not MI6. And certainly not the CIA. It was one case amongst many that the consul dealt with."

"You're talking about the Muhsen sisters?"

"Yes. I remember there was great difficulty locating the village where they were taken, because the Yemeni military held the only official maps that existed of Yemen."

"This case is not a consular issue. After the disappearance of the Peace Corps volunteer, her fellow Peace Corps friends informed the US Embassy that she had become romantically involved with a young, Yemeni man. CIA were alerted, because the Yemeni is a returning *mujahideen*, who fought in Afghanistan, but they are unaware of which group he is affiliated with."

"This sounds so different to when I was there. I knew some of the Peace Corps females and they felt safe. The only hostages taken, when I was there, were tourists by the tribal leaders."

"Well, I can assure you many groups were active then but of course John was not at liberty to tell you about them and now, after the Iraq/Kuwait invasion, the extremist groups are becoming increasingly militant and their influence across the Arabian peninsula is growing. As of now, the volunteer's whereabouts are still unknown. As you are well aware, the search is hampered by the lack of knowledge of the terrain in Yemen.

"As a result of this case, you need to be vigilant about any relationships that women in the school have. There is no evidence that any militant group is operating in Syria, but intelligence analysts cannot validate whether students from Britain and other European universities are being targeted. Your presence in the school is an extremely important asset to us now."

"But what if I get caught, or I am presumed to have done something? Do I have diplomatic status, even though I'm not a diplomat anymore?" I started to worry about the false accusation that was made against Naguib and how quickly it escalated out of control. I did not want to end up in prison like him.

"Yes. Your clearance is complete with London, and so as an operative for MI6 you are immune. Remember you also have a backup. Your cover as a Damascus student is authentic."

I smiled weakly. I was beginning to feel I was getting out of my depth.

"Just remember, no heroics and stay out of drama."

I thought of Hussein and the girls. I had originally wanted to tell Adrien about him, but I felt silly. I was just some little, English girl with a jealous ex-boyfriend, and Adrien had real issues to resolve.

As he spoke, he drew his chair away from his desk and held out his hand for a firm handshake.

"Miss Booth, thank you. I'm sorry to finish, but I have another meeting."

As I made my way to the door, I remembered I wanted to ask about making a phone call home. Now, I felt a greater need to touch base with home. I was thrown off guard by the gravity of the conversation.

Even though Adrien made out that it was business as usual, I felt trepidation. I stuck my head back into Adrien's office.

"I meant to ask, may I call my parents while I'm here?"

"Sure. You can have a few minutes to speak with them."

He took me to the receptionist's room, who had already left for the day, and said I could call from there.

I dialled home and prayed that someone would answer.

"Plymouth 8652110. Who's speaking please?"

"Mother? It's me." My heart lightened, as I heard the familiar greeting.

"Oh, hello darling. How are you?" Mother sounded cheerful, just as always.

"I just have a few minutes to let you know that everything is going so well. I'm studying hard." The line was not very good and my mother's voice was not completely audible.

"That's wonderful dear." I could just make out what she said. "Where are you living now?

"I'm living with two Norwegian girls in the Old Christian Quarter. They are really good friends." I was almost shouting to make sure she heard me at her end.

"That's good to know."

"Have you received any of my letters?"

"No, not yet. I expect they will take a long time coming from there."

"That's probably true."

"I look forward to reading them when they do come."

"Thanks mother. Is everyone well at home?"

"Apart from a cold, your father is well, and I'm hoping not to catch it. It's very cold and wet here."

Adrien appeared at the door and I knew it was time to leave.

"That's no surprise being wet in England." Mum and I laughed together. "I hate to, but I have to go. Give my love to everyone."

"Love to you, dear."

"Love you too. Bye, Mother."

"Bye, darling."

I hung up the phone and brushed tears from my eyes. I turned to Adrien and smiled.

"Thank you for letting me call home."

"You're welcome, Elizabeth. Anytime."

We shook hands and his was as firm as always.

Twenty-eight

Soon, Astrid and Elina offered me a permanent place in their house, albeit I slept in Astrid's room.

Each morning, I was excited to explore more of the neighbourhood near my new abode. It was great to take my time. I had not been able to do that with Hussein.

Initially, I felt like a tourist, but gradually I blended into life as a pseudo resident, learning to navigate the labyrinth of alleyways back and forth to Baab Touma to catch the bus to the Institute. Eventually, I became familiar with the local street vendors: the baker, the juicer, the grocer and the like.

I visited the other gates, the most notable of which was Baab Sharqi, at the east end of Straight Street. The gate had a large, central arch, possibly for Roman chariots to enter and two smaller ones on the side for the market people and inhabitants. A minaret towered above it, which dated back to the thirteenth century. At every step, I found myself in a different era, immersed in the pages of all the history books I had read at Durham. It was a melting pot of architecture, civilisations and religions. Around every corner, the city revealed its bygone days. It was possible to come across pagan, Muslim, Christian, Roman, Omayyad, or Greek treasures, all within the Roman grid plan.

I remembered a few bible stories from my Catholic education, and especially the pictures. A vivid image of Salome with John the Baptist's severed head on a tray, as depicted in the painting by Caravaggio, had haunted me for many years. A small, ornate, framed picture was mounted along with others beside the rosewood mantelpiece at my Grandma's. As children, we rarely went into her formal living room, which mostly was used only to receive visitors.

One time, while playing hide-and-seek with Jacob, I was in pursuit of the perfect hiding place and entered the room through the glass French doors. I ran behind the heavy, satin, blue drapes, drawn to the sides of the doors and waited to see if Jacob would find me. I peeked out several times to check if Jacob was coming by. It was then that I saw the painting. I ran from my spot, giving myself away. I had nightmares for weeks about the head, slowly opening its mouth to speak, but thankfully, always woke before I heard its voice. If I ever went back into the room, I averted my eyes from that side of the mantelpiece.

Astrid occasionally accompanied me on my ramblings. She was a veritable tourist book and had incredible knowledge of the Old City and its history. The more time we spent together, the more I enjoyed her company. As we walked along the street lined with shops selling textiles, spices, imported objects and other sundry things, she rattled off historical facts. She pointed out another of the ancient gates that was part of the fortified city.

"This is Baab Kisan. This is where Christians believe St. Paul was lowered from in a basket through a window in the wall." I was enthralled.

We passed by a mosque, which Astrid told me was the house of Judas, where the Bible mentions that Saul was baptised by Ananais.

"Christians say that this mosque was built upon the foundations of that ancient church. The nearby Chapel of St. Ananias is now the sacred place, where they can commemorate that event."

I envied her encyclopaedic knowledge.

Back at the house, sitting in the living room, we continued our discussion.

"You know so much about the history of Damascus. Did you learn it at school?"

"I learnt much of it in church. My priest was a traveller and was here many years ago."

"So, you're Catholic?" I asked.

"I am interested in all religions. Kaleem gave me his Qur'an, which is such a beautiful gift." She handed me the book.

It certainly was a beautiful book. It was bound in mottled leather, with ornate, golden calligraphy on the cover and gold-edged pages. I would never have guessed that Kaleem would own something so beautiful and expensive-looking. Kaleem was very conscious of the money he spent, in a way that implied his caution was a necessity.

"He gave me this, as a token of his appreciation for letting him stay here."

"That's very kind of him."

"I know," she said, with a rare smile. "He's so nice. I really like him."

She opened it to the first page where there was an Arabic inscription.

"Look what he wrote." Astrid eagerly pushed the book under my nose.

"*Enti sadiqki fi al dunya wa fi al akhira.* You are my friend in this world and in the next." My voice trailed off as the meaning sunk into me. "Gosh, that's heavy. Sounds like he likes you an awful lot."

"Yes. I think it comes from a surah in the Qur'an." Astrid beamed. "I like him a lot too."

I wondered whether Astrid was falling in love with Kaleem, as I had done with Hussein. I wished I wasn't so tainted, but I couldn't help but feel that perhaps Astrid was being played like I had been.

I knew I needed to mention this to Adrien, when we next met.

***

Days passed, but I had not gone to Adrien, and Kaleem faded from the front of my mind. It was getting chillier in Damascus, as the winter season loomed. I hadn't brought a coat with me and knew I would need one soon. Astrid mentioned that she needed one too, so we went shopping. Astrid and I passed a shopkeeper selling used army jackets.

The rack of coats stood outside a scruffy shopfront. All were second-hand and all different: different shades of green and khaki, different zips, different buttons, different pockets and different lengths. I tried some on, and the shopkeeper smiled at me, probably amused that a westerner was interested in looking like a soldier.

I had chosen a short, dark-green coat with silver buttons. It was big on me, but it was thick and comforting. I looked at myself in a small, dirty mirror the shop keeper had mounted inside his stall. I looked strange to myself. I was in jeans and a tee shirt with the big coat draped over me. I was still wearing the *hijab* that Hussein had given me. Looking at it, I was reminded of him and that first day in the *souq* – clinging to him for protection. I was not the same girl. I carefully unpinned the scarf and shoved it into one of the coat's pockets. I shook out my hair, which was getting long. The girl in the mirror still didn't look like me, at least not the me in the mirrors back home, but she was someone I wanted to be.

***

Each afternoon, my friends and I caught the bus to the Institute for our classes at 2p.m. It became a routine—one I looked forward to each day. Matthew started to catch the bus with us, and I often chatted to him about home.

"So, you live in Exeter? That's so near to my home town, Plymouth."

"You're a Janner." We laughed as that was slang for a local person from Devon.

"Don't you miss pasties?" he asked with a smile in his eyes.

"Yes. And clotted cream."

"Funny, how you miss the comforts of home and local food—even the bad ones."

"So true!" I shrieked. "I've been craving food that I never even ate when I was actually home."

"At this point, I'd even settle for a blood sausage," Matthew said and we descended into quite a laughing fit.

We often reminisced about home. I enjoyed getting to know Matthew. He was such an interesting person and so smart. He had graduated from Cambridge University in Political History and spoke fluent Italian, as his grandparents were from Italy. His favourite sport was deep-sea diving, and he said one day he would take me to dive. One dive site he wanted to go to was called Shark Cove near the Raouché Rocks in Beirut. He had already done some dives in Aqaba, Jordan, and the Great Barrier Reef in Australia. I was amazed and thought him so fearless, having faced sharks and sting rays at close quarters.

Matthew often asked me for help with his Arabic, both verbal and written. I could remember how hard it had been for me at the beginning, when the learning curve was very steep. With the script looking so completely different, one couldn't always believe that there were only two more letters in the Arabic alphabet than in the English one. That, reading from right to left, and the back of the book to the front, made for only the very beginnings of that steep curve.

The numerical rules of Arabic have a logic of their own. I often amused myself with the thought that the early Arabists must have chewed *qat* to dream up those rules. For numbers from 3 to 10, the noun is plural, but from 11 to 99, it's singular which gives eight toys but fifteen toy. But just to add utter confusion, different rules apply in the construction of the numbers and nouns of one or two.

I told Matthew some of my best techniques for learning the complex grammar rules and tips on remembering vocabulary by labelling everything with a piece of paper. My room at university had been absolutely plastered with labels attached to furniture and objects: bed, table, drawer, notebook.

***

Winter temperatures truly arrived in November. The mornings were icy cold. Astrid showed me how to use the oil stove that we had in our room. It was a lethal method of heating a cold room. The little stove had a glass door that was completely black with soot. She placed a couple of small logs of wood inside, then filled a metal bulb above the stove with paraffin oil. Once she opened the pipe, the oil dripped onto the wood. She lit the oil and a flash of fire leapt out, as the flame raced down from the bulb to the stove. It was instant heat, but at the same time I noticed how quickly the room smelled of burning oil and smoky wood.

Before long, the aroma had saturated our clothes and skin completely.

Early one morning before the sun came up, I woke to find Astrid kneeling on the floor. She was bundled up in a blanket with her bare feet peeking out. At first, I wondered if she had fallen out of bed accidentally. I leant over the side of the bed to check on her and saw she was praying on a small prayer mat. The air was so frigid I could see her breath, as she whispered her prayers.

"Astrid, I—I thought you were Catholic," I quietly interrupted her, my breath also showing in the freezing air. She didn't respond immediately, but finished reading from the open Qur'an laid by her side.

"I've decided to convert, so I'm teaching myself about the rituals. I'm not sure I'm going to like these dawn prayers." She tugged the blanket tightly around her body.

It startled me that she hadn't shared that she was considering converting to Islam. I wondered idly, if her conversion had anything to do with Kaleem. I was still half asleep, but something about that thought stuck at the back of my mind. I shook it off, turned over and went back to sleep.

Twenty-nine

Classes were going well, and in the evenings, Astrid and I often worked together on our translations. Sometimes it was three of us, with Kaleem joining in to complete coursework.

Astrid seemed to be closer to Kaleem with each passing day, while I felt more and more like a third wheel. Kaleem and I were polite and friendly to each other, but it was strained. At the back of my mind was the belief that his motives for being with Astrid were the same as Hussein's. I tried to brush my mistrust of him to one side, as I had no proof and they were clearly besotted with each other. So, I tried to get to know him in the hope that he might give away some clues, but he was difficult to talk to. His avoidance of conversations with me only served to enhance my suspicions of him. although I kept telling myself that perhaps it was just that his English was not the best. It wasn't just me. Everyone noticed how, when we were in a crowd, he and Astrid would seclude themselves, quietly and intimately talking in whispers. When I finally broached the subject of my concern privately to Astrid, I was surprised by her response.

"Are you and Kaleem serious about each other?"

"We're soulmates."

"So, do you think you'll stay together even when you finish school?"

"Maybe, but that's none of your business." She raised her voice and glared at me.

"I'm sorry. I just hope you're careful and know what you're doing."

"I don't need you to tell me what to do." Astrid shouted angrily at me.

After this incident, it became difficult to talk to Astrid as well as Kaleem.

***

I enjoyed our lessons with Professor Ad-Din, but the same could not be said for Matthew and his teacher. He was struggling with his teacher, who also didn't speak English, which in a beginner's class made it almost impossible to explain grammar and vocabulary. Charades is not a skill everyone commands, and apparently, his teacher was dramatically challenged. I often spent time helping Matthew.

"For all the help you gave me, I wondered if you would like to go to a movie with me this evening?" Matthew asked the day after a particularly daunting study session.

"A movie? Here in Damascus? What film would that be?"

"Actually, *The Bodyguard* with Whitney Houston is showing in the cinema at the Sheraton Hotel."

"I didn't even know the Sheraton had a cinema. I'd love to go."

After we left school that evening, we grabbed a quick bite to eat in a small cafe. I had a falafel sandwich and fruit juice, and Matthew ordered the same.

We caught a taxi to the hotel. Matthew kindly bought both tickets.

What we were not expecting were the crowds of men who showed up for the film. We were crushed in the foyer as we waited for the door to open to the auditorium. I got irritated, when I was nudged and brushed, it seemed on purpose by men behind me, who could have given me a little more space. Matthew got upset too when he saw how much it was really bothering me. It seemed a long time before the doors opened and the compacted mass could move forward.

"Here, let's sit on the end of an aisle," Matthew said as we made our way into the theatre. "That way, any man will have to sit next to me and you can be on the end." I was touched by his thoughtfulness.

We were amongst the first to enter the spacious and empty auditorium, and moved down on the left side to find a seat. A stream of men poured into the cinema and sat also on the left side. To begin with I thought it was odd that very few men sat on the right side. I turned to Matthew.

"Is it just me, or is our side filling up rather rapidly?"

Matthew looked around.

"You're right. I think you are a bit of a spectacle."

A man sat beside Matthew and I was relieved that I was in the aisle seat so no one could sit next to me, but men sitting in front of and behind us, showed no embarrassment at turning round to look at me. It gave me a glimpse into how a celebrity might feel being stalked by fans.

"Are you sure you want to stay to watch the movie? This is intimidating even for me." Matthew was concerned.

"I feel fine," I said, shrugging my military coat up around my shoulders. I glared at a man who had turned to gawk, and he broke his gaze.

"Okay. As long as you're fine." Matthew smiled. "I would ask if you want a drink, but I'm not leaving you alone for a second."

"That would be a terrible idea." We laughed.

"It's pretty tough for women in Damascus, isn't it?" He was overwhelmed by the reaction I had amongst the Syrian men, who acted more like teenagers than grown men.

"It's been hard at times, that's for sure," I replied.

We settled down to watch the film, which was well worth all the trouble once the lights went down.

"I really had a great night," I said as we made our way out. "Thank you so much Matthew."

"Do you want to get a drink together? The lounge here does very nice tea."

"Yes, that would be lovely."

Once we were seated in the tea room, I wanted to ask Matthew more about his studies. "I never asked, but why are you learning Arabic now, after already graduating from Cambridge?"

"I'm only learning Arabic for something to do."

"What do you mean?"

"I'm studying my doctorate at Cambridge. My thesis is on the Syrian Socialist National Party, the SSNP, during the bloody coups of the 1950s and 1960s in Syria. While I'm doing my research here, I thought it would be helpful to learn Arabic at the same time."

"Well, you must be good at languages, if you are already fluent in Italian."

"That's an easy language. I'm struggling with Arabic."

"I'm struggling with modern Syrian history and politics. We haven't got to that period yet at university. We started with the pre-Islamic period and have got to the Ottoman Empire."

"Well, it's important that any traveller to Syria understand the recent history here, to get a sense of the environment that the Syrian people experience."

"I've learnt a lot about the people just living here, and from what you and Astrid have told me. She's taught me a lot about the Old City and ancient history. I still need to catch up with the current history."

We sipped our tea.

"So, who is the SSNP?" I asked.

"It's a sectarian, nationalist party based on fascist politics. It has a very brutal and secret history, often using terror tactics to gain political control. Since President Hafez Al-Assad came to power, the SSNP, which was once banned, is now tolerated."

"That's scary that he has no problem with their tactics." I swallowed a gulp of tea.

"Yes, the Assad government is not a regime you want to oppose. Many members of an opposition party called the Muslim Brotherhood were murdered. Some were lucky and were expelled from Syria. To be a member of the Brotherhood is now considered a capital offence in Syria."

"What do the SSNP fight for?"

"Their main call is for a 'Greater Syria' with the belief that Lebanon is part of Syria."

"Are they a terrorist organization? I've heard of Hezbollah and Abu Nidal." I wanted to mention the horrific terrorist event that happened while I was serving in Sana'a, but I knew I needed to keep my

222

background confidential. In December 1988, the expatriate community was in shock when the news broke of the bombing of a Pam Am flight over Lockerbie in Scotland. Some of the expatriates knew people who were traveling home for Christmas on that passenger airline. I hadn't thought about the incident since I had been here, but the memory sent chills up my spine.

"The SSNP was established back in the early 1930s, earlier than either of those groups and the PLO. Some consider its organizational structure and militia wing a precursor to terrorist groups operating today."

What Matthew said was unnerving. I had seen first-hand what the Assad government did to people and the paranoia and fear that it sowed in its own people.

"The Syrians have lived with the systematic fear for decades. It is a matter of being a victim, or a perpetrator in this country," added Matthew.

My heart faltered as I thought of what happened to Naguib.

Matthew was generous and paid for our tea at the lounge, which was much more expensive than any tea I had bought from a street trader. We left in a taxi.

"I wanted to ask how it was going living with the Norwegian girls."

"I really like living in the Old City, but I have to admit it's getting a little uncomfortable, as Astrid is quite involved with Kaleem now, and I have found them in the bedroom, which I share with her."

"That sounds awkward. I noticed how close they were becoming."

"Yes, I think I may have to find another place to stay soon."

"Well, that is what I was leading to. I have a spare room at my flat and you could stay there, if you like."

"I am interested, but is it okay for us to live together in Syria?"

"I think the authorities turn a blind eye to it, as so many foreigners have done so in the past. Hans and Ingrid have been living together since they arrived without incidence."

"That's true."

"Would you like to take a look at my flat?"

"Yes, I'd like that."

Matthew redirected the taxi driver to his home.

When we arrived, Matthew showed me around. The kitchen was very basic, and had a small European toilet and shower in a cubicle to the side of the kitchen. It was hardly big enough to turn around, but I wasn't going to complain. At least there was no need to heat water to fill a bucket and no need to hand flush the toilet.

"I'll show you *La pièce de résistance*. Follow me."

He led me back out the front door and then up some narrow steps to a heavy, metal door. The door opened out onto the roof of the building.

For a moment, I gazed at the view from his rooftop. The building was five floors and stood above the roofs of other buildings strewn with television aerials and washing lines. It had a clear view of an immense roundabout called the Omayyad Square, with a beautifully manicured lawn and ornate fountain in the centre. The Assad library stood prominently to the side of the roundabout. It reminded me of a multi-storey car park with its ugly, ochre, stone walls and black windows. At the top of the large, concrete steps, a huge, cast-iron statue of Hafez Al-Assad sitting on chair, holding an open book in his hand, welcomed visitors to the library.

I ducked under a washing line with Matthew's clothes drying and sat on a plastic chair beside him.

"This is where I like to sit to de-stress from the day."

"With your tea." I smiled knowingly.

"Yes." He paused. "I brought you out here also, because there's a little more to my PhD than the research here in Syria."

"Okay?"

"My thesis is not just concentrated on the politics of the SSNP. I am also researching the Muslim Brotherhood. Because they were the Islamist opposition to the Assad regime, the library holds no information on them. Instead, I've collected research on them from the American University of Beirut, and interviewed retired Brotherhood members, who are now living there."

"You've travelled already to Lebanon?"

"Yes, before school started, but I need to go back at some point. I didn't finish going through what I need."

"I'd like to go there some time."

"Well, that's a possibility as I need to finish some research at AUB."

"When you go next time, let me know."

We watched cars circle around the Square, continuing daily life. Few people appeared to frequent the Assad library.

"Do Syrians use the library much?" I asked, looking at the deserted, massive steps at the entrance.

"Actually, I have registered at the library, where I found some research."

"It's no problem for foreigners to register there?"

"No. The library is accessible to any foreign student. They ask questions like why you are registering, and I had to write the parameters of my research. Of course, not entirely the whole truth."

"Is that why we're out here talking?"

"I guess the paranoia gets to everyone," he nervously admitted. "I'm sure I'm targeted for observation because of my time in Beirut. Because my research is not complete without reviewing those papers and books they have banned, they would have tracked my movements to Lebanon, checking on what I researched there."

"So, the Syrian secret police would have been in Lebanon too?"

"Yes, but they cannot track what I did at the AUB. My work is safe, as I have left it all with the consular officer in the Beirut Embassy there. I didn't want to chance bringing it back to Syria."

He paused and folded his arms and then rubbed his chin in thought.

"I'd like you to register at the Assad library."

"You need me to translate?"

"Yes. Some research in Arabic. Not much I promise. Are you up for it?"

"So, if I registered, I would say it's for my research in Durham?"

"Yes. Does that mean you're interested?"

"As long as you honestly know that this will not draw attention to me."

"No. Like I said, Hans and Ingrid are registered and many other students I'm sure."

"If you take me up on the offer, I was thinking, in return for your help, you can stay in the spare room. You won't have to pay anything and I have an international phone."

"Let me think about it and I can let you know soon."

"Yes. Certainly."

I thought of Adrien and his warning to stay out of the limelight.

Thirty

A few days later at school, Matthew invited me and some others to go carol singing with him. It was myself, the Norwegian girls, Kaleem, Magnus, Hans and Ingrid. At first, I thought he was joking, as it seemed an odd thing to do in Damascus, even though it was Christmas, but everyone was keen to join in with the seasonal tradition by gathering at one of the British diplomats' houses to sing together and then celebrate Mass at a Greek Orthodox church in the Old City.

The carol singing was joyful and festive, if a little off key, in the diplomat's home, which was all decked out with a Christmas tree and decorations. Singing "Oh Holy Night" and "Away in a Manger" reminded me of the story of the birth of Jesus, and I thought about how moving and wondrous it was that I was in such an historic city, where disciples and saints had walked the same streets I was walking.

Matthew introduced us all to the host of the party.

"This is Vice Consul, Mark Anthony Franklin."

"Thank you for inviting us all here," I said politely.

Matthew took me by the hand, as the Vice Consul began to lecture the students good naturedly. Matthew led me to another crowd of guests and tapped on the shoulder of another man. The man turned around and it was Adrien.

"Elizabeth, let me introduce you to Adrien Osbourne, the information officer."

"Hello, Elizabeth," Adrien said and raised his eyebrows pointedly.

"Do you two know each other?" Matthew asked.

"We met when Elizabeth registered at the consular section some weeks ago," Adrien replied. "So, you both met at the Institute, I presume?"

"Yes, Elizabeth is going to help with my thesis."

"It's a very interesting doctorate. When was that decided?" Adrien was looking at me.

"It hasn't been, yet." I frowned jokingly at Matthew, who laughed.

"Will you help with my thesis, Ms. Booth?" Matthew asked with a little flourishing bow. I giggled.

"If you want my opinion, I think it's a marvellous idea," Adrien interjected. "It'll be good for your degree too, Elizabeth."

I had the feeling the decision had been made for me.

"Of course, I'll help."

"Have you decided where to live yet, Elizabeth?" Adrien continued, sipping a club soda.

"Funny you should ask. I've also asked Elizabeth to officially become my flatmate."

"Well, that sounds like a good arrangement too."

At that moment, I looked over and saw Kaleem and Astrid almost joined at the hip. They had become inseparable.

"You know what, Matthew? I accept both your kind offers."

"I'm glad," he smiled.

The Christmas party spilled out of the diplomat's house and into the Christian quarter. We walked along Straight Street to the main crossroads with Cardo Maximus and entered the Greek Orthodox church, which stood above the ancient ruins of a Byzantine church called Knisset al-Mariam-yeh, the St. Mary's Church. The Mariamite Cathedral of Damascus had held the seat of the Greek Orthodox church of Antioch since the fourteenth century.

The church was lofty, with vast ceilings. My eyes had to adjust to my surroundings, with its pictures and statues adorning the walls and covered in gold, gems and astonishing lights. The smell of frankincense was stronger and more natural than I remembered from Christmases back home. I suspected that the resin had been freshly picked that day from one of the beautiful trees in the gardens nearby. In the front of the church before the altar, a choir was assembled and sang Greek Christmas hymns. I saw the front pews were full of nuns and priests in black habits. They prayed in silence.

Matthew, Hans, Magnus, Ingrid, the others and I filed down through the side aisle of the church, until we reached the middle where others were already standing, as the pews were full. I felt like an intruder trespassing on a private ceremony. I stood in awe and wonder at the ceremony, as a parade of Greek priests in white and gold robes walked in procession down the central aisle. They swung silver chalices, filled with incense. Little puffs of smoke rose upward to the vaulted ceiling. The ceremony had probably not changed in centuries.

I couldn't remember the last time Christmas had felt so meaningful and reverent. I had lost my closeness to my faith and had come to think of Christmas as just a commercial holiday, but this experience was special. There was nothing crass or commercial about anything around me.

That evening, I collected my things from the Norwegian girls' house and left with Matthew for my next place. I was deep in thought about the coincidence of Matthew and Adrien also knowing each other. I knew it was not likely planned, but I was beginning to wonder if things were always the way they presented themselves.

Did Matthew only know Adrien as a diplomat or did he know he was also the spook? As someone outside the Damascus Embassy, neither of us should have had access to that information. Even other diplomats in any given embassy don't necessarily have clearance for it.

In Sana'a, I was one of the diplomats cleared to know the identity of the MI6 agent, because I worked in the Chancery Office Building, but I had also had to be cleared because John accidentally left Baudot-coded paper tape, a tape punched with hundreds of holes depicting letters, on the floor of the radio communications room. He was usually careful to collect all his papers and tapes. I had found a roll of tape and picked it up thinking it was mine, as by the end of my shift I would often have a mile of punched tape to shred. I fed his tape accidentally through my teleprinter, which printed out the message. As soon as I read it, I knew it was his, as it referred to an American agent he was coordinating with in Sana'a. I had no choice but to come clean with him, before he discovered that part of his tape was missing and came looking for it. As a result of my knowledge of that one piece of intelligence, he had to report his oversight to his officers back in London. He never spoke to me again about the incident and we kept as much distance as possible between our work in such a confined space. Knowing that the MI6 now had a file on me in their offices made me feel important when in fact it was probably very insignificant.

In normal practice, the spooks have as little exposure as possible. Surely, Adrien would not have told Matthew about his MI6 position? Of course, he had told me.

Thirty-one

The January mornings were cold, but sunny and bright. I became used to Matthew's almost quintessential, English-morning breakfasts. On sunny mornings, there was a suntrap on the roof by a high-brick wall to the side of the entrance, which acted as a windbreak. There we would sit and drink our morning tea. I usually enjoyed a yogurt, even though the local variety had lumpy curds, with a sliced banana. Matthew loved his tea and normally wouldn't eat until later.

After breakfast, I either studied some vocabulary or translated passages from the Institute textbook. Either way, I had my *Hans Wehr* dictionary always ready by my side. Matthew tended to prioritise his research above his studies. It explained his placement in the beginner's class at school.

We were taking our regular break from our studies for a second cup of tea of the day, when I could tell that Matthew had something on his mind. He tended to pace slowly when something was bothering him. He had made quite a few rounds this morning.

"I'm planning on going to Beirut next week, when we're off school." He looked at me expectantly.

"Would you like me to come with you?" I asked, sipping my tea.

"I could definitely do with your help." It was a very English response.

"I want to see Lebanon, now that I'm so close. My parents won't be too happy, especially my mother."

"Then don't tell them. Why is it different from Syria anyway?"

"They are concerned about the hostage taking."

"The hostage crisis has ended."

"I wish they would believe that. They still worry."

"Well, it's a mother's prerogative to worry," Matthew admitted. "My mother is the same. I keep as much from her as I can."

The Lebanese hostage crisis had occurred during the Lebanese Civil War between various clans within Hezbollah. It was during that time that Hezbollah achieved notoriety in the West. The last of over a hundred, western hostages had been released in December of the previous year, including Terry Anderson, an American, Middle-East correspondent for the Associated Press, who had been kidnapped in 1985 during the height of the war. Many hostages didn't make it, as some were murdered, or died in captivity.

I vividly remember the day I heard about Hezbollah for the first time. News broke about the abduction of Charles Glass in the summer of 1987. I was working in the news department in the Foreign and Commonwealth Office in London, when there was a huge ruckus and a sudden, feverish atmosphere. The department had to issue an F.C.O. statement for its daily, midday press conference, owing to the breaking news from Lebanon.

Normally, the usual news correspondents from *the Guardian, the Telegraph* and the BBC arrived each day at noon, to receive a standard F.C.O. press release. On that day though, the conference room was crowded. I recognised the regular news reporters, when I prepared the conference room laying out pencils, notepaper, cups and water on the huge table. If the

F.C.O. statement were newsworthy, it would often appear in that evening's edition of the papers. I got a kick out of reading the evening *London Standard* and seeing the F.C.O. spokesperson's statement on the front page. It made me feel important that I knew it hours before the public did.

On that particular June 17th, the breaking news was that another western hostage had been taken on the streets of Beirut. Charles Glass, an American journalist, was now held captive by Hezbollah. The crisis created an electric atmosphere in the news department. The desk officer, Bill Evans, who worked on Middle Eastern news, was busier now than the desk officer covering the crisis in Korea. The media was eager to get the Foreign Secretary, Sir Geoffrey Howe's statement. The phone lines on Bill's desk all lit up with calls from various media outlets hoping for the freshest news on the hostage. I monitored the Reuters and Associated Press tele-printers on an hourly basis, as reports spewed out from correspondents on the ground in Beirut.

That evening, it wasn't fun to read the evening edition. It made me feel sick thinking of how scared the American must have been. I had been able to shrug it off though. After all, I was in no real danger myself.

***

Not long after we decided to go to Beirut, Matthew and I returned to the flat after a long day at school. Upon entering, I sensed that something was wrong. It was that small prickle at the back of your neck that tells you someone else had inhabited the air just before you came in. Initially, it was difficult to put a finger on. I dismissed the feeling.

I threw my bags into my bedroom, then I went into the kitchen to get some water. Matthew went to the living room to sit down and relax. Matthew was the first to notice something.

"Elizabeth, did you move the table?" Matthew called to me, over the sound of the running tap.

"Sure," I replied sarcastically. "I moved it last time I vacuumed." It had become a joke between Matthew and I that neither of us was any good at keeping house. The flat was often cluttered and dusty, although never actually dirty.

"I'm serious. The table has been moved and I didn't do it." There was an edge to his voice that brought the prickling sensation back to my neck. I put down my glass and walked into the living room. Matthew's eyes were big.

The ornately carved, wooden coffee table, which was always in the middle of the Turkish carpet had, indeed, been moved. The table was so heavy it left indents in the carpet, which were visible now.

We checked the rest of the flat, looking for other signs that it had been searched and then we went to the door that led out to the roof and found it hard to open. The carpet had curled over by the threshold and jammed the door.

"By the looks of it, they pulled the carpet back here."

Matthew simply nodded.

"Could it have been the secret police?" I asked looking around. I felt exposed.

"I'm sure it was them."

For a moment, he was like Rodin's *The Thinker*, with his hand on his chin. I was waiting for his thought.

Then Matthew moved slowly across the room. He stopped dead in the middle, next to the coffee table.

"What were they looking for?" I was rubbing my ear and my face had flushed hot.

"Obviously, they were looking for papers on my research, but they couldn't have found anything. They won't have found anything, except for stuff from their own library here."

"Shouldn't we report the break in to the Embassy?"

"I'm not sure what difference that will make. Adrien knows that the *mukhabarat* watches foreigners."

"True, but isn't it unusual for them to be searching your flat?"

"It's a warning. They're telling me to watch myself."

Matthew spent the next few hours going over the books and papers he had accumulated, checking to see if he had written anything incriminating. I thought about Naguib and pictured Matthew with his head roughly shaved.

You wouldn't be here, if they had found something, my friend.

Charles Glass, the American journalist who was missing in Lebanon for 62 days, celebrated his freedom with his family here today after a debriefing by United States diplomatic and intelligence officials.

—New York Times, *Freed Hostage Rejoins Family*
August 20, 1987

Thirty-two

The next morning, I let Matthew know I had to get some stamps from the Post Office and slipped out of the flat, telling the taxi driver to take me to the British Embassy.

"Elizabeth?" Adrien said, as I entered his office. "I suspect you have something for me being back so soon."

"Yes. We were searched by the secret police." I seated myself opposite his fastidious desk. "We discovered obvious signs that they had been in our flat turning over carpets and searching around who knows where. Honestly, I felt burglarised."

"Well, I'm glad you came in, because the search was not for Matthew, it was you that they wanted information on."

"On me?" I was shocked. I didn't understand what Adrien was implying. How did they even know where I was staying? "Why would they want information on me?"

"Unfortunately, it was overlooked for some time by our consular admin staff. There's no doubt that the Syrian government knows that you were formerly a British diplomat in Sana'a."

"How would they know that? I gave up my diplomatic passport. I've just got a regular one now."

"Here." He picked up the photocopy of my passport. I was puzzled as to what my passport had to do with this situation. He opened it on his desk, turning to the page with my Egyptian visa, dated in March the previous year.

"Did you travel to Cairo directly from Sana'a when you did that Arabic course there?"

239

"Yes." I felt sick. I pulled at my ear.

"Well, the Egyptian diplomat who stamped your passport, also wrote all over the visa and made a notation along the side of that page."

He pointed to Arabic letters and numbers scribbled along the spine of that page. He had deciphered the messy Arabic handwriting.

"It says, 'She worked covertly in the British Embassy in Sana'a.'"

I was infuriated. That sly, Egyptian diplomat assumed I was a spook in the Embassy.

"This is a development that may jeopardise your entire presence in this country. The Syrian visa they issued you is on the very next page and they would have scrutinised your entire passport, while it was in their hands at their London embassy. In addition to keeping track of all foreigners, they would have had increased surveillance on you since your arrival." He lay the papers down on his desk and took a deep breath.

"Tell me, what airline did you fly with when you came?"

"Syrian Arab Airlines."

"And you were befriended by the steward?"

"Yes, Asim introduced me to many people on the plane."

"And afterwards? Did you say you stayed with a Syrian couple?"

"Yes. Abu Kersch and Umm Nadeen. He introduced them to me."

"Asim was most certainly secret police and used the couple as means to keep surveillance on you."

I was speechless. It was all an organised ruse for the Syrian government. I had been played. Was everything a trick? The Syrian couple? The girls? Hussein? Most of all, Hussein. I was still hesitant to tell Adrien about Hussein. It was too embarrassing.

"Unfortunately, when I asked you to report on the students, I was not aware that the Syrian government knew that you were a British diplomat in Yemen. When they broke into Matthew's flat, they must have been looking for proof that you have a cover as a student, but are still working, either for the Foreign and Commonwealth Office, or MI6. It's a very precarious situation for you. If they find any evidence of spying, or working on anything sensitive to their government, you'll be arrested. Are you sure there's nothing in your belongings?"

"I'm sure I didn't write anything anywhere." I squirmed at the thought of a man's hands going through my clothes and personal items.

"What about Matthew? Has he written anything pertaining to your former job?"

"No. I haven't told him. I know he's careful about everything, anyway. Matthew told me all his research that he did in Beirut has been kept at the embassy there, in the consular section."

"Yes. He told me that too."

"Could I be arrested?" I was starting to feel frantic. "They couldn't do that, if I have diplomatic immunity, could they?"

"Elizabeth, you do. We will protect you, but they will keep you under surveillance, so we must remain vigilant."

"Matthew has asked me to go to Beirut to translate books for his research at the AUB."

"I want you to go. Don't change anything: plans, routines, anything. Besides, you will be safer there anyway."

I was floored.

"How will I be safer there?"

"Although the Syrian Army is occupying Lebanon, it is less likely you will be tracked."

I breathed heavily. Adrien put a fatherly hand on my shoulder.

"You will be fine, Elizabeth, but you have to stay calm."

The weight of his hand on my shoulder was reassuring and I sighed. He was right of course.

Thirty-three

For the journey between Damascus and Beirut, Matthew and I shared a taxi with two Syrians, who smoked continuously during the ride. I wrapped myself up in my army coat against the cold, February morning. I sat next to the window and had a choice to either open the window for some fresh air and get frostbite on my nose and cheeks, or inhale thick cigarette smoke. In the end, Matthew opened his window as he already had a terrible cough and could barely breathe.

Lebanon was still recovering from a civil war, which had ended in 1990. The Lebanese Civil War raged between the Christian and Muslim militias, but also involved Israel, and Syria. Initially, Syrian forces were brought in to reestablish peace, but ultimately they established an occupation of large regions of Lebanon. The war also helped to form Hezbollah, which means Party of God. It became the most organised and powerful group in Lebanon. The world classified it as a terrorist organisation, although some would argue that it was a legitimate political party.

Normally the journey should have taken two hours, but it became closer to three because we had to stop whenever we approached one of the numerous barriers across the road. Some barriers looked hastily erected, as they only consisted of a few oil drums, with a pole balanced between them. Dirty, shredded flags hung on the poles by the drums.

Other checkpoints were more permanent, with a dozen or so oil drums piled two or three high and cemented together. The flags snapped in the wind. At one, several soldiers were hanging out by small huts, drinking coffee made in their portable, blackened stoves. The checkpoints were frequent and it wasn't clear to me which faction or country each represented.

"It all depends on a few observations," Matthew said, reading the question on my face. "Look at the badges on their uniforms, their head gear, or the flags."

"So, what was the last one?"

"Our last checkpoint was the South Lebanese Army, the SLA. They were wearing black berets, which had the Lebanese flag on the front with the cedar tree."

"So, which checkpoint are we at now?" I looked out the window and saw men in red berets and camouflage uniforms.

"This is the Syrian Army. Most checkpoints will be the Syrian Army."

The person at the Syrian checkpoint behind sandbags asked for passports. The soldiers looked bored.

"How long have the Syrian Army been here?"

"Since 1976. It's a sore point for Lebanon. Initially, the Syrian Army were in Lebanon as peacekeepers, but they never left."

"Does Hezbollah ever have checkpoints?"

"No. They would be easy targets for the SLA or Israeli shelling. We've just travelled through Beqaa Governorate, which is one of their strongholds, but there was no sign of Hezbollah."

This country appeared full of sundry men in fatigues. Thinking that I had been driven through Beqaa Valley was sobering. I thought back to the news department, when there had been a flurry of activity when Charles Glass had been taken, and now, here I was travelling through the territory, where former hostages had been held for years by Hezbollah. I thought about Adrien's reassurances and took a deep breath.

I sat silently afterwards, watching the landscape change from arid lands to a mountainous region covered by forests. Soon, we headed down towards the coast. Beirut was sprawled below us. Even though it was a cold and grey day, the sight of the city was chilling and thrilling at the same time.

In comparison to Damascus, my first impressions of Beirut were of a city in shambles. All around, there was evidence of the Civil War. Even though it had ended a few years ago, the city was still struggling to repair its infrastructure, roads and buildings. The streets had many potholes, diversions and roadworks. The traffic was always heavy, with hundreds of taxis in addition to private vehicles. Public transport barely existed.

Our taxi pulled up in a huge parking lot that looked like it may have been a bus station, although there were hardly any buses there. It was teeming with taxis and pedestrians. The noise of engines, horns and the throng was all around. The air smelled of obnoxious exhaust fumes, with the occasional waft of food from roadside stalls. The two Syrian men left us hastily, after negotiating a price with the driver. I heard them argue over a few pounds before they struck a deal. Even though Matthew had already negotiated our price, I realised the two Syrians did not equally share the cost of our four-hour drive.

"We're going to stay in a hotel not far from the British Embassy," Matthew informed me, as we stepped out of the cab. "I stayed there the last time I was here."

At the bus station, Matthew flagged down another taxi and gave it the address of the hotel.

At the hotel, I relished a moment of stillness, after the onslaught of the noise. I lay stretched out on the soft bed with glorious white linen and tried to regain my peace of mind and balance, as the cacophony of urban life continued below my window.

"We have nothing on the agenda today, so you can relax. I'll be in the room next door to this," Matthew informed me.

I unpacked and thought about nothing in particular for the rest of the day.

***

I spent a restless night and woke up the next morning feeling drained. Somewhat revived after drinking coffee in the hotel lobby, Matthew and I caught a taxi to the American University in Hamra, west Beirut, not far from the demarcation line, known as the Green Line, that separated east and west Beirut, and where most of the conflict during the Civil War took place. West Beirut was where, some would say, Muslim fundamentalists and terrorists had taken control, and east Beirut was the pro-Western, prosperous, Christian section.

The road outside the American University catered almost exclusively to students. It had bookshops, coffee shops, fruit sellers and small grocery shops. There was no denying that we were in the Shiite Muslim section of Beirut, when I saw large posters of Ayatollah Khomeini, the former leader of Iran. But I was shocked to also see graphic pictures of slaughtered

Muslims in mass graves in Bosnia. It was hard to look at the dead bodies piled up on each other, discarded like garbage. At first I didn't understand the connection between these murdered Muslims in Bosnia and Iran until Matthew explained that Bosnian Serb leaders went to Iran to seek support from the Ayatollah.

Before entering the University, we wandered around some of the bookshops. Browsing through books, I came across a T-shirt with a cartoon of Garfield the Cat with a military helmet on and the words "I survived Beirut" printed in bold lettering. In the face of all the carnage that the city had undergone in recent years, the depiction of a fun-loving cartoon character surviving the shelling and terror of war was odd to say the least. I smiled, in spite of myself.

We walked towards the demarcation line and soon reached Martyrs Square. A statue stood in the middle created by the Italian sculptor, Marino Mazzacurati. It was heavily marked by bullet holes and the remnants of war. All around us, buildings were demolished. Some buildings, that had originally had many storeys, were now destroyed. Floors cascaded down upon each other. Piles of rubble metres high lined the roads. Burnt out cars littered the streets. It was hard to imagine the square in its heyday. Most of the rubble had been swept to one side to clear a small road around the square. There was no vegetation, except for weeds and the occasional sapling that had managed to cling onto the dust and sand. I looked around some of the buildings which were more intact, although that wasn't saying much. One was the Holiday Inn. Its sign was still visible on the upper side of the building. Almost all the tinted windows had blown out. I noticed that families were squatting in the rooms. There were washing lines and misshapen drapes pulled over the window frames.

We walked into the University compound. The remnants of the clock tower from when it had been bombed killing American marines was still evident. Nearby, the library was covered in sections with tarpaulin. Parts of the building were under construction and, as I worked away in a small room, I could hear heavy-machinery drilling and hammering on the reconstruction. It was strange to sit and study in a place one associates with silence, when I was actually in the midst of a construction site.

"The students are on holiday, so there's hardly anyone here," Matthew mentioned offhand. "I know it's going to be hard to study in this noise. We can try to do a couple of hours, before we break."

Matthew and I browsed the bookshelves, searching for the titles of the books Matthew wanted to pull out. He collected various English, German, Arabic and Italian articles, books and publications. We settled on a large enough table to spread out. He stacked the Arabic books in front of me. I was in disbelief at the amount he had found.

"You can't want me to go through all these books."

"There's only certain chapters I need translating. I have the details." He handed me a sheet of the book titles and the page references of the texts he wanted to me to read.

We spent the first two hours of the morning in the library. Translating page after page of Arabic was extremely tedious. The books were historical and political in nature. I did not completely grasp the relevance of what I was translating, as they were only paragraphs and small excerpts from each book, but I knew they were pertinent to Matthew's research in an important way. I started to familiarise myself with some of the key players in the many Syrian coup d'états of the 1950s: Colonel Adib Shishakli, Al-Malki, Atassi and the like. Honestly, I had a hard time staying awake, especially after a night of tossing and turning.

At last Matthew said, "Let's take a lunch break."

"Yes, I need one desperately."

We picked up a sandwich and a drink in the university cafeteria and followed a path for a few minutes through some lush gardens to a small tunnel, which exited out onto a rocky coastline. I realised how much more liberal the dress-code was at AUB, compared to the students I had seen coming and going into the Damascus University, when we came across some students sunbathing in shorts and T-shirts.

After taking in the view of the Mediterranean Sea and the sea breeze, we settled upon a rock to eat our small picnic and soaked in some mid-morning sun. We started to chat.

"Have you heard of Ronald LeBrun?"

"No," I said honestly.

"He's a Middle East correspondent for *the Guardian*."

"Well I've heard of *the Guardian*, although I don't read it much."

"He's also an accomplished author. You need to read his book, *Lebanon's Quagmire*. It's all the history you need to know about Lebanon's Civil War."

"I will. Thank you."

Matthew paused.

"Well, he lives here on the Corniche," he said with a glint in his eye.

"He actually lives here?"

"Yes. He's been here for many years. During the hostage crisis, he was the only western journalist who stayed in Beirut and wasn't kidnapped.

"That's crazy."

"Some people think he's a bit crazy, although some say brave. But he's definitely known to be the reporter who reports on the front line and not from the safety of a hotel room." He paused and then smiled. "I have a surprise. I called him from the hotel last night and he's agreed to meet us this afternoon."

"That's brilliant!" I beamed.

Thirty-four

A taxi took Matthew and I to a narrow street, just behind the Corniche, where many of the two-storey houses were in bad condition. The taxi pulled over to a walled house with large palm trees in the garden. We opened the gate and ducked to miss the large fronds blowing in the sea wind. Matthew rang the doorbell and a middle-aged man answered.

"Ronald. It's good to see you again." The two shook hands, as if they were old school friends reuniting.

"Come in, come in." Mr. LeBrun ushered us into his house. "Matthew, how's your research going?"

"Going well." We entered his small living room. "This is Elizabeth Booth. She is helping me with my research at the AUB."

"Pleased to meet you, Elizabeth. Come this way." Ronald led me to his balcony.

"You can see the Corniche from my house." He pointed out the view. "And over here, he turned inland and pointed, "that's the closest rocket that landed near my house."

Sure enough, there was an enormous crater, where a house used to be. He started to describe the logistics of the war in great detail.

"What was it like living here during the Civil War?" I ventured to enter the conversation, because it seemed Ronald was keen to talk, regardless of my interaction.

"Have you read my book? Those are the horrors I lived." Ronald LeBrun's response was direct. It was a trait that I was sure made him such a great journalist. "It was hair-raising at times, but there were no other journalists covering the war on the Green Line."

He spoke with a loud, robust voice, which made me wonder if his hearing was compromised by the noise and shelling of the quotidian horror he experienced in the war zone.

"So, Matthew, are you travelling down to the UN compound again?"

"Yes, I spoke to Abdullah yesterday. He's got a contact for me, possibly an interview in the Rashidiyeh Camp." Matthew seemed sheepish, when he answered.

"That sounds promising. Do you know who the contact is?"

"Al-Aynayn." Matthew wiped his nose and coughed slightly, as if he was trying to end the conversation.

"The Commander of Fatah? He's a militant, a member of the Sunni organisation, and the founding and dominant force of the PLO. I'm impressed."

"I'd like you to come with me again," Matthew said.

"I can't this time, although I wish I could. He's not easy to interview. Sadly, I'm leaving for the US."

"It's a shame you can't."

"I agree, but I've also got lectures where I am speaking, and book signings."

It seems Matthew had some plans that I didn't know about and I was not sure what they had to do with the United Nations, who Abdullah al-Aynayn or Fatah were.

I looked at Matthew directly, waiting for him to explain what he was talking about, but Ronald didn't stop talking.

"Matthew, it's a good time to go down, as the skirmishes have subsided and the Israelis have made assurances that they will not conduct a land invasion into Lebanon." Ronald continued to elaborate with a story of his, when he went down to the Fiji UN battalion in the Security Zone, but I wasn't paying much attention.

"I'm sorry, but what's going on? Matthew, am I going with you?"

"I wasn't planning on taking you. I think I have some explaining to do. It's research that I'm doing, but this isn't for my doctorate per se."

"He's got a commission with the UN to write a report on covert intelligence and terrorist activities." Ronald took control of the conversation.

Matthew coughed behind his hand, as if expressing his protest.

"Which reminds me, you left your UN, press identity card here." Ronald scrambled around a bunch of papers on a side table near the sofa and picked up a bright orange, index-size card and handed it over to Matthew.

"Thanks." Matthew sat back in the sofa and seemed to settle himself. He shot a look of embarrassment at Ronald. "Elizabeth, the UN got wind of my thesis and were interested in all the fieldwork that I am conducting, the interviews with intelligence agencies, the political members of Syrian groups, and also in Jordan and Egypt, where I've already completed my fieldwork."

"So, you're not exactly who you said you were," I said, raising an eyebrow.

"I am a postgraduate doing my PhD," Matthew said defensively. "But also, I am working as a freelance researcher for the United Nations."

"Well, I'd like to go with you to do the interview with al-Aynayn. Don't you need someone still to translate?"

"Abdullah, the contact from the United Nations Relief and Works Agency, went with me to translate last time."

"I'd like to go. I don't want to stay in the hotel all day."

"I don't see why she can't go," Ronald interrupted again. "Like I said, it's quiet down there."

"Okay, I'll need to get you a UN press pass at the Tyre compound," Matthew conceded. "We can travel tomorrow morning."

"When will we be back? Is it overnight?"

"No. We'll easily be back by the evening. Tyre's only 80 miles south from here."

"Well, Matthew, let me know how it goes. I look forward to reading your research."

"When are you flying out Ronald?"

"Tomorrow." Ronald turned to me. "Nice to meet you, Elizabeth. Good luck with this guy." He smiled and firmly shook my hand.

JERUSALEM, Feb. 16

Israeli forces killed the leader of the pro-Iranian Party of God in Lebanon today in a lightning strike by helicopter gunships that reportedly also left his wife, his son and at least four bodyguards dead

—New York Times, February 17, 1992: Haberman, Clyde. *Israelis Kill Chief of Pro-Iran Shiites in South Lebanon*

Thirty-five

The morning after meeting Ronald LeBrun, Matthew and I got ready to go to Tyre. The night before, Matthew had been close-lipped about how he had become involved with the UN, or Ronald LeBrun in the first place. He went to his room early.

At first, I was upset. I was tired of all the lying and omissions, but then I thought about all the things I hadn't necessarily mentioned to Matthew. *I'd call it a draw.*

We caught a taxi to the main, Beirut central bus station — the focal point for all destinations — and then jumped into another to head to Tyre, the last southern city before the UN Security Zone and where the United Nations headquarters was situated. We rode for an hour along the Lebanon coast. Along the way, I decided it was a good time to grill Matthew again about what he had been talking about with Ronald.

"So, who is this man we're going to interview?"

"His name is Sultan Abu al-Aynayn. He's the commander of Fatah in Lebanon."

"Isn't Fatah a faction of the PLO?"

"Yes, it was the Palestinian National Liberation Movement. Arafat is the founder of Fatah, and al-Aynayn is the commander in Lebanon."

"Aynayn lives in Rashidiyeh?"

"Yes," Matthew said, opening up thanks to the chance to talk political intrigue. "Rashidiyeh is a Palestinian camp, under the auspices of UNRWA. Not many people realise that Lebanon has Palestinian camps — twelve in fact. Most associate Palestinian camps with the West Bank, or Gaza Strip."

When we arrived in Tyre, we found the compound was bustling with UN soldiers and international news crews. It was a mad house. Having been on the road, Matthew and I had not heard the news. Matthew often listened to the BBC Arabic Services on his short-wave radio, but he had packed it in his rucksack in the boot of the taxi.

"What's happened?" Matthew asked one of the journalists, who was standing outside having a cigarette.

"The leader of Hezbollah, Sheikh Abbas Musawi, was killed by an Israeli airstrike in Jibchit." He spoke with a thick, Parisian accent and was from the French *Le Monde* newspaper. He pulled out a box of Gitanes and offered Matthew a cigarette.

"No, thank you. So, when did this happen?"

"Yesterday. Did you not hear about it?"

"I guess not."

"What press are you with?"

"We're not press."

"You'd better be press, if you're going anywhere now."

"Why's that?"

"Israelis have mounted air strikes into the Hezbollah strongholds, because Hezbollah is shelling the border in retaliation for Musawi's death. It's escalating every hour. Everyone's trying to get down to the action."

I spotted a Japanese news team, who were wearing bulletproof jackets and press arm cuffs with their flag on it. Many journalists and their camera operators were scrambling for rides further into the incursion zone. Most taxi drivers were hesitant to go, because the Israeli air strikes hadn't ceased. The competition between the international press associations was fierce. Many were bribing and bargaining with drivers to take them any distance south. I recognised some of the American and British press corps: Associated Press, CNN and Reuters.

"Elizabeth, come with me and we'll get that UN press card for you," Matthew said, tapping me on the arm.

We walked over to a hut by the side of the large, crowded, dusty car park with a sign outside that read: 'United Nations Relief and Works Agency.' Matthew and I stepped into the office.

"Hello, Abdullah."

A young, Middle Eastern man sat at a desk inside. The room was full of maps and papers, randomly pinned on the walls, as if it were a police incidence room.

"Hey, my friend. You made it." Abdullah was smiling broadly.

"Yes. We just heard the breaking news."

"Yes. Musawi, along with his wife and child, were killed in their car by an Israeli rocket, on their way to Beirut."

"Does that mean that the interview with Fatah is postponed?"

"No. It's still on. Who's this with you?"

"This is Elizabeth, my official assistant researcher and translator." I liked that title and nodded, smiling. "Can you make her a UN press card, as she'll be coming to the interview with me and will need it by the looks of the chaos this incident has caused? You're still coming, aren't you?"

"Unfortunately, I'm needed here, as you can see," Abdullah replied. He opened his desk drawer and took out an orange card, identical to the one Matthew had.

"What's your full name?"

"Elizabeth Booth."

He wrote my name in Arabic and English with the dates and then handed it to me.

"It expires a week from now."

"Thank you." I swelled with an odd feeling of pride.

As we left the hut, I still needed to know how we were getting to the Camp and whether it was safe, given the situation.

"Matthew, we're not going into the incursion zone, are we?" Having heard that this was a grave situation, I did not want to leave the safety of the United Nations compound.

"No, the interview is in Rashidiyeh Camp, which is just four miles outside of Tyre. These journalists are all trying to head down to the United Nations Interim Force in Lebanon (UNIFIL) Buffer Zone, where the villages may be hit by the Israelis."

He flagged down a taxi outside the compound. I saw the cabbie's fearful reactions. I began to wonder how safe I really was.

The taxi driver declared that he was not heading out of Tyre, until we told him we were only going to Rashidiyeh, to which he agreed.

It was early afternoon as we travelled down the coastal road. The sandy beaches were deserted, except for migratory birds wading at the shoreline. We passed by flat grasslands, where the wildlife thrived in the abundant, dense flora. It was a beautiful, idyllic scene, which under normal circumstances would have been a tourist destination.

A little further we passed small, one-storey buildings that looked temporary, but they had small gardens, with mature olive, mulberry, and fig trees, proving that they had been there for some time.

We arrived at the camp. It was a stark contrast to the landscape we had just passed through. The camp was a mass of cement-brick buildings with corrugated roofs. As we stepped out of the taxi, a stray dog was slouched in the shade of a bare olive tree. We faced a metal, rusted archway with Palestinian flags, and walls with painted graffiti on them. One slogan read 'Palestine from the sea to the river.' One wall had a huge, colourful mural of a veiled, Palestinian woman embracing the walled city of Jerusalem in her arms, with a white dove flying above the symbol of Islam. The symbolism was not lost on me.

We waited by the arch. Not long after we were approached by a small group of Palestinian men. Four of them were armed and wearing army uniforms. They had bullet belts slung around their shoulders and automatic weapons in their hands. They looked the same age as my brother and yet they were weary and war-torn. They stood behind a tall soldier who was obviously in charge. He had a Palestinian *kefiyah* scarf around his head, a full beard and moustache and was also in camouflage fatigues.

"*Yalla.*" He spoke gruffly, as if he was hoarse from shouting orders.

We walked in single file towards the cement buildings with barred windows, like those in a prison.

A chicken ran across our path, as we turned into the alleyway. Each narrow alleyway had an open ditch in the centre to drain rainwater and sometimes even sea water when the high tide came in, but mostly they were filled with dirty water, sewage and rubbish. Turn after turn, we followed two armed men in front and were followed by another two armed men behind. Each turn was a sharp right or left, as we disappeared into the camp grid.

I began to feel anxious about the distance we were from the entrance. Heads popped up from the rooftops and I saw small, dirty faces of children, occasionally brave enough to say "Hello, bonjour." The living conditions looked miserable. These people lived in intense poverty, and a paucity of the most basic services. The houses were like sieves, with bullet holes all over the walls, as Rashidiyeh is the closest camp to the Israeli border and the most hit by airstrikes.

Finally, the soldiers stopped. The bearded one pulled back a thin curtain, on the front door of a house.

"*Yalla*. Come."

We stepped inside into a smoke-filled room. More soldiers lingered inside. All motion and noise stopped, as they gawked at us. The bearded soldier headed straight to another door, this one was shut. He knocked and then opened it and stepped to one side.

"*Ruha*. Go," he ordered.

Seated at a large desk was al-Aynayn. Behind him was a large picture of Arafat and himself shaking hands. Next to that picture was a headshot of George Habash, whom I recognised immediately with his white hair and bushy, black moustache.

During the many work hours John and I spent in the radio communications box, he liked to expound on the politics and history of the Arabian Peninsula. It was his soapbox, and I imagined he often debated competitively with his peers at Cambridge. I only paid attention occasionally. However, one discussion I keenly listened to, came up after our trip to Aden.

Visiting the communist Yemen was prohibited for us, and the first time we could make such a trip south to Aden was when the two Yemens unified in May 1990. We travelled to the British Embassy there to meet the chief radio engineer, who was on an official business trip to Aden to teach a crash course on basic radio repairs. One evening, John took myself and the engineer to a well-known, hole-in-the-wall Adeni restaurant to eat. They served blackened red snapper on newspaper with no cutlery. I remember that the burnt fish was the most delicious I had ever eaten. I was also amused, when John told us the legend about Aden, that unless a traveller climbs the dormant volcano, in whose crater the city sits, they will always return to Aden. I was agreeable to the idea of going up the volcano, but it was a work, not a pleasure trip for us all.

Other than that, the two-day trip was uneventful. I was not enthralled by Aden. It was a sandy, rocky and dirty city. The sand wasn't the same as beach sand that I loved as a child, but volcano sand that got everywhere like dust: up my nose, in my eyes and into my pores.

It wasn't until we were back in Sana'a and in the box that John disclosed that there was a small table beside ours in that tiny restaurant that had three men sat at it. One of those men was George Habash, the leader of the Popular Front for the Liberation of Palestine, PFLP. At the time, I had no idea who the PFLP, Habash or the Doctor, which John said he was commonly known as by his members, were. John was the very first person I knew to talk about the PFLP and the PLO. For an MI6 officer it must have warranted reporting to London, but for me I almost felt like I had bumped into a celebrity in Soho.

And now, sitting in front of the leader of Fatah in Lebanon, there was George Habash's image, with his white hair and bushy, black moustache.

Al-Aynayn was a middle-aged officer with broad shoulders. He had large, bulbous eyes, and was clean-shaven with a bald head.

"*Ahlan wa sahlan*. Hello." He didn't get up from his seat behind the desk. He leaned forward and folded his hands before him on his desk. His voice was commanding and deep as he eyed each of us.

The younger soldiers filed into the room and stood behind us, as we took a seat in front of him.

Shivers went down my spine. The room grew dark, as the daylight started to fade and no one switched on the bare, bulb light in the centre of the ceiling. Only one, barred window lit up the room. I could feel my heart beat in my throat. Al-Aynayn began to speak, but I couldn't focus on his words. I thought of whether we were going to get kidnapped. It's probably not something you expect, until it is already too late, and in this case, it would be too late as the entrance seemed so far, far away. Every step into the quagmire, I thought, I was stepping further into a nightmare waiting to happen. I heard the men behind me shift their feet and the clinks of metals filled the air. I remembered John had said the PFLP abducted American journalists and even hijacked planes to draw attention to its movement.

I tried to focus on the speech. Al-Aynayn's speech was an unrelenting, furious, labyrinthine argument. I recognised some of his rant. He extolled on the hardships his peoples were suffering.

"Living conditions are difficult."

"There's no help from the NGOs or the UN."

"We are crowded, we have no materials to repair our houses, we cannot build, we cannot expand."

Finally, he pointed to one of the young soldiers behind us. "That man there is twenty, married with children and he can't get a house, or a job. Unemployment is too high."

"Do you want to ask me anything?" he asked, after he had exhausted himself and wiped spit away from his mouth.

Matthew looked at me expectantly and I was like a deer in headlights. I had no questions. Suddenly, I remembered that Bill Clinton had just been elected President of the United States.

"What do you think of Bill Clinton being the new President of the United States?"

He became red in the face and I realised my question was a mistake. We sat for more excruciating minutes, as he ranted about America. I was worried that I had made him so angry he was going to kill us, but finally he stopped. This time he looked breathless, and waved his hand at us. The men stood to attention and we got the message to leave, or perhaps escape.

We were escorted out of the camp. We waited for a taxi to pass by. On the verge of the road, in the fading sunlight, I snapped a photo of a pile of used missiles. I wondered if they were fired at, or from, the camp.

Matthew and I were silent in the taxi on the way back to the Sheraton hotel. The gravity of the situation washed over me. I had made it into the most militarized Palestinian camp in Lebanon and made it out unscathed. If it weren't for my mental and physical exhaustion, I would be gleefully smiling to myself at pulling off such an escapade but instead I closed my eyes and longed to sink into the most comfortable hotel bed I had ever felt.

Thirty-six

The next day, the day before we were due to leave Lebanon, Matthew informed me that he had some more interviews with officials for his thesis.

"I've arranged to meet a former member of the Muslim Brotherhood. He's been in exile in Cyprus, but has come to Beirut for a few days. It's not a good idea for you to accompany me and apparently, he speaks English perfectly."

"That's okay. I think I'll go to the hotel lobby and pick up a newspaper and relax."

I was happy to be left alone and took my time waking up, having breakfast in the lobby restaurant. I went to the newspaper stand to pick up *the Telegraph* newspaper. I read about the Israeli gunships bombarding the southern villages in Lebanon. Hopefully the attacks were not escalating into a crisis, but already, there were many civilians killed or injured.

An Arabic newspaper, *Al Jazeera*, caught my eye, as I recognised a photograph of a woman. I leaned forward and picked it up for a closer look. In numb disbelief, I realised the photograph was of my friend, Fatima. The heading of the article was 'Martyrdom in Southern Lebanon'. She was wearing combat clothes, with a black beret and holding a Kalachnikov. Her eyes were dead, and her mouth was a grimace. Over her left shoulder, there was a man who could have been Hussein. Tears silently streamed down my face.

Hussein did this to her. He murdered her for betraying him.

My mind started to unravel, as I was tormented by the thought that I caused her death. She had saved me from marrying him. Somehow, he had decided that she had to be disposed of. I was sure it was him in the picture.

He's a monster. Is Hussein in Lebanon? Why she was brought to southern Lebanon? Who forced her to be a suicide bomber? Is he Hezbollah?

I desperately needed to distract myself, as a knot of anger formed in my gut. After picking at, but not eating breakfast, I decided to revisit the bookstores near the university, along Bliss Street. I wasn't sure why. I needed to do something though.

The street was buzzing with students. I wandered in and out of a few shops, browsing through books. I stumbled across the Garfield T-shirt, but it didn't seem funny anymore. Despite myself, I felt tears welling up in my eyes.

I stepped out of the shop. I looked at my watch and was surprised it was already 3 p.m. I figured I should flag down a taxi and go back to the hotel. Matthew might be finished with his interviews and we could have a cup of tea together. I was going to tell him everything when we got back.

A car drew up alongside me and for a moment I thought it was a taxi, but it didn't have the usual writing on it. I stepped away from it. The car doors opened and two men rushed out and grabbed me. Within seconds, all went black as a cloth came over my head and I was shoved into the back of the car. I wrestled and screamed, but I was forced further along the back seat. One man got in beside me and tied my hands tightly in front of me with coarse rope. The car doors slammed as it sped off.

"Keep your head down." He yelled in Arabic.

I lay across the backseat, my body rocked involuntarily back and forth as the car swerved and accelerated through the gears. After some time, I noticed the brakes were not applied as often, as we reached a faster cruising speed.

"Where are you taking me?" I screamed.

Immediately, I was jabbed sharply on my right side. It felt like one of my ribs broke. I cried out.

"Shut up!" he yelled again in Arabic.

After what seemed like forever, we stopped. Cold, fresh air rushed into the car. I anticipated my exit and didn't resist this time. My arms were pulled violently to the left. I cried out in pain again, as my ribs felt as if they pierced my chest.

Still blindfolded, I was dragged up some steps. I lost my balance and fell onto my knees. Immediately two men grabbed me by the armpits and hauled me up the remaining steps.

The crisp, February fresh air turned into a smoky, stale air. Like a ragdoll, I was dragged along the floor and then it all stopped.

"Stand up."

I felt blood trickle down my knees underneath my torn jeans after being dragged up the flight of stairs.

Hands patted me shamelessly and stroked my body all over. They removed my watch from my wrist and took my bumbag from my waist, which had my passport and money in it and then took my army coat, leaving me in my sweatshirt and jeans. I stood still, stripped of my identity, my protection and my security.

"You're going to die here," one of the men taunted, as he searched me for things to steal.

I will probably die here.

"Please, *min fadlak*, let me go."

More hands reached around my head. I stiffened, bracing myself to be strangled.

"Never, you filthy animal." He growled, pulling and tugging at the hood before lifting it roughly over my head.

The extreme brightness was blinding. I kept my face bowed as I didn't want to look at whoever was breathing on me. Blinking rapidly and squinting, as my eyes adjusted to the light, I focused on a sand-coloured, military style boot which kicked a metal plate towards my legs. Then he bent over me and with a knife he slashed the rope away from my wrists. I flinched when the rope fell near to me realising that his knife ripped through a thick rope like it was cutting butter.

"Try to escape and you will be shot," he threatened. Then, he grabbed my chin, pulling it up, forcing me to make eye contact. His breath smelt of smoke and alcohol. I expected to see bared teeth, snarling at me, but he was smiling. Before exiting, he took a few moments to fondle and grope me. I did nothing, but bow my head again.

Escape?

I was in a state of unremitting terror.

Will anyone ever find me? Is this really happening to me?

I looked at the plate of food and saw he had spat in it. I retched seeing his phlegm and at the thought that he touched me. Even if I were hungry, I could not have eaten the scraps in front of me. Small pieces of gristle and bread were covered in a mix of sand and dirt. I felt like a stray dog getting the meagre leftovers of his abuser.

Shivering, I crouched on a dirty, thin mattress on the floor. Daylight faded as the slits in the window darkened and the room filled with shadows. The hours became monotonous.

The electric light and fan worked intermittently—a few hours here, a few hours there. Flies landed on me, but I was too numb to feel them. The TV in the next room was blaring Egyptian soaps and comedy shows all night. My captors laughed and talked loudly, uncouth and rude to each other. I could smell the food they were cooking and still I had no appetite, but my stomach spasmed with hunger pains.

In the room, there was a small nightstand. I pulled the drawer open and I was surprised to find a pen amongst the discarded chewing gum wrappers and rubbish. I also smoothed out an old paper bag, crumpled and slightly torn, but good enough to use. I needed to write. I prayed the pen worked, as I began to write. My hand was shaky and cold. I wrote as best I could.

I was feeling frantic to write more, but was running out of space and wrote half of it around the edges. I hoped it was legible.

While writing the letter, the reality hit hard. Salt dried on my cheeks from my tears, as I sat in a heap on the mattress. I thought of my parents and my brother and prayed that they would know I was alive and that I loved them dearly and missed them terribly.

I put my hands together and knelt on my knees to pray.

"Please Lord, let my mother and father and brother know that I love them. Let them know that I miss them. Please tell them I am sorry for causing them so much pain and that I am alive and will be back with them soon. Lord guide my rescuers to my captors. Please forgive me for my sins. Forgive me, Lord Jesus, for my selfishness, not thinking of others and causing suffering to my family by my actions. My Saviour Jesus Christ, save me."

My eyes stung from lack of sleep. I didn't think I had caught any sleep, but I must have lapsed from exhaustion. I was roused when a harsh light shone directly onto my face through the gaps in the boarded window. Within a few seconds, I was conscious of my pain and the horror of my situation. A soldier brought me more scraps and some water, which I ate and drank little of. I was allowed to leave the room to use the bathroom. As I made my way to the bathroom, a soldier in fatigues leaning against the wall in the hallway, spat on me as I shuffled by.

"*Sharmouta*. Whore."

I kept moving, my eyes lowered. The toilet was a traditional hole in the floor. The ceramic tile all around it was soiled, but I was numb to the disgust I faced. I looked at a cloudy reflection of me in a small shaving mirror and saw my bloodshot eyes staring back. I cleaned the spit from my cheek with a piece of soap that was left in a stained sink in the tiny water closet.

Back in my cell, I returned to the sanctuary of my threadbare mattress. I strained to make out any news on the TV about my abduction. My heart sank when I heard nothing.

Hopelessness crept in, as I feared that I would never be rescued. I was sure that Matthew would have told the Embassy of my disappearance that afternoon when I didn't come back to the hotel. But I was more concerned that they wouldn't know where I was taken, nor who had taken me. I glanced at the men who occasionally checked on me to see if they had any badges on their uniforms. Having passed through so many checkpoints with Matthew, I was now able to identify Hezbollah or the South Lebanese Army (SLA), but I didn't recognise the badge that this soldier wore; a red and white badge, with a circle with an arrow in it.

Who has taken me?

I feared it had something to do with the Syrians, because of the raid in Matthew's flat. Perhaps they had found additional, incriminating evidence about my activities in their country? Why else would I be kidnapped? Perhaps I was going to be taken back to Syria by the Syrian security forces and detained like Naguib. A glimmer of hope washed over me, as I recalled that Adrien had guaranteed I had diplomatic immunity, which meant I would be released. The Syrian authorities would not dare to detain a British diplomat, jeopardising international relations with many countries as a result.

In the solitude, I blamed myself for my recklessness. Now, the real consequences of my actions were staring at me. I held tight to the slippery optimism of my own survival.

It's all my fault.

February 20th, 1992

To my Father,
In those hours, I reflected on all the small things that you had done for me. I had failed to treasure so many memories that got forgotten during my tumultuous teenage years. They showed your enduring love and how you had coped with those times that I ignored you or acted insolently.

Memories like the time you stood behind me, as I struggled to keep my balance on my first bicycle and then encouraged me to ride without stabilisers. You were so happy, when I rode solo for the first time.

You taught me how to do things, so I could be independent. You helped me to fix a puncture in my bicycle tyre and later how to wire a plug for my hairdryer.

You were the one who taught me to drive and bought my first car, The Banger. When I dented it on the garden wall, your only concern was that I was okay.

And when I applied to the Foreign and Commonwealth Office, you were the one rushing off to the central Post Office in town to catch the last delivery, because I had almost missed the submission deadline.

I never appreciated your patience, as you coped with my standoffish moody years. When you offered me pragmatic and sound advice, I turned you down.

When I left home, you were not demonstrative. You were not someone who showed your emotions easily, but you were steadfast and concerned for my welfare and safety, although I wasn't able to see it at the time.

Your impact shaped me to live a life of honesty and integrity, and to be able to admit my shortcomings. I have not always made the best choices, but you have allowed me to carve my own path. When I fell, you showed me how to be resilient and jump back up.

You set your goals high, setting me an example, so I would always aim to achieve my best.

You have always stayed faithful to Our Lord God and I admire that about you. It was one of the most valuable strengths I had to turn to, during my hour of need.

I love you father.

Thirty-seven

I sensed it was the early hours of that morning, when some of my captors came crashing into the room, battering me with threats and saying I was going to die. I was exhausted and paralysed with fear. There was nothing I could do but be pushed around. They grabbed my bruised arms and half carried and half dragged me outside, as my legs were weak.

They put the black sack over my head again and tightened the drawstring. It was difficult to breathe without the cloth going into my mouth. It tasted of soil and dirt.

My arms were pulled behind my back this time and then tied with a rope.

I heard an onslaught of insults directed at me. "*Shoo haya*. Here's a snake."

"Hussein?" I thought I recognised his voice.

"*La!* No!" I was kicked in the back of my knees.

I was pushed to walk forward. I stumbled. My shins hit what I thought must be the step into a car. Someone pushed my head down and shoved me forward into the back seat. The doors slammed shut. I was driven away from an unknown room to another unknown destination. I was gripped with fear. I prayed again.

I believe in you, My God Almighty. Please Lord Jesus save me. Please let me be on my way to Damascus.

The men threw a blanket over my body. I lay underneath it, in silence, for miles. I could hear their voices in the front seat, talking above the sound of a crackly radio playing music. For an instant, I thought I recognised Hussein's voice again, but it was hard to discern with the background noise.

My arms were aching at my shoulders twisted tight around the back of my body, pulling the joints forwards and backwards, with the movement of the car. Occasionally, it seemed as if the car was driven off-road, as we changed from a smooth road to a heavily bumpy ride.

They are avoiding SLA checkpoints.

I felt as if I was journeying into an abyss. I could tell it was not the main road that the taxi had taken from Damascus. I feared that I was far off the beaten track, and far from Damascus and Beirut. Images of normality came to me — my family eating at the breakfast bar in the kitchen. I yearned to be back in the safety of my family. My hope that someone, somewhere, would somehow know where I was, was almost gone. I concentrated on my hearing, and heard gravel crunch under the car wheels. A bush brushed and scratched the side of the car door near my head. Then, the tyres rolled smoothly, as they hit tarmac again.

The car stopped and I was pulled up and heaved out of the car. Fresh, cold air stung my face, which had been stained by fresh tears. They guided me up some steps.

Elizabeth, you have to try to escape.

I could clearly hear my mother's voice.

Elizabeth?

The thought of escaping terrified me. I would surely die trying.

How?

I answered my mother's voice.

I'm too scared.

I was at their mercy.

I peered through the tiny holes in the material and momentarily saw the pink sky and then I disappeared once again into the darkness of an unknown building. I could make out the sound of a car horn and other traffic nearby. I hoped that meant someone might see me walking outside and report it to the police.

They left me in a room. I panted into the hood, feeling claustrophobic. It was freezing and I shivered, perhaps from the cold, but also from fear. In between my heavy breaths, I heard a quiet, shaky voice.

"Hello?" I tried to steady my breathing and listen again. It was a female voice.

"Hello?" she said again. She didn't sound Arabic. I vaguely recognised the muffled voice through the thin wall.

"Hello," I answered. "Who's there?"

"I'm Astrid." I could hear her accent now.

I shuffled over to the side of the room, where the voice came from. I felt a doorway—an adjoining door.

"Astrid? Is it really you?"

"Yes. Is that you, Elizabeth?" I could hear her more clearly.

"Yes."

"I'm not sure how long I've been here. Days, weeks perhaps."

"Astrid. We will get out of here. Matthew knows I was abducted. We will be rescued."

We have to be rescued.

I thought back. Astrid's disappearance hadn't registered with me, with other student friends, the school, or her family back home. No-one was looking for her. Elina, her friend hadn't even notified the university. Elina brushed it off when we asked, "She used to disappear all the time back home. She'll be back. She could have eloped to Kenya with Kaleem. She even mentioned that once." We all agreed she was besotted with him and aloof so we hadn't worried.

"Kaleem brought me here," she sniffled.

"Kaleem abducted you?" I said incredulously.

"Yes. He lied to me."

"But we all thought you had gone away somewhere with him."

"I did. We were going to Kenya for our honeymoon. After we got married, he completely changed. He took my passport. He took everything. I didn't realise until it was too late."

I heard sobs.

"I'm so stupid."

"No, Astrid. You're not stupid."

I could have stopped this.

I thought of how stupid I was for not warning Astrid about my suspicions of Kaleem. Maybe if I had said something, like Fatima had done to me, Astrid would not have stayed with him. "We will get out of here. Matthew knows I was abducted. We will be rescued."

We stopped talking, as we heard footsteps. A few minutes later, when they walked away, Astrid spoke again.

"Elizabeth," she paused. "The Arab man you were with at the registration at the Institute. He's here."

"Hussein?"

"Yes. He's here. I recognised him."

His name rang in my ears. I hadn't heard it in months.

Hussein. I did hear his voice.

The thought echoed in my brain like a church bell. I buried my head between my knees, in utter despair.

"Are you sure it's Hussein?" I asked, hoping for a moment that we were both wrong.

"Yes. I recognised him from the Institute, when he used to drop you off and once came in with you. It's him. I'm sure. Doesn't he have blue eyes?"

Yes. Those damned blue eyes.

I fell silent. My mind was ablaze with questions about Hussein and Kaleem and how these were connected.

Somewhere in the building, a heated discussion broke out. Chairs were scraped across the floor and those heavy boots walked back and forth, as loud rants infiltrated my room. I strained to hear what they were saying.

"I hear something about the airport. Someone is coming from Yemen." Astrid had been listening too.

"Yes. I heard that too."

There was a series of quick responses between a small group of men. All the voices were yelling, as if no one was in control. It was unnerving to hear, as whatever it was, it appeared to be escalating.

21st *February 1992*

Dear Mother and Father,
I never thought that I would be writing a letter to you under these circumstances. I thought my time in Syria would be full of adventures and studying. I hope this letter never needs to be sent and that I can just carry it home myself, when I am released. I will never give up hope that I will see you again. I have put myself in a bad situation and ignored my own safety. If I have caused you pain, I am sorry. I never wanted to hurt you by making foolish mistakes. I remember mother telling me that everyone makes mistakes and that's how you learn to become better. I can't lose hope and I believe I will learn a lot from this huge mistake.

I am so thankful that you are the kind of parents who encourage their children to travel and broaden their horizons. You have always been there for me even when I didn't appreciate you. I haven't always shown it, but I love you both so much. Please forgive me for my recklessness.
Your daughter, always and forever with love,
Elizabeth

Thirty-eight

Snippets of information rang out of the rants of the men.

"*Al-Hakim.* The Doctor."

"Sana'a"

"Flight YR760."

It was alarming to piece together the jigsaw of words. Whichever way the pieces fell, the picture it formed was vile.

"A doctor is coming, but why would a doctor come?" Astrid whispered. "Someone is coming from Yemen."

I slumped against the door.

I was glad Astrid couldn't see my terror-stricken reaction to learning that The Doctor was involved in our abduction.

"Elizabeth, are you still there?"

I had fallen silent, unable to answer Astrid for fear of my voice revealing the terror inside me.

"When did you meet Hussein?" she asked, as if she was reading my mind.

I summoned up the courage to speak. I didn't want Astrid to lose all hope, which had slipped away from me.

"I met him soon after arriving, through a friend. But I discovered that the friend was an informant for the Syrian government."

I kept going over and over the events of my journey, since arriving. Adrien had confirmed that Asim and Naguib were informants for the Assad government.

Adrien may have known who Hussein was. I should have told him.

"Do you think Kaleem and Hussein are in Hezbollah?"

"I don't think so." I stayed intentionally vague as I didn't want to heighten Astrid's fear.

The truth was I feared a worse terrorist group than Hezbollah—a group with no intention of releasing their hostages.

"Whoever has us will release us." I remained steadfast and put my hands together in prayer.

"Are we going to die, Elizabeth?" Astrid's voice was barely audible.

"No Astrid, we are going to survive," I said, trying to convince myself as much as Astrid that survival was possible. I tried to push away the thought of death, but allowed myself to pray that when and if it happened, that it would be swift.

The room became colder and colder and I presumed the sun was setting. I heard every sound, from within or outside the building. I wanted to stay alert, but I was barely maintaining wakefulness. No moment was silent. No moment was without fear.

Doors slammed and feet marched towards us. Within minutes, my door burst open and I was pulled up off my feet. The hood was ripped from my head so violently it almost choked me. The rope was cut from my hands. My eyes adjusted to the light in the room and I made out a heavily set, white-haired man, with a full beard and green fatigues, standing just two feet away from me.

"*Ya*, Elizabeth." George Habash spoke within inches of my face. I could see his yellow teeth and chapped lips, under his moustache which was now more grey than black.

I stared at him, confused by his comment.

"You know my name?"

"You were a British diplomat in Sana'a." I wasn't sure if it was a question or a statement.

Blood drained from my body. I felt the prickly tingle run through me and a cold reality struck me.

How could he know that?

I opened my mouth, but only a gasp came out.

"Our paths crossed in Aden, a few years ago. You are a diplomat, aren't you?"

I could not look at him.

A soldier grabbed my chin.

"Answer."

"Or perhaps you are British Intelligence?"

"No. I'm a student."

"Why are you here?"

"I'm doing research at the AUB. Please believe me. I'm not a diplomat."

My lips were still split and cracked. I could taste blood on my tongue. I hadn't drunk anything for hours.

"You were with two other British diplomats, eating in a restaurant on the Main Street. I never forget a face." His voice was threatening.

I daren't answer him, as I had no idea what would happen if I denied his statement.

My legs buckled and I collapsed in front of him.

"Get rid of her."

Two men dragged me, my knees scraping across the floor. I didn't even scream. I looked sideways, at each of them. They both wore black *kefiyahs* covering the entire head, nose and chin. They looked like medieval executioners. The only things visible were their eyes. The soldier to my right had unremarkable brown eyes and the one to my left had cornflower, blue eyes, with long, black lashes. I knew those eyes…

"Hussein." I could barely draw my breath as my arms were stretched pulling my ribcage apart. The pain was piercing.

Astrid was right. He is here.

"Hussein. I'm not a spy. You know me. Please don't do this."

He gave me a cold, steel look, as he carried me away.

I couldn't keep my head up and slumped between them both, as my feet dragged. Wordlessly, he stuffed me into a car. I knew this time, I was going to be executed.

How could I ever have trusted him? God, please help me.

I fell into a heap on the back seat of the car and awaited the end of my journey.

My family will never find me. They will never know my story. Please Lord, tell them I love them all.

Hussein slid into the driver's seat, started the car and pulled away. With a start, I realised they hadn't hooded me. I was going to be killed, so they didn't bother to cover my head.

I looked out the window, as the blue sky, broken by billowing clouds, flashed by. The car rolled over railway tracks and shuddered. A military plane was flying low enough for me to see. The road was smooth, as we travelled into an urban area and the scenery became more and more built up. We slowed down as we stopped behind traffic and at lights. "It must be some sort of main road," I thought to myself.

Elizabeth. You must escape. Your hands are free.

I didn't want to escape. My body was broken. I had no strength. What will happen to Astrid, if I get away? Surely, she will be killed.

Then it hit me. If I die, no one will know that Astrid is being held hostage. It was like coming up for air. Something inside my chest broke open and gushed adrenaline through my veins. The moment the car slowed down to the next stop, I sat up and pulled at the car door handle.

Run.

From the corner of my eye, I saw the man in the passenger seat reach for his gun. He flung his door open, on the opposite side to me.

"*Iitlaq alnnar ealayh,*" Hussein yelled.

Shoot her. He is telling him to shoot me.

I ran for my life, with the energy of a fleeing gazelle. A gun fired behind me, but I kept running without looking back. I dodged the people who were milling around the pavements, shopping for their everyday necessities and going about their normal business. Things began to come into sharper focus. I saw huge banners portraying Hassan Nasrallah, Hezbollah's new Secretary General. Posters of martyrs were plastered all over the sides of buildings. Then a billboard of Khomeini faced me from across the street. I was in the Shiite neighbourhood in West Beirut. I recognised my surroundings. We were near the American University.

This is Al Hamra district.

I saw the bakery, where we once grabbed lunch. My timing could not have been better. The midday sale of fresh bread always attracted a large, unruly crowd, anxious to get their order after the dawn batch had sold out a few hours after it was baked. The large, flat breads were being passed over their heads, as they yelled to the baker how many they wanted, holding up the number of fingers. Then the money was passed back to the window. I pushed through the men and women.

I ran down the next street and came out by the main dual carriageway opposite the bus depot. There was a line of taxis waiting for customers. It was easy to flag one down, although I looked like a beggar, in my torn and dirty clothes and nothing like a western tourist that the taxi driver would expect from hearing my British accent.

"*'Ila as-safara al-biritanniya*. To the British Embassy." I begged the driver to drive as quickly as he could.

As we drove out of the bus depot, I peered out of the tinted windows of my temporary sanctuary. The shooting had created a crowd. Bus passengers, drivers, bystanders and soldiers were clogging up the road. The police and ambulance were on the scene. We drove within feet of the foray. I saw that the police had detained someone in handcuffs. I let out a sigh of relief and prayed that my captors had been caught.

I was still running on adrenaline, incapable of shutting down, even in the midst of exhaustion. I just hoped I would be in the hands of safety, when that eventually happened.

Thirty-nine

I stumbled from the taxi to the entrance of the Embassy.

"Please help me," I pleaded.

The Lebanese, armed security guards who were on patrol, immediately came to my side. Initially, I was scared by the familiar camouflage and black berets and my pulse raced, poised to flee again if I needed to, but when one of them was yelling into a walkie-talkie, I realised they were not going to take me back to the hell I had just come from. They held me up and guided me through the security gate.

When I stepped into the British Embassy compound, I finally felt some relief. I could have collapsed there and then from pure exhaustion, dehydration and hunger, but I had Astrid on my mind. It sickened me to think what our captors would do to her, when they discovered I had escaped.

The doors of the building flew open. Three diplomats came running out. One was carrying a walkie-talkie, still communicating with the security guards.

"Yes. I confirm it is Elizabeth Booth. She is here in the Embassy."

Then I saw Matthew rushing towards me.

"Elizabeth, I can't believe it. You're safe." He took my arm from the guard and pulled it around his shoulder, propping me up. I winced from the shooting pain piercing me underneath my ribs.

"I'm so sorry for bringing you to Beirut. I feel responsible for this."

"Matthew. Listen. I was with Astrid. She's still there." I breathlessly spoke as I held my ribcage. "The PFLP will kill her now."

"Oh, my God." Matthew was aghast. "Let's get you inside."

I walked as best I could with Matthew.

"Take her into the Ambassador's Office. It has a couch she can lie on." A female diplomat instructed Matthew.

"Adrien's on his way," Matthew said frantically. "I know this is hard, but we must get you taken care of first. Where are you hurting? How were you treated?"

I wanted to answer all his questions, but it was too much. I felt I was slipping into unconsciousness as voices became distant as if I was listening to them under water.

"We need to get her inside so the doctor can assess her." A female diplomat was talking to Matthew trying to get him to stay calm.

"Rest here." I lay my head on soft cushions and Matthew gently picked my legs up and stretched me out along a couch. "Do you have a blanket? She's freezing." He turned to the woman, who also noticed I was shivering so profoundly my teeth were chattering in my thin dishevelled clothes.

"I'm Dr. Mitchell. I need to do a quick medical assessment of you, in case there's anything that requires immediate medical attention." I barely heard another person who came to my side.

Dr. Mitchell checked my vitals.

"Let me look at those wounds," I squirmed, when she touched my ribcage.

"I believe you may have a broken rib, but we won't know for sure, until we get you to the hospital. The bruising is also significant."

"Please, you need to find Astrid," I muttered.

Dr. Mitchell walked away to receive a phone call. No one seemed to be listening to me, as I strained to be heard. When she put the receiver down, she approached me again.

"She needs to go to hospital," she said to someone standing by my bed.

"Please, save Astrid." I was only just hanging on to consciousness. I felt a prick in my arm, as the doctor withdrew a needle.

***

In the distance, I heard a male voice.

"Do we know who took her yet?" I strained to hear it.

"No, there has been no contact with her kidnappers." A deeper voice responded.

"Is she going to be okay to interview?"

"I have known her for some months and know her background. She is resilient and strong. I know she will be."

I opened my eyes, but everything was out of focus.

"Elizabeth?"

Is that my father?

"Elizabeth?" Again, the voice quietly called.

"Father?" I asked, but my mouth was tacky and dry.

"Can you hear me?" It was Adrien.

"Where am I?"

"You're in hospital."

"How long have I been here?"

"Not long. Dr. Mitchell ordered your transport to the American University of Beirut Medical Centre to take care of you better."

I tried to lift my head, but it was so heavy it dropped immediately back into a soft pillow.

I still desperately needed to sleep. I peered out of my swollen eyes. A drip was attached to my arm. My ribcage was bandaged up and wires on my chest drooped from machines above my head. I could hear the constant noise of the machines, beeping to the sound of my heartbeat.

I'm alive.

I shut my eyes, but could still hear Adrien talking to me.

"I'm so sorry for what you have been through." He warmly squeezed my hand.

"Adrien?" I recognised his voice, but I was so weak I didn't know if my voice was audible.

"Yes. It's me." I could feel his hot breath close to my ear.

My body was not in pain anymore, but I was groggy. The soft mattress beneath me and the smell of clean laundry was soothing and comforting.

I'm safe. But Astrid. She's still in danger.

"Have you got Astrid?"

"We are still searching for her." Adrien patted my arm gently.

I looked across the room and saw a compact man, in his late forties, with a little paunch. He wore a dark blue suit, light blue shirt and red tie. The other man was intense with deep furrows above the bridge of his nose and across his forehead and a stout structure, with a double chin, in his late fifties. He looked like a seasoned agent, who had seen many clandestine cases out in the field. He was dressed impeccably, with a similar dark suit, white shirt and navy blue tie.

"Elizabeth, these men are here to get critical information to help locate Astrid." Adrien was by my side, calmly reassuring me.

"Thank you, Agent Osbourne." The younger-looking officer switched places with Adrien and stood at my bedside.

His voice was baritone. "I'm Agent Arrowsmith from TIB, the Terrorist Investigation Branch in MI6. I'm so sorry for your ordeal and I apologise that we have to do this interview now, but as Agent Osbourne stated we need to conduct it immediately."

"I understand," I replied weakly.

The other man stepped forward.

"Good morning, Miss Booth. I'm Officer Townsend in charge of Homeland Security in London's Scotland Yard and I will be recording the interview. We are grateful for your willingness to do this considering what you have been through." He glanced at the drip above my head. "We will try to be out of your way as soon as we can as you have a long recovery ahead of you." He took a seat in the corner of the room, placing a large cassette recorder and a stack of files on the table beside him.

Officer Townsend hit the play and record button on the cassette player and the tape started to turn.

"Let us begin the interview," Agent Arrowsmith said. "We have to start with formal questions, before we can get to updating you about recent events."

"I understand."

"Today is 23 February 1992. I am Agent Roger Arrowsmith. In the room with me is Officer Sean Townsend and Agent Adrien Osbourne. Please state your full name."

"Elizabeth Booth."

"Are you compliant and willing to be interviewed?" Agent Arrowsmith waited for my response.

"Yes."

"Do you understand that what is said here is confidential, in accordance with Her Majesty's Official Secrets Act?"

"Yes."

"Please answer all questions with as much information as you can. What may appear incidental information may be integral to our investigation."

I heard Officer Townsend shuffle papers around inside one of the files. He cleared his throat and pulled a hanky out of his pocket to wipe his nose.

"Sorry," he coughed.

"Do you remember anything about the location where you were held? The buildings, the surrounding noises, like children, airplanes or traffic?"

"I was held in two places. I don't remember much from the first one, but on the way to the second one I saw low-flying military planes. I think we passed a military airport and shortly afterwards crossed railway tracks. After half an hour or so, we entered Beirut from the east. I escaped in Al Hamra district, near Bliss Street."

"This is very significant." Arrowsmith seemed pleased with my recall.

"Thank you," Officer Townsend scribbled down some notes and passed them to Adrien, who left the room.

"Was Astrid Van Der Horst in captivity with you?"

"Yes."

"Were there other women in captivity?"

"I don't think so."

"Do you know who held you?"

"Yes. They were with the PFLP. George Habash was there. Kaleem and Hussein."

"Are you sure it was George Habash?"

"Yes. I recognised him. John Ellis and I encountered him in a restaurant in Aden."

"And he recognised you?"

"Yes. He must have. When he came into my cell, he said my name."

"When were you in Aden?"

"It was shortly after the unification. Maybe September or October 1990."

"Who is Hussein?"

Tears welled in the corners of my eyes, just at the mention of his name. They ran down the side of my temples and pooled in my ears. I tried to regain my composure, but it was impossible to control my emotions. A torrent of sobs erupted.

Adrien, who had come back in the room, reached over with a tissue and dried my face.

"I know this must be difficult to talk about."

"I can do it. I need to help Astrid."

"I was in a relationship with him, when I first arrived in Damascus."

"What's Hussein's full name?" Arrowsmith continued with the questioning.

"Hussein Ali Al-Hambali." I clenched my jaw.

Why didn't I ever tell Adrien? Maybe he's a known terrorist. This might have all been avoided.

"And you're sure of his name?"

"Yes. I saw it on the marriage contract he wanted me to sign." I was shaking.

"So, did you marry him?"

"No," I said emphatically. "My friend, Fatima, told me he wanted a visa to reach England. That ended my relationship with him. She was killed for saving me."

"What do you refer to?"

"Fatima was forced to be a suicide bomber in southern Lebanon. I saw her in the *Al Jazeera* newspaper."

Officer Townsend coughed again.

"I want him caught." I lashed out.

"When was this?"

"It was in the newspaper on 21 February."

"I recall that the suicide attack had all the hallmarks of the Syrian Socialist National Party, who used two, female suicide bombers, Sana'a Mahaidli and Ibtissam Harb in 1985, who also targeted the Israeli occupation in Lebanon," Officer Townsend chimed in with a haughty tone.

"We believe the suicide bomber was SSNP. Are you saying it was the PFLP?" Arrowsmith continued.

"I don't know, but I lived with Fatima during my relationship with Hussein. She was like a sister to me. They knew each other." Tears streamed down my face.

"What is her full name?"

"I don't know."

"Perhaps it is a different Fatima?" Agent Arrowsmith questioned.

"We can determine many reasons why women have been recruited as suicide bombers. The organisations may consider women are a soft recruit, as they believe women are easier to manipulate and indoctrinate. Women are definitely seen as 'valuable assets', as their action shows more stealth and ultimately strikes fear in their enemy, who then have to suspect everyone once women are recruited in their operations. Most importantly though is the media coverage, which will be more extensive for a woman, and more embarrassing to the enemy, showing them how powerless they are even to the fairer sex." Officer Townsend was unapologetic about his verbosity and male chauvinism, and didn't even look our way as his brows creased deeper, in full concentration on the articles laid in front of him.

His presumption that I didn't recognise, or know Fatima annoyed me. He hadn't even acknowledged Fatima as a person – let alone as my friend.

"Tell us about her. We would like to understand her motivation. Was she a devout Muslim, or did she have nationalistic beliefs? Perhaps she was avenging a family member's death? Anything you know may help us."

"No." I was seething. "Fatima is dead, because she helped me. She's a hero, not a martyr. She would never become a suicide bomber. He's a murderer."

Agent Arrowsmith lay his hand on my shoulder waiting for a few moments for the shudders to subside.

"I am so sorry. I know this must be difficult for you."

"Yes. She was like a sister to me."

"If Hussein was affiliated with the PFLP, then he is responsible for ordering her death," he continued. "We will get him," he promised. "Are these girls Syrian?"

"Fatima was Syrian. I think they were all Syrian except one — Nadia, she was Jordanian. Who knows she may be dead too." My throat hurt as I fought the urge to cry. Nadia in my mind was also a hero for helping me. I had no idea what became of her.

I cleared my voice and added, "Hussein is also Syrian."

"No. Hussein Ali Al-Hambali is not Syrian. He's Palestinian, with a Syrian residency. We had surveillance on him last year, but lost track of him."

"You know of him?"

"Yes. He is associated with a previous terrorist incident."

His name was known all along to MI6. I want to scream.

"Do you feel like you need a break?" Adrien rubbed my arm.

"Her attention span is short, but we need to gather as much of her perishable memory as possible," Officer Townsend reminded us all. "Otherwise some may be lost."

Adrien reluctantly stepped away from my bed.

"It's okay," I said. "I want to continue."

Officer Townsend shuffled more files around on his table. He produced a photograph and held it up.

"Is this the man you saw in your cell?" His cough was throaty.

"Yes. That's George Habash." I was shaking, unable to look at the picture for more than a few seconds. "I remember one of the soldiers had a red and white badge with a circle and arrow."

"That sounds like the PFLP emblem," Adrien interrupted.

"I'm sorry, but I have another photograph that is more disturbing," Officer Townsend continued. "One of the men in the car that you escaped from was killed at the scene by the police. We need to know if you recognise him."

He held it up and I saw the bloody body of a man in camouflage fatigues. The black *kefiyah* was pulled off his head and turned to one side, but I knew that ashen, deathly face.

"That's Kaleem." I looked away from the picture. "It's Astrid's husband."

"Thank you."

"What about Hussein? He was driving." My heart raced, hoping that he was also shot by the Lebanese police.

"The driver got away," Agent Arrowsmith said.

I gasped. A feeling of intense insecurity overwhelmed me, even though I was miles away from him.

"The Lebanese and Syrian police are still searching for him. They will search his residence in Duma, his places of work and anyone who knows him."

I wiped my sniffling nose.

"So, his intention was to travel to England?" Adrien asked.

"I believed he wanted a visa. When I didn't marry him, I never saw him again. I never thought I would see him again. I went on to live with Astrid and then Matthew."

"Do you know if he suspected that you were a former diplomat? Maybe he saw your passport, you know, with the Egyptian diplomat's comment in it?"

"He could have seen it, when I extended my visa at the Ministry of Interior."

"We are almost certain he must have seen it." Officer Townsend was examining a photocopy of my passport.

"Did he try to convert you to Islam?"

"Yes, but what difference does that make?"

I thought of the Muhsen sisters' kidnapping in Yemen and how their mother desperately tried to get the Foreign and Commonwealth Office involved. They were only fourteen and fifteen years old. There was a public outcry and eventually the consular section stepped in to help. It took eight years to get permission from Yemen to allow them to return to England, although one of them, Nadia, never returned. I never imagined that I could have been in a similar situation: married, with no help from my country in the event I needed it.

Townsend grunted.

"Astrid is married and a Muslim." I clenched my fists and pounded the bed. "You have to get her out of there. What about her embassy? Can't they do anything?"

"No. She is at the mercy of the husband's family."

"What about the Peace Corps woman in Sana'a?" She popped into my head.

"Mary Sharp was killed by her Yemeni boyfriend. The boyfriend was caught by the Sana'a police and hanged in the main square for the murder."

"Mary?" The name jolted me. "Hussein mentioned a Mary. Maybe she was charmed, like Astrid and I."

I heard Officer Townsend harrumph under his breath, and Agent Arrowsmith muttered back to him.

"It was hard to access information about Mary's case, as the Yemeni government executed him as a criminal. The Americans investigated and found out that the Yemeni boyfriend was called Nasir Al-Gibtar. He made a visa application at the American Embassy, but was denied." Officer Townsend flicked through his files again.

"Astrid told me while in captivity that she and Kaleem had plans to fly to Kenya via Frankfurt."

"Do you know which date?"

"She didn't mention any departure date."

"The American Embassy in Sana'a gave us Nasir Al-Gibtar's intended date of travel from their air tickets. His departure is tomorrow." Officer Townsend blew his nose.

"Tomorrow?" I gasped. "Do you think that date has a significance?"

"What do you mean?"

"I wonder if Kaleem intended on travelling that same date with Astrid."

There was a lull in the room when all the men stopped what they were doing and turned to stare at each other. It was just a moment and then Agent Arrowsmith made a quick nod towards Officer Townsend who abruptly left the room.

"We will find out if she's booked on any flight," Agent Arrowsmith said reassuringly.

"I don't know, if I've done enough. She must be rescued. I don't know if I'll ever forgive myself, if she's killed as well." I wrapped my arms tightly around my body and choked a cry. "I wish I could do more to help."

"Listen, Elizabeth, we have gathered priceless intelligence from you. You have been like an undercover agent in the field. Along with your Arabic skills, we don't know of a better agent. It'll be because of you that we uncover a terrorist plot larger than we had anticipated." Adrien put his arms around my hunched shoulders and gave me an enormous bear hug.

Adrien held me tightly, his warm body comforting me while I soaked the front of his jacket.

"As my mother always said 'Let it all out.' Let's get you on your way home, as family is what you need to begin mending from this horrific experience."

I heard the cassette recorder loudly stop.

"Agent Osbourne is right. You are an admirable woman and we are indebted to you for your service. You know, I wouldn't be surprised if you are asked to work here. You'll put us all to shame." Agent Arrowsmith came to Adrien and I as we embraced. I thought he was going to hug me too, as his eyes were watery. He held out his hand. His grip was strong and he squeezed my knuckles together so hard I winced. "We are so grateful to you for your immense courage and tenacity."

Adrien released me and I lay back in my bed.

I was exhausted. I knew the nurse was hovering to get the officers out.

"Will you let me know what happens tomorrow?"

"We will be in touch." Agent Arrowsmith grinned as he left the room.

"Adrien, can I call my parents?"

"Yes, but of course, keep it brief. Let me remind you, it's confidential information."

"I'll think of a story to tell them."

I thought of John, when he shared with me how hard it was to be an MI6 officer, as many accolades and patriotic missions are never shared, nor even written in the history books. He once told me to tell a truth, but bend it or wrap it with a story, then it's not so much a lie but artistic license.

I drifted off to sleep.

At the time when this research was conducted, in the early 1990s, the Assad faction of the Ba'ath party was at the height of its powers. It was therefore impossible to do serious academic research that covered the period of the emergence – too many of the players were still active and had too many skeletons to hide. Indeed, during fieldwork for this book, even when interviewing the "retired" Ba'athists and other political actors, I had to deal with thinly veiled warnings from the ubiquitous Syrian *mukhabarat.*

— Andrew Rathmell (permission given) *Secret War in the Middle East: The Covert Struggle for Syria 1949 - 1961*

Forty

When I woke up, Matthew was sitting in a chair in the corner of my room, reading a newspaper.

"You've been asleep for hours. You had some bad nightmares."

"I'm not surprised."

"I'm so sorry for what happened to you. I feel responsible for your capture."

"No. Matthew, it wasn't your fault. I was careless to go to Hamra. I should have known better than to wander around alone."

"At least you're safe now."

"Yes. I can't believe how foolish I was."

"Don't be so hard on yourself. I don't think I would have been as strong as you."

"Thank you, Matthew."

"Adrien told me they are sending you home."

"I need to make a call home," I said, having been reminded of my parents.

"Yes, hold on. I'll get that sorted."

He left the room momentarily. When he returned, he had a black phone, which he plugged into the wall near my bed.

"Adrien said that they have been trying to get in touch with you. I don't think he elaborated on anything, so it'll be up to you to explain something benign to them."

"Yes, I understand."

It was hard to speak to my parents. I dialled their number, which I had known since I was five years old. The phone rang and mother answered in the same way she, and the whole family, always answered the phone.

"Plymouth 8652110. Who's speaking please?" she answered sweetly.

"Hi, Mother. It's me." I was trying to talk with a normal voice, but the moment I heard her, my throat constricted, and it was hard not to sound as if I was about to cry, which I was. I thought about the letter I wrote on the torn paper bag. I had left it in the room when I was hastily carried off by the kidnappers.

"We are so glad you are safe. We have been worried sick about you."

"I'm fine. I'm sorry I worried you," I paused, as my voice was cracking up. "I'm heading home."

"Thank goodness. Did you go to Beirut?" she paused… "Don't worry, you can tell us when we see you. We just want you home, as soon as possible."

"I can't wait to be home. I've missed you all."

"We have missed you terribly, and can't wait to see you."

I could tell mother was crying.

"Here's your father. He wants to have a word."

"Okay. I love you."

"Yes. We love you too."

I wanted to cut the conversation short because I was on the verge of crying. Unfortunately, it didn't work. Mother had handed the phone over to father.

"Hi, Elizabeth."

"Hi, Father." I lost it. My father, my protector. All I wanted was to be home in his arms, the only man who loved me unconditionally.

"Father, I'll see you soon,"

"Yes. Dear. See you soon." I could tell that he was emotional too.

We hung up.

Matthew came to me, with the box of tissues. I blew my nose and wiped my cheeks.

"I hope to be home soon."

"You will."

I turned to Matthew and knew that we had experienced something that neither of us would ever forget and would forever tie us together.

"I'll see you in London, then?"

"Well, actually you don't get rid of me that easily, as I'm on the flight with you."

"I'm so glad for the company."

I was relieved, that I wasn't travelling home alone.

Forty-one

The flight from Beirut was long and I was anxious to see my parents. Matthew and I sat together. We were greeted by the sweetest-smiling air hostess, offering us some peanuts and a drink. I remembered back to how I was taken in by friendly smiles that hid shadowy characters, on my outbound flight.

"I wonder if my parents will recognise me, when we see each other. My hair is blonder and longer and I've lost weight, as my captors weren't very good cooks." I tried to joke, thinking it might make things easier to deal with, but I knew I had a long way to go to mend the nightmares and flashbacks I had on a daily basis.

"Humour is definitely a good remedy," Matthew grinned.

"I'm sure they will notice I'm far more grown up than when I left."

"You're probably the only student going back to Durham, who has been through as much as you have."

"I'll just be a regular student."

"Do you know what you'll do, after your degree?"

"I think I'll have a quiet life."

"I think it's in your blood now. You'll be drawn to the excitement again."

"What about you? Have you finished with your research for your PhD?" I asked curiously.

"Yes. I still have to write it up, but I have good news. I have been offered a job with MI6, because they were impressed with the work I had done on the counter-intelligence."

"You are the one who can't leave danger alone."

"You might be right there," he nodded.

***

We exited the aircraft and headed to baggage claim.

"Here's an Evening Standard." Matthew walked over to a newspaper lying on a bench. "I wonder if there's any news about Lebanon."

He flipped quickly through the pages and then stopped.

"Here it is," He smacked the page. "Two paragraphs hidden on page thirteen."

"What does it say?"

"Norwegian student's ill-fated marriage almost resulted in an abduction. Beirut – The Lebanese authorities were able to locate a Norwegian national who had been reported missing to the Norwegian Embassy. An Embassy spokesman has confirmed that the Norwegian female, Astrid Van Der Horst, was abducted by a Kenyan national after marrying him.

The Foreign and Commonwealth Office has issued a reminder to travellers to register at the consular section in their Embassies worldwide to ensure their safeguard." Matthew smiled broadly. "Astrid's safe."

"Yes, she's safe." I hugged Matthew in sheer excitement of the news and cried with joy.

"It's all thanks to you." He squeezed me tightly.

A heavy weight lifted from my shoulders knowing that she was probably home with her parents or at least on her way soon.

I collected my trusty rucksack from the conveyor belt. Then we passed through customs towards the receiving line in the concourse.

"This is it. Our families await us. Time to say our goodbyes." We gave each other one last hug, before we made the final steps of our journey together.

"I hope we can meet up again soon." I wiped a tear. "I will miss you."

"Yes, I hope so. Let's have some tea and cakes at the Ritz next time you are in London. After all, we deserve to treat ourselves with the best after what we have been through."

"That would be lovely. I've never been." I smiled.

The receiving area was crowded with people waiting for loved ones. I saw them before they saw me. I rushed into my mother's arms. It was the safest place I had been since leaving.

We wept together. It was hard to let go and we swayed from side to side in our embrace.

"Elizabeth," she wept.

"Mother." I held onto her and felt her body shudder. "It's so good to be back."

I looked over at father. He still looked the same, with his stocky body and balding head, but now he seemed demure. The formal and lofty father I had known was gone. I faced him as an equal, and I could tell he was cognizant of that.

He was standing beside us. For the first time in my life, he was unafraid to show his fatherly love. He stepped forward and hugged me. His strong arms wrapped around my back and he squeezed me hard. When he pulled away, he had tears in his eyes. It was a hug of the like I had never had, and yet yearned from him, for many, many years.

"It's so good to see you." He wiped away a tear.

"Father, I've missed you so much." I wiped my eyes and hugged him again, as my wet cheeks moistened his shirt.

"We were listening to Radio 4 on our way here. Did you hear about the Norwegian girl who went missing? Thankfully she was found."

"Perhaps she was at the school you went to?" Dad speculated.

"I didn't hear about it, but at least she is safe now," I added as calmly as I could. Meanwhile, my heart was bursting with joy.

"That is why I didn't want you to go to Lebanon. I'm so relieved you are safe." Mother kissed my head.

"What on Earth happened to you?" Father asked anxiously.

"It's a long story, but nothing to do with marrying anyone. I have to confess I was in Beirut and got stranded there without any money."

"In Beirut?" Mum piped in.

"I'm sorry, Mum. I had to go, as I was so close. It wasn't my fault I ran out of money. Lebanon accepted credit cards, but I found out mine was cancelled by my bank, because I hadn't paid a stupid, late fee of £12. It was a nightmare. They didn't realise the difficulty they put me in, with no way other way to access money there."

"So, why didn't you call us?"

"I couldn't. I barely had any money and needed it for my taxi back to Damascus."

"What did you do?" Dad asked, even more anxiously.

"I had friends there who could help me."

I felt terrible to cover up, but I knew I had to keep all of it confidential. "I'm sorry, Dad, I know you must have tons of questions, but I'm exhausted. Can we talk about it later? I am just so happy to be going home."

"Let's go home." Mother patted us both on our backs.

We headed towards the revolving door and out onto the pavement towards the car park. I knew we had time to talk about all my experiences in the days to come, but for now I was content to be in the arms of my family. The vision I had during my captivity, that I would be reunited with my family had finally come true. Heading home was the only destination I wanted to go for a long time to come.

10 March 1993

Dear Diary,

Today I woke up in my old bedroom. I can't find the words to write how good it feels to be home with my family. Seeing familiar odds and ends scattered around the house is so comforting. It's as if nothing has changed except for me.

Before I left I was happy to put as much distance as possible between my parents and I, but when I saw them, I hugged them both so tightly I didn't want to let go. I never imagined my homecoming would be so emotional. Dear God, thank you for delivering me safely home into the arms of my parents and brother.

I still can't bring myself to talk to them about what happened. I think it will take some time and even then I can't tell them everything. When they asked about it in the car I told them I'll talk about it later. I don't think anybody will ever know the whole story of what I have been through.

I know they are concerned as they see how depressed I am. I'm not who I was anymore. I feel different. It's hard to explain. I have no idea how to do this on my own, but I have my family now.

Right now, I have no interest in life. I am happy to just curl up and block out the world. Watching black and white movies on the telly, curled up on the leather sofa with the curtains drawn is the safest I have felt in a long time. I know I will eventually step back into the world, but for now I am in no hurry to venture out.

It's too painful to think about everything that has happened. I try not to think about Hussein, but I do in regards to how much I loved him, and if I'll ever love again. The hardest thing is that he is still out there somewhere and it scares me to death that he could be seducing another innocent woman, leading another woman to her death.

I was thinking about his nickname for me, 'my gazelle' he would call me, and the symbolism of it in Arabic literature. It struck me how apt it really was because when I arrived in Damascus, I was like a yearling gazelle; unsteady and dewy-eyed. I was preyed upon and then caught in the mouth of a lion. Only with my agility and swiftness was I able to escape. Now, I bound forward with my eyes wide open in search of those lurking in the shadows.